*FIEND*ISH RAVES

"View *The Fiend* as a superb thriller, as a model of craftsmanship, or as a deeply disturbing psychological novel. From any viewpoint, it is a masterwork."

—Anthony Boucher, *The New York Times*

"[Margaret Millar's] novels qualify her to rank with the likes of Dorothy L. Sayers and Agatha Christie . . . A mistress of mystery of the first rank."

—*John Barkham Reviews*

When they let him out, they warned him: stay away from little girls. But then he fell in love.

MARGARET MILLAR

THE FIEND

INTERNATIONAL POLYGONICS, LTD.
NEW YORK CITY

For Jewell and Russ Kriger,
with deep affection, as always

INTRODUCTION

There is no fiend in this book, only Charlie, a good-looking, rather bewildered young man who suffers from an illness for which no cause or cure has been found. Charlie was treated for this illness, and was, according to the authorities who released him, rehabilitated. The term means, roughly, that he indicated remorse and promised not to repeat his offense. (It may also mean that the correctional facility is overcrowded and room must be made for newcomers.) Charlie's remorse and promise were sincere. Then both are forgotten when he falls in love with a nine-year-old girl. He watches her play in the school playground, he follows her home, he drives up and down the street where she lives.

Shortly before starting this book, I attended the trial of a child molester. While the defense lawyer did his best to portray the victim as a deliberately provocative figure, the nine-year-old girl on the stand was pitifully innocent. The accused had also molested her younger sister and other children in the neighborhood. He was found guilty and given the full penalty allowed by law. As of this writing, years later, he has probably been rehabilitated three or four times, gone through a dozen psychiatrists and social workers. He will be back. The odds on that are about 100 to 1.

My husband once suggested that I sub-title this book *After Psychiatry, What?* It's a good question. Some day there might be a good answer, and one of the most baffling problems facing judges and law enforcement officials might be solved.

M. Miller

Santa Barbara, CA
September 1983

The fiend with all his comrades
Fell then from heaven above,
Through as long as three nights and days . . .

Caedmon

It was the end of August and the children were getting bored with their summer freedom. They had spent too many hours at the mercy of their own desires. Their legs and arms were scratched, bruised, blistered with poison oak; sea water had turned their hair to straw, and the sun had left cruel red scars across their cheekbones and noses. All the trees had been climbed, the paths explored, the cliffs scaled, the waves conquered. Now, as if in need and anticipation of the return of rules, they began to hang around the school playground.

So did the man in the old green coupé. Every day at noon Charlie Gowen brought his sandwiches and a carton of milk and parked across the road from the playground, separated from the swings and the jungle gym by a steel fence and some scraggly geraniums. Here he sat and ate and drank and watched.

He knew he shouldn't be there. It was dangerous to be seen near such a place.

"—where children congregate. You understand that, Gowen?"

"I think so, sir."

"Do you know what *congregate* means?"

"Well, not exactly."

"Don't give me that dumb act, Gowen. You spent two years at college."

"I was sick then. You don't retain things when you're sick."

"Then I'll spell it out for you. You are to stay away from any place frequented by children—parks, certain beach areas, Saturday afternoon movies, school playgrounds—"

The conditions were impossible, of course. He couldn't turn and run in the opposite direction every time he saw a child. They were all over, everywhere, at any hour. Once even at midnight when he was walking by himself he'd come across a boy and a girl, barely twelve. He told them gruffly to go home or he'd call the police. They disappeared into the darkness; he never saw them again even though he took the same route at the same time every night after that for a week. His conscience gnawed at him. He loved children, he shouldn't have threatened the boy and girl, he should have found out why they were on the streets at such an hour and then escorted them home and lectured their parents very sternly about looking after their kids.

He started on his second sandwich. The first hadn't filled the void in his stomach and neither would the second. He might as well have been eating clouds or pieces of twilight, though he couldn't express it that way to his brother, Benjamin, who made the lunches for both of them. He had to be very careful what he said to Benjamin. The least little fanciful thought or offbeat phrase and Ben would get the strained, set look on his face that reminded Charlie of their dead mother. Then the questions would start: Eating clouds, Charlie? Pieces of twilight? Where do you get screwy ideas like that? You're feeling all right, aren't you? Have you phoned Louise lately? Don't you think she might want to hear from you? Look, Charlie, is something bothering you? You're sure not? . . .

He knew better, by this time, than to mention anything about clouds or twilight. He had said simply that morning, "I need more food, Ben."

"Why?"

"Why? Well, because I'm hungry. I work hard. I was wondering, maybe some doughnuts and a couple of pieces of pie—"

"For yourself?"

"Sure, for myself. Who else? Oh, now I see what you're thinking about. That was over two years ago, Ben, and the Mexican kid was half starved. Everything would have been fine if that busybody woman hadn't interfered. The kid ate the sandwich, it filled him up, he felt good for a change. My God, Ben, is it a crime to feed starving children?"

Ben didn't answer. He merely closed the lid of the lunchbox on the usual two sandwiches and carton of milk, and changed the subject. "Louise called last night when you were out. She's coming over after supper. I'll slip out to a movie and leave you two alone for a while."

"Is it? Is it a crime, Ben?"

"Louise is a fine young woman. She could be the making of a man."

"If I were a starving child and someone gave me food—"

"Shut up, Charlie. You're not starving, you're overweight. And you're far from being a child. You're thirty-two years old."

It was not the command that shut Charlie up, it was the sudden cruel reference to his age. He seldom thought about it on his own because he felt so young, barely older than the little girl hanging upside down from the top bar of the jungle gym.

She was about nine. Having watched them all impartially now for two weeks, Charlie had come to like her the best.

She wasn't the prettiest, and she was so thin Charlie could have spanned her waist with his two hands, but there was a certain cockiness about her that both fascinated and worried him. When she tried some daring new trick on the jungle gym she seemed to be challenging gravity and the bars to try and stop her. If she fell—and she often did—she bounced up off the ground as naturally as a ball. Within five seconds she'd be back on the top bar of the jungle gym, pretending nothing had happened, and Charlie's heart, which had stopped, would start to beat again in double time, its rhythm disturbed by relief and anger.

The other children called her Jessie, and so, inside the car with the windows closed, did Charlie.

"Careful, Jessie, careful. Self-confidence is all very well, but bones can be broken, child, even nine-year-old bones. I ought to warn your parents. Where do you live, Jessie?"

The playground counselor, a physical education major at the local college, was refereeing a sixth-grade basketball game. The sun scorched through his crew cut, he was thirsty, and his eyes stung from the dust raised by scuffling feet, but he was as intent on the game as though it were being played in the Los Angeles Coliseum. His name was Scott Roberts, he was twenty, and the children respected him greatly because he could chin himself with one hand and drove a sports car.

He saw the two little girls crossing the field and ignored them as long as possible, which wasn't long, since one of them was crying.

He blew the whistle and stopped the game. "O.K., fellas, take five." And, to the girl who was crying, "What's the matter, Mary Martha?"

"Jessie fell."

"It figures, it figures." Scott wiped the sweat off his forehead with the back of his hand. "If Jessie was the one who fell, why isn't she doing the crying?"

"I couldn't be bothered," Jessie said loftily. She ached in a number of places but nothing short of an amputation could have forced her to tears in front of the sixth-grade boys. She had a crush on three of them; one had even spoken to her. "Mary Martha always cries at things, like sad events on television and people falling."

"How are your hands? Any improvement over last week?"

"They're O.K."

"Let me see, Jessie."

"Here, in front of everybody?"

"Right here, in front of everybody who's nosy enough to look."

He didn't even have to glance at the sixth-graders to get his message across. Immediately they all turned away and became absorbed in other things, dribbling the ball, adjusting shoelaces, hitching up shorts, slicking back hair.

Jessie presented her hands and Scott examined them, frowning. The palms were a mass of blisters in every stage of development, some newly formed and still full of liquid, some open and oozing, others covered with layers of scar tissue.

Scott shook his head and frowned. "I told you last week to get your mother to put alcohol on your hands every morning and night to toughen the skin. You didn't do it."

"No."

"Don't you have a mother?"

"Of course. Also a father, and a brother in high school, and an aunt and uncle next door—they're not really blood relations but I call them that because they give me lots of things, etcetera —and heaps of cousins in Canada and New Jersey."

"The cousins are too far away to help," Scott said. "But surely one of the others could put alcohol on your hands for you."

"I could do it myself if I wanted to."

"But you don't want to."

"It stings."

"Wouldn't you prefer a little sting to a big case of blood poisoning?"

Jessie didn't know what blood poisoning was, but for the benefit of the sixth-grade boys she said she wasn't the least bit scared of it. This remark stimulated Mary Martha to relate the entire plot of a medical program she'd seen, in which the doctor himself had blood poisoning and didn't realize it until he went into convulsions.

"By then it was too late?" Jessie said, trying not to sound much interested. "He died?"

"No, he couldn't. He's the hero every week. But he suffered terribly. You should have seen the faces he made, worse than my mother when she's plucking her eyebrows."

Scott interrupted brusquely. "All right, you two, knock it off. The issue is not Mother's eyebrows or Dr. Whoozit's convulsions. It's Jessie's hands. They're a mess and something has to be done."

Flushing, Jessie hid her hands in the pockets of her shorts. While she was playing on the jungle gym she'd hardly noticed the pain, but now, with everyone's attention focused on her, it had become almost unbearable.

Scott was aware of this. He touched her shoulder lightly and the two of them began walking toward the back-exit gate, followed by an excited and perspiring Mary Martha. None of them noticed the green coupé.

"You'd better go home," Scott said, "Take a warm bath, put alcohol on your hands with a piece of cotton, and stay off the jungle gym until you grow some new skin. You'd better tell your mother, too, Jessie."

"I won't have to. If I go home at noon and take a bath she'll think I'm dying."

"Maybe you are," Mary Martha said in a practical voice. "Imagine me with a dying best friend."

"Oh, shut up."

"I'm only trying to help."

"That's the kind of help you ought to save for your best enemy," Scott said and turned to go back to the basketball game.

Out of the corner of his eye he noticed the old green coupé pulling away from the curb. What caught his attention was the fact that, although it was a very hot day, the windows were closed. They were also dirty, so that the driver was invisible and the car seemed to be operating itself. A minute later it turned onto a side street and was out of sight.

So were the two girls.

"We could stop in at my house," Mary Martha said, "for some cinnamon toast to build your strength up."

"My strength is O.K., but I wouldn't mind some cinnamon toast. Maybe we could even make it ourselves?"

"No. My mother will be home. She always is."

"Why?"

"To guard the house."

Jessie had asked the same question and been given the same answer quite a few times. She was always left with an incongruous mental picture of Mary Martha's mother sitting large and formidable on the porch with a shotgun across her lap. The real Mrs. Oakley was small and frail and suffered from a number of obscure allergies.

"Why does she have to stay home to guard the house?" Jessie said. "She could just lock the doors."

"Locks don't keep him out."

"You mean your father?"

"I mean my *ex*-father."

"But you can't have an *ex*-father. I asked my Aunt Virginia and she said a wife can divorce her husband and then he's an *ex*-husband. But you can't divorce a father."

"Yes, you can. We already did, my mother and I."

"Did he want you to?"

"He didn't care."

"It would wring my father's heart," Jessie said, "if I divorced him."

"How do you know? Did he ever tell you?"

"No, but I never asked."

"Then you don't know for sure."

The jacaranda trees, for which the street was named, were in full bloom and their falling petals covered lawns and sidewalks, even the road itself, wth purple confetti. Some clung to Jessie's short dark hair and to Mary Martha's blond ponytail.

"I bet we look like brides," Jessie said. "We could pretend—"

"No." Mary Martha began brushing the jacaranda petals out of her hair as if they were lice. "I don't want to."

"You always like pretending things."

"*Sensible* things."

Jessie knew this wasn't true, since Mary Martha's favorite role was that of child spy for the FBI. But she preferred not to argue. The lunch she'd taken to the playground had all been eaten by ten o'clock and she was more than ready for some of Mrs. Oakley's cinnamon toast. The Oakleys lived at 319 Jacaranda Road in a huge redwood house surrounded by live oak and eucalyptus trees. The trees had been planted, and the house built, by Mr. Oakley's parents. When Jessie had first seen the place she'd assumed that Mary Martha's family was terribly rich, but she discovered on later visits that the attic was just full of junk, the four-car garage contained only Mrs. Oakley's little Volkswagen and Mary Martha's bicycle, and some of the upstairs rooms were empty, with not even a chair in them.

Kate Oakley hated the place and was afraid to live in it, but she was even more afraid that, if she sold it, Mr. Oakley would be able by some legal maneuver to get his hands on half of the money. So she had stayed on. By day she stared out at the live oak trees wishing they would die and let a little light into the house, and by night she lay awake listening to the squawking and creaking of eucalyptus boughs, and hoping the next wind would blow them down.

Mary Martha knew how her mother felt about the house and she couldn't understand it. She herself had never lived any other place and never wanted to. When Jessie came over to play, the two girls tried on old clothes in the attic, put on shows in the big garage, rummaged through the cellar for hidden treasure, and, when Mrs. Oakley wasn't looking, climbed the trees or hunted frogs in the creek, pretending the frogs were handsome princes in disguise. None of the princes ever had a chance to become undisguised since Mrs. Oakley always made the girls return the frogs to the creek: *"The poor little creatures. . . . I'm ashamed of you, Mary Martha, wrenching them away from their homes and families. How would you like it if some enormous giant picked you up and carried you away?"*

The front door of the Oakley house was open but the screen was latched and Mary Martha had to press the door chime. The sound was very faint. Mrs. Oakley had had it muted shortly after Mr. Oakley moved out because sometimes he used to come and stand at the door and keep pressing the chime, demanding admittance.

"If she's not home," Jessie said hopefully, "we could climb the sycamore tree at the back and get over on the balcony of her bedroom and just walk in. . . . What's the matter with your doorbell?"

"Nothing."

"Ours is real loud."

"My mother and I don't like loud noises."

Mrs. Oakley appeared, blinking her eyes in the light as if she'd been taking a nap or watching television in a darkened room.

She was small and pretty and very neat in a blue cotton dress she had made herself. Her fair hair was softly waved and hung down to her shoulders and she wore high-heeled shoes without any backs to them. Sometimes, when Jessie was angry at her mother, she compared her unfavorably with Mrs. Oakley: her mother liked to wear sneakers and jeans or shorts, and she often forgot to comb her hair, which was as dark and straight as Jessie's own.

Mrs. Oakley kissed Mary Martha on the forehead. "Hello, lamb." Then she patted Jessie on the shoulder. "Hello, Jessie. My goodness, you're getting big. Each time I see you, I truly swear you've grown another inch."

Whenever Mrs. Oakley said this to her, which was at least once a week, Jessie felt highly complimented. Her own mother said, "Good Lord, do I have to buy you another pair of shoes *already*?" And her brother called her beanpole or toothpick or canary legs.

"I eat a lot," Jessie said modestly. "So does my brother, Mike. My father says he should get double tax exemptions for us."

As soon as she'd made the remark Jessie realized it was a mistake. Mary Martha nudged her in the side with her elbow, and Mrs. Oakley turned and walked away, her sharp heels leaving little dents in the waxed linoleum.

"You shouldn't talk about fathers or taxes," Mary Martha whispered. "But it's O.K., because now we won't have to tell her about your hands. She hates the sight of blood."

"I'm not bleeding."

"You might start."

Charlie wrote the name and address on the inside cover of a book of matches: Jessie, 319 Jacaranda Road. He wasn't sure yet what he intended to do with the information; it just seemed an important thing to have, like money in the bank. Perhaps he would find out Jessie's last name and write a letter to her parents, warning them. Dear Mr. and Mrs. X: I have never written an anonymous letter before, but I cannot stand by and watch your daughter take such risks with her delicate bones. Children must be cherished, guarded against the terrible hazards of life, fed good nourishing meals so their bones will be padded and will not break coming into contact with the hard cruel earth. In the name of God, I beg you to protect your little girl. . . .

(2)

For many years the Oakley house had stood by itself, a few miles west of the small city of San Felice, surrounded by lemon and walnut groves. Most of the groves were gone now, their places taken by subdivisions with fanciful names and low down payments. Into one of these tract houses, a few blocks away from the Oakleys, Jessie had moved a year ago with her family. The Brants had been living in an apartment in San Francisco and they were all delighted by the freedom of having their own private house and plot of land. Like most freedoms, it had its price. David Brant had been forced to renew his acquaintance with pliers and wrenches and fuse boxes, the children were expected to help with the housework, and Ellen Brant had taken over the garden. She bought a book on landscaping and another on Southern California flowers and shrubs, and set out to show the neighbors a thing or two.

Ellen Brant was inexperienced but obstinate. Some of the shrubs had been moved six or seven times and were half dead from too much attention and overfeeding. The creeping fig vine, intended to cover the chimney of the fireplace, refused to creep. The leaves of the jasmine yellowed and dropped from excess dampness, and Ellen, assuming their wilting was due to lack of water, turned on the sprinkling system. Bills from the nursery and the water department ran high but when Dave Brant complained about them Ellen pointed out that she was actually increasing the value of the property. In fact, she didn't know or care much about property values; she simply enjoyed being out-of-doors with the sun warm on her face and the wind smelling mysteriously of the sea.

She was busy snipping dead blossoms off the rosebushes when Jessie arrived home at one o'clock.

Ellen stood up, squinting against the sun and brushing dirt off her denim shorts and bare knees. She was slim and very tanned, like Jessie, and her eyes were the same unusual shade of grayish green.

"What are you doing home so early?" she said, pushing a strand of moist hair off her forehead with the pruning shears. "By the way, you didn't straighten up your room before you left. You know the rules, you helped us write them."

It seemed to Jessie a good time to change the subject as dramatically as possible. "Mary Martha says I may be dying."

"Really? Well, you wouldn't want to be caught dead in a messy room, so up you go. Start moving, kiddo."

"You don't even believe me."

"No."

"I bet if Mary Martha went home and told *her* mother she was dying, there'd be a terrible fuss. I bet there'd be ambulances and doctors and nurses and people screaming—"

"If it will make you feel any better I'll begin screaming right now."

"No! I mean, somebody might hear you."

"That's the general purpose of screaming, isn't it?" Ellen said with a smile. "Come on, let's have it, old girl—what's the matter?"

Jessie exhibited her hands. A dusting of cinnamon hadn't improved their appearance but Ellen Brant showed neither surprise nor dismay. She'd been through the same thing with Jessie's older brother, Mike, a dozen times or more.

She said, "I have the world's climbingest children. Where'd you do this?"

"The jungle gym."

"Well, you go in and fill the washbasin with warm water and start soaking your hands. I'll be with you in a minute. I want to check my record book and see when you had your last tetanus booster shot."

"It was the Fourth of July when I stepped on the stingray at East Beach."

"I hope to heaven you're not going to turn out to be accident-prone."

"What's that?"

"There were at least a thousand people on the beach that afternoon. Only you stepped on a stingray."

Although Jessie knew this was not intended as a compliment, she couldn't help taking it as such. Being the only one of a thousand people to step on a stingray seemed to her quite distinctive, the sort of thing that could never happen to someone like Mary Martha.

Half an hour later she was ensconced on the davenport in the living room, watching a television program and drinking chocolate milk. On her hands she wore a pair of her mother's white gloves, which made her feel very sophisticated if she didn't look too closely at the way they fitted.

The sliding glass door was partly open and she could see her mother out on the lawn talking to Virginia Arlington, who lived next door. Jessie was quite fond of Mrs. Arlington and called her Aunt Virginia, but she hoped both women would stay outside and not interrupt the television movie.

Virginia Arlington's round pink face and plump white arms were moist with perspiration. As she talked she fanned herself with an advertisement she'd just picked up from the mailbox.

Even her voice sounded warm. "I saw Jessie coming home early and I was worried. Is anything the matter?"

"Not really. Her hands are sore from playing too long on the jungle gym."

"Poor baby. She has so much energy she never knows when to stop. She's like you, Ellen. You drive yourself too hard sometimes."

"I manage to survive." She dropped on her knees beside the rosebush again, hoping Virginia would take the hint and leave. She liked Virginia Arlington and appreciated her kindness and generosity, but there were times when Ellen preferred to work undisturbed and without someone reminding her she was driving herself too hard. Virginia had no children, and her husband, Howard, was away on business a great deal; she had a part-time gardener and a cleaning woman twice a week, and to open a can or the garage doors or the car windows, all she had to do was press a button. Ellen didn't envy her neighbors. She knew that if their positions were reversed, she would be doing just as much as she did now and Virginia would be doing as little.

Virginia lingered on, in spite of the sun which she hated and usually managed to avoid. Even five minutes of it made her nose turn pink and her neck break out in a rash. "I have an idea. Why don't I slip downtown and buy Jessie a couple of games?—you know, something absorbing that will keep her quiet."

"I thought Howard was home today."

"He is, but he's still asleep. I could be back by the time he wakes up."

"I appreciate your offer, naturally," Ellen said, "but you've already bought Jessie so many toys and books and games—"

"That won't spoil her. I was reading in a magazine just this morning that buying things for children doesn't spoil them unless those things are a substitute for something else."

Ellen had read the same magazine. "Love."

"Yes."

"Jessie gets plenty of love."

"I know. That's my whole point. If she's already loved, the little items I buy her can't harm her."

Ellen hesitated. Some of the items hadn't been so little—a ten-gear Italian bicycle, a cashmere sweater, a wrist watch—but she didn't want to seem ungrateful. "All right, go ahead if you like. But please don't spend too much money. Jessie might get the idea that she deserves an expensive gift every time something happens to her. Life doesn't work out that way."

There was a minute of strained silence between the two women, like the kind that comes after a quarrel over an important issue. It bothered Ellen. There had been no quarrel, not even a real disagreement, and the issue was hardly important, a two-dollar game for Jessie.

Virginia said softly, "I haven't offended you, have I, El? I mean, maybe you think I was implying that Jessie didn't have enough toys and things." Virginia's pale blue eyes were anxious and the tip of her nose was already starting to turn red. "I'd feel terrible if you thought that."

"Well, I don't."

"You're absolutely sure?"

"Don't go *on* about it, Virginia. You want to buy Jess a game, so buy it."

"We could pretend it was from you and Dave."

"I don't believe in pretending to my children. They're subjected to enough phoniness in the ordinary course of events."

From one of the back windows of the Arlington house a man's voice shouted, "Virgie! Virgie!"

"Howard's awake," Virginia said hastily. "I'll go and make his breakfast and maybe slip downtown while he's eating. Tell Jessie I'll be over later on."

"All right."

Virginia walked across the lawn and down her own driveway. It was bordered on each side with a low privet hedge and small round clumps of French marigolds. Everything in the yard, as in the house, was so neat and orderly that Virginia felt none of it belonged to her. The house was Howard's and the cleaning woman's, and the yard was the gardener's. Virginia was a guest and she had to act like a guest, polite and uncritical.

Only the dog, a large golden retriever named Chap, was Virginia's. She had wanted a small dog, one she could cuddle and hold on her lap, and when Howard brought Chap home from one of his trips she had felt cheated. Chap was already full-grown then and weighed ninety pounds, and the first time she was left alone with him she was frightened. His bark was loud and ferocious; when she fed him he nearly gobbled her hand; when she took him out on a leash he'd dragged her around the block like a horse pulling a wheelless carriage. She had gradually come to realize that his bark was a bluff, and that he had been underfed by his previous owners and never taught to obey any orders.

From the beginning the dog had attached himself to Virginia, as if he knew she needed his company and protection. He was indifferent to Howard, despised the cleaning woman, and held the gardener in line with an occasional growl. He slept inside at night and kept prowlers away not only from Virginia but from the immediate neighbors as well.

Howard had gotten up and let the dog out. Chap came bounding down the driveway, his plumed tail waving in circles.

Virginia leaned down and pressed her cheek against the top of his huge golden head. "You silly boy, why the big greeting? I've only been away for ten minutes."

Through the open kitchen window Howard overheard her and said, "A likely story. You've probably been over at the Brants' gabbing with Ellen all morning."

She knew he intended it mainly, though not entirely, as a joke. Without replying, she went in the back door, through the service porch to the kitchen. The dog followed her, still making a fuss, as if she were the one, not Howard, who'd been gone for two weeks.

Howard had made coffee and was frying some bacon on the grill in the middle of the stove. When he was home he liked to mess around the kitchen because it was a pleasant contrast to sitting in restaurants, being served food he didn't enjoy. He was a fussy eater for such a large man.

A head taller than Virginia, he had to lean way down to kiss her on the mouth. "You're a sight for sore eyes, Virgie."

"Am I?" Virginia said. "The bacon's burning."

"Let it. Did you miss me?"

"Yes."

"Is that all, yes?"

"I missed you very much, Howard."

He flipped the bacon expertly with a spatula, all four slices at once. "Still want me to quit my job, Virgie?"

"I haven't brought that subject up for over a year."

"I know. It makes me wonder how you've been spending your time while I'm away."

"If you want to know, ask me."

"I'm asking you."

"All right." Virginia sat down at the kitchen table, her pale pretty hands folded in her lap. "I start off each day with a champagne breakfast. After that, it's luncheon with the girls, with plenty of drinks, of course. We play bridge for high stakes all afternoon and end up at a cocktail party. Then I have dinner at a nightclub and carouse until dawn with a group of merry companions."

"Sounds rigorous," Howard said, smiling. "How do you manage to stay so beautiful?"

"Howard—"

"Put a couple of slices of bread in the toaster, will you?"

"Howard, were you serious when you asked me how I spent my time?"

"No."

"I think you were. Perhaps you'd like me to keep a diary. It would make fascinating reading. Juicy items like how I took some clothes to the cleaners, borrowed a book from the library, bought groceries—"

"Cut it out, will you, Virgie? Something popped into my head and I said it and I shouldn't have. I'm sorry. Let's forget it."

"I'll try."

He brought his plate of bacon to the table and sat down opposite her. "I hope I didn't wake you when I came in this morning. Chap made a hell of a fuss, he almost convinced me I had the wrong house. You'd think he'd know me by this time."

"He's a good watchdog," she said, adding silently: *You'd think I, too, would know you by this time, Howard, but I don't.* "How was the trip?"

"Hot—103 degrees in Bakersfield, 95 in L.A."

"It's been hot here, too."

"I have an idea. Why don't we head for the beach this afternoon? We'll loll around on the sand, have a walk and a swim—"

"It sounds nice, Howard, but I'm afraid I can't. You know how badly I sunburn.

"You could wear a wide straw hat and we'll take along the umbrella from the patio table."

"No."

He stared at her across the table, his eyes puzzled. "That was a pretty definite no, Virginia. Are you still sore at me?"

"Of course not. It's just that—well, the umbrella's no good any more. It was torn. I threw it away."

"It was practically brand-new. How did it get torn?"

"The wind. I intended to tell you. We had a big wind here Tuesday afternoon, a Santa Ana from the desert. I was downtown when it started and by the time I got home the umbrella was already damaged."

"Why didn't you take it to one of those canvas shops to have it repaired?"

"The spokes were bent, too. You should have see it, Howard. It looked as if it had been in a hurricane."

"The bougainvillaea beside the garage usually blows over in a Santa Ana. I didn't notice anything wrong with it."

"Salvador may have tied it up."

She knew this was safe enough. Salvador, who spoke or pretended to speak only Spanish, wasn't likely to deny or confirm anything. He would merely smile his stupid silver-toothed smile and crinkle up his wise old eyes and go right on working. *You speak, señor, but if I do not hear you, you do not exist.*

There had been no Santa Ana on Tuesday afternoon, just a fresh cool breeze blowing in from the ocean. Virginia had not been downtown, she'd been sitting on the front porch watching Jessie and Mary Martha roller-skate up and down the sidewalk. It was Jessie's idea to borrow the umbrella to use as a sail, and it had worked all too well. The two girls and the umbrella ended up against the telephone pole at the corner. Over cookies and chocolate malted milks Virginia told the girls, "There's no need to go blabbing to your parents about this. You know your mother, Jessie. She'd insist on paying for the umbrella and she can't really afford to. So let's keep this our secret, shall we?"

Virginia got up and poured Howard some coffee. Her hands were shaking and she felt sick with fear that Howard suspected her of lying. "I'm terribly sorry about the whole thing, Howard."

"Come on now. I hardly expect you to apologize for a Santa Ana. As for the umbrella, it was just an object. Objects can be replaced."

"I could go downtown right now and buy one, while you're reading the newspaper."

"Nonsense. We'll have one sent out."

"I'm going down anyway."

"Do you have to? We've hardly had a chance to talk."

We've had a chance, Howard, she thought, *we just haven't used it to very good advantage.* She said, "You'll be reading the paper anyway. It seems silly for me merely to sit and watch you when I could be accomplishing something."

"Since you put it like that," Howard said, taking her hand, "go ahead. Do you need money? What do you want to accomplish?"

"An errand."

"Ah, we're playing the woman of mystery today, are we?"

"There's no mystery about it," she said bluntly. "Jessie's sick. I want to buy her a little game or two to keep her quiet."

"I see."

She could tell from his tone that what he saw gave him little pleasure.

"I'm sorry the kid's sick," he added. "What's the matter with her?"

"According to Ellen, Jessie's hands are sore from playing on the jungle gym."

"It hardly sounds catastrophic."

"I know, but Ellen tends to minimize things like that. Sometimes I think she's not sympathetic enough with the child."

"Sympathy can be overdone and children can take advantage of it."

"Not Jessie. She's really a wonderful girl. You know, when she and I are alone together, I never have the least trouble with her. The problem of discipline doesn't even come up."

"Why should it?" Howard said dryly. "She calls the shots."

Virginia looked shocked. "That's not true."

"All right, it's not true. I'm just imagining that she comes barging in here without knocking, helps herself to whatever is in the refrigerator, bangs on the piano, feeds the dog until he's too stuffed to move—"

"It so happens that she has my permission to feed both the dog and herself and to come in here when she feels like it. She has no piano of her own so I'm giving her lessons on ours because I think she has talent."

"Listen, Virginia, I've wanted to say this before but I hated to cause trouble. Now that trouble's here anyway, I might as well speak my piece. You're getting too bound up with Jessie."

"I won't listen to you."

She put her hands over her ears and shook her head back and forth. After a moment's hesitation, Howard grabbed her by the wrists and forced her hands to her sides.

"You'll listen, Virginia."

"Let go of me."

"Later. It's natural enough for you to be fond of the kid since we don't have any of our own. What isn't natural is that she's taken everybody's place in your life. You don't see your friends any more, you don't even seem to want to spend much time with me when I'm home."

"Why should I, when all you do is pick on me?"

"I'm not picking on you. I'm warning you for your own good not to make yourself vulnerable to a heartbreak. Jessie doesn't belong to you, you have no control over her. What if something happens to her?"

"Happens? What?"

"For one thing, Dave Brant could lose his job or be laid off and forced to move away from here."

Virginia was staring at him bleakly, her face white. "That would suit you fine, wouldn't it?"

"No. I happen to like the Brants and enjoy their company. They're not, however, my sole interest in life. I'm prepared to survive without them. Are you?"

"I think you're jealous," Virginia said slowly. "I think you're jealous of a nine-year-old girl."

He let go of her wrists as if the accusation had suddenly paralyzed him. Then, with a sound of despair, he walked away into the living room. She stood motionless in the middle of the kitchen, listening to the rustle of Howard's newspaper, the sighing of his leather chair as he sat down, and the rebellious beat of her own heart.

(3)

At 12:50 Charlie Gowen went back to the wholesale paper supply company where he was employed. He was always punctual, partly by nature, partly because his brother, Benjamin, had been drumming it into him for years. "So you have your faults, Charlie, and maybe you can't help them. But you can be careful about the little things, like being on time and neat and keeping your hair combed and not smoking or drinking, and working hard— A bunch of little things like that, they all add up, they look good on a man's record. Employment record, I mean."

Charlie knew that he didn't mean employment record but he let it go and he listened to Ben's advice because it sounded sensible and because, since the death of his mother, there was no one else to listen to. He felt, too, that he had to be loyal to Ben; Ben's wife had divorced him on account of Charlie. She'd walked out leaving a note in the middle of the bed: "I'm not coming back and don't try to find me. I'm sick of being disgraced."

Charlie worked at the paper supply company as a stock boy. He liked his job. He felt at home walking up and down the narrow aisles with shelves, from floor to ceiling, filled with such a variety of things that even Mr. Warner, the owner, couldn't keep track of them: notebooks, pens, pencils, party decorations and favors, brooms and brushes and mops, typewriter ribbons and staplers and stationery, signs saying No Trespassing, For Rent, Private, Walk In, erasers and bridge tallies and confetti and plastic lovers for the tops of wedding cakes, huge rolls of colored tickets to functions that hadn't even been planned yet, maps, charts, chalk, ink, and thousands of reams of paper.

The contents of the building were highly inflammable, which was one of the main reasons why Charlie had been hired. Though he carried matches for the convenience of other people, he hadn't smoked since the age of fourteen when Ben had caught him trying it and beaten the tar out of him. Mr. Warner, the owner, had been so delighted to find a genuine nonsmoker, not just someone who'd quit a few weeks or months ago, that he'd given Charlie the job without inquiring too closely into his background. He knew in a general way that Charlie had had "trouble," but there was never any sign of it at work. Charlie arrived early and stayed late, he was pleasant and earnest, always ready to do a favor and never asking any in return.

In the alley behind the building Charlie found one of his co-workers, a young man named Ed Hines, leaning against the wall with an unlit cigarette in his hand.

"Hey, Charlie, got a match?"

"Sure." Charlie tossed him a packet of book matches. "I'd appreciate having them back, if you don't mind. There's an address written on the cover."

Ed grinned. "And a phone number?"

"No. Not yet."

"You gay old dog, you!"

"No. No, it's not like that actually—" Charlie stopped, realizing suddenly that Ed wouldn't understand the truth, that there was a family at 319 Jacaranda Road who were neglecting their pretty little girl, Jessie.

Ed returned the matches. "Thanks, Charlie. And say, the old man's in a stew about something. You better check in at the front office."

Warner was behind his desk, a small man almost lost in the welter of papers that surrounded him: order forms, invoices, sales slips, bills, correspondence. Some of this stuff would be filed, some would simply disappear. Warner had started the business forty years ago. It had grown and prospered since then, but Warner still tried to manage the place as if he personally knew, as he once had, every customer by name, every order from memory. Many mistakes were made, and with each one, Warner got a little older and a little more stubborn. The business continued to make money, however, because it was the only one of its kind in San Felice.

Charlie stood in the doorway, trying to hold his head high, the way Ben kept telling him to. But it was difficult, and Mr. Warner wasn't watching anyway. He had the telephone perched on his left shoulder like a crow. The crow was talking, loud and fast, in a woman's voice.

Mr. Warner put his hand over the mouthpiece and looked at Charlie. "You know anything about some skeletons?"

"Skeletons?" The word emerged from Charlie's throat as if it had been squeezed out of shape by some internal pressure. Then he went dumb entirely. He couldn't even tell Mr. Warner that he was innocent, he had done nothing, he knew nothing about any skeletons. He could only shake his head back and forth again and again.

"What's the matter with you?" Warner said irritably. "I mean those life-size cardboard skeletons we have in stock around Halloween. Some woman claims she ordered a dozen for a pathologists' convention dance that's being held tomorrow night." Then into the telephone, "I can't find any record of your order, Miss Johnston, but I'll check again. I promise you you'll get your skeletons even if I, ha ha, have to shoot a couple of my employees. Yes, I'll call you back." He hung up, turning his attention to Charlie. "And believe me, I meant everything but the ha ha. Now let's start searching."

Charlie was so dizzy with relief that he had to hold on to the doorjamb to steady himself. "Yes, sir. Right away. If I knew exactly what to search for—"

"A package from Whipple Novelty in Chicago."

"That came in this morning, Mr. Warner."

"It did? Well, I'll be damned." Warner looked pleasantly surprised, like a man who doesn't expect or deserve good news. "Well, I hand it to you, Charlie. You're getting to know the business. I ask for skeletons, you produce skeletons."

"No. No, I—"

"I saw you at the drive-in the other night, by the way. You

were with a nice-looking young woman. Funny thing, I could have sworn I've seen her before. Maybe she's one of our customers, eh?"

"No, sir. She works at the library, in the reference department."

"That explains it, then," Warner said. "So she's a librarian, eh? She must be pretty smart."

"Yes, sir."

"It pays to have a smart wife."

"No, no. She's not—I mean, we're not—"

"Don't fight it, Charlie. We all get hooked sooner or later."

Charlie would have liked to stay and explain to Mr. Warner about his relationship with Louise, but Mr. Warner had picked up the phone and was dialing, and Charlie wasn't sure he could explain it anyway.

He felt sometimes that he had known Louise all his life and at other times that he didn't know her at all. In fact, he had met her about a year ago at the library. Charlie was there at Ben's insistence: "You don't want to be a stock boy forever, Charlie. I bet there are careers you never even heard about. One of them might be just down your alley but you've got to investigate, look around, find out what's available."

And so, night after night, Charlie went to the library and read books and magazines and trade journals about electronics, photography, turkey farming, real estate, personnel management, mining engineering, cartooning, forestry, interior design, cabinetmaking, raising chinchillas, mathematics. He barely noticed the woman who helped him locate some of this material until one night she said, "My goodness, you certainly have a wide range of interests, Mr. Gowen."

Charlie merely stared at her, shocked by the sudden attention and the fact that she even knew his name. He thought of a library as a warm, safe, quiet place where people hadn't any names or faces or problems. The woman had no right to spoil it, no right—

But the next time he went, he wore a new shirt and tie, and a very serious expression which befitted a man with a wide range of interests. He took out an imposing book on architecture and sat with it open on the table in front of him and watched Louise out of the corner of his eye as if he had never seen a woman before and wasn't sure what to expect from the strange creature.

He guessed, from the way her colleagues deferred to her, that she was head of the department and so must be at least in her late twenties. But she had a tiny figure like a girl's with the merest suggestion of hips and breasts, and her movements were quick and light as if she weighed scarcely anything at all. Every time Charlie caught her glancing at him, something expanded inside of him. He felt larger and stronger.

He was only vaguely aware that it was getting late and people were leaving the library.

Louise came from behind the desk and approached the table where he was sitting. "I hate to disturb you, Mr. Gowen, but we're getting ready to lock up."

Charlie rose awkwardly to his feet. "I'm terribly sorry, I didn't notice. I—I was absorbed."

"You must have great powers of concentration to study in a noisy place like this."

"No. No, I really haven't."

"I wish I could let you take this book home but it's from the reference shelves and isn't allowed out. Unless, of course, there are special circumstances—"

"No. No, there aren't." Charlie hung his head and stared down at the floor. He could almost feel Ben behind him, telling him to square his shoulders and keep his head up and look proud. "I mean, I'm not an architect or anything. I don't know anything about architecture."

He hadn't planned on telling her this, or, in fact, talking to her at all. He'd intended to let her think he was a man of some background and education, a man to be respected. Now he could hear his own voice ruining everything, and he was powerless to stop it.

"Not a thing," he added.

"Neither do I," Louise said cheerfully. "Except about this building, and here I qualify as an expert. I can predict just where the roof will be leaking, come next January."

"You can? Where?"

"The art and music department. You see, last year it was the children's wing, they patched that up. And the year before, it was here, practically above my desk. So next time it's art and music's turn."

"I'll have to come back in January and find out if you were right."

There was a brief silence; then Louise said quietly, "That sounds as if you're going away some place. Will you be gone long, Mr. Gowen?"

"No."

"We'll miss you."

"No. I mean, I must have given you the wrong impression. I'm not going anywhere."

"You didn't give me the wrong impression, Mr. Gowen. I simply jumped to a wrong conclusion. My dad says I'm always doing it. I'm sorry."

"Even if I wanted to, I couldn't go anywhere."

Charlie could feel Ben behind him again: *Stop downgrading yourself, Charlie. Give people a chance to see your good side before you start blabbing. You've got to put up a front, develop a sense of self-preservation.*

"In fact," Charlie said, "I can't even leave the county without special permission."

Louise smiled, thinking it was a joke. "From whom?"

"From my parole officer."

He didn't wait to see her reaction. He just turned and walked away, stumbling a little over his own feet like an adolescent not accustomed to his new growth.

For the next three nights he stayed home, reading, watching

television, playing cards with Ben. He knew Ben was suspicious and Charlie tried to allay the suspicion by talking a lot, reminiscing about their childhood, repeating jokes and stories he heard at work.

Ben wasn't fooled. "How come you don't go to the library any more, Charlie?"

"I've been a little tired this week."

"You don't act tired."

"A man needs a change now and then. I've been getting into a rut spending every night at the library."

"You call this a nonrut?" Ben gestured around the room. Since their mother's death nothing in the house had been moved. It was as if the chairs and tables and lamps were permanently riveted in place. "Listen, Charlie, if anything happened, I have a right to know what it was."

"Why?"

"Because I'm your older brother and I'm responsible for you."

"No. No, you're not," Charlie said, shaking his head. "I'm responsible for myself. You keep telling me to grow up. How can I, with you breathing down my neck? You won't allow me to do anything on my own."

"I won't allow you to make a fool of yourself if I can help it."

"Well, you can't help it. It's over. It's done." Charlie began pacing up and down the room, his arms crossed on his chest in a despairing embrace. "I made a fool of myself and I don't care, I don't give a damn."

"Tell me about it, Charlie."

"No."

"You'd better. If it's not too serious I may be able to cover up for you."

"I keep uncovering and you keep covering up. Back and forth, seesaw, where will it end?"

"That's up to you."

Charlie paused at the window. It was dark outside, he could see nothing on the street, only himself filling the narrow window frame like a painting that had gotten beyond control of the artist and outgrown its canvas. A layer of greasy film on the glass softened his image. He looked like a very young man, broad-shouldered, slim-waisted, with a lock of light brown curly hair falling over his forehead and twin tears rolling down his cheeks.

Ben saw the tears, too. "My God, what have you done this time?"

"I—I ruined something."

"You sound surprised," Ben said bitterly, "as if you didn't know that ruining things was your specialty in life."

"Don't. Don't nag. Don't preach."

"Tell me what happened."

Charlie told him, while Ben sat in the cherrywood rocking chair that had belonged to his mother, rocking slowly back and forth the way she used to when she was worried over Charlie.

"I don't know why I said it, Ben, I just don't *know*. It popped out, like a burp. I had no control over it, don't you understand?"

"Sure, I understand." Ben said wearily. "I understand you've got to put yourself in a bad light. Whenever things are going all right you've got to open your big mouth and wreck them. Who knows? This woman might have become interested in you, a nice relationship might have developed. God help you, you could use a friend. But no, no, you couldn't keep your trap shut long enough even to find out her name. . . . Don't you *want* a friend, Charlie?"

"Yes."

"Then why in hell do you do these things?"

"I don't know."

"Well, it's over with, it's finished. There's not much use discussing it." Ben rose, heavily, from the rocking chair. "I suppose this means you won't be going to the library any more?"

"I can't."

"You could if you wanted to. If it were me, I'd just sail in there one of these nights with a smile on my face and pretend the whole thing was a joke."

"She knew it wasn't a joke."

"How can you be sure? You said you turned and walked out. If you didn't stick around to watch her reaction, you can't tell what it was. She might have gotten a big laugh out of it, for all you know."

"Stop it, Ben. It's no use."

"It's no use always looking on the black side, either. You're a good-looking man, Charlie. A woman could easily flip over you if you gave her a chance. If you held your head up, squared your shoulders, if you thought white instead of black for a change, if you put on a front—"

Charlie knew all the if's, including the one that was never spoken: If you got married, Charlie, some of your weight would be lifted off my back.

The following afternoon, when Charlie got home from work, there was a letter waiting for him, propped up against the sugar bowl on the kitchen table. Charlie received few letters and he would have liked to sit with it in his hands for a few minutes, wondering, examining the small neat handwriting. But Ben came out of the bedroom where he had changed from his good gabardine suit into jeans and T-shirt.

"There's a letter for you."

"Yes."

"Aren't you going to open it?"

"If you want me to."

"If *I* want you to?" Ben said irritably. "For Pete's sake, what have *I* got to do with it? It's your letter."

Charlie didn't argue, though he knew the letter wasn't really his. He had nothing that was privately, exclusively his own, any more than a five-year-old child has. The letter might as well have been addressed to Ben, because Ben would read it anyway, just as if Charlie, in his times of trouble, had lost the ability to read.

Charlie slit the envelope open with a table knife and unfolded the small sheet of stationery:

Dear Mr. Gowen:

I wanted to tell you this in person, but since you haven't appeared at the library, I must do it by letter. I was deeply moved by your courage and forthrightness on Monday evening. Very few people are capable of such honesty. Perhaps I'm being too presumptuous but I can't help hoping that what you did was an act of trust in me personally. If it was, I will try to deserve this trust, always.

Very sincerely yours,
Louise Lang

P.S. About that reference book on architecture, I have arranged for you to borrow it for a month, if you'd like to.

"Well," Ben said, "who's it from?"

"Her."

"Her?"

Charlie's left hand was clenched into a fist and he kept rubbing it up and down his jaw as if he were testing it for a vulnerable place to strike a blow. "She—she misunderstood. It wasn't like that. I'm not like that. I'm not any of those things she said."

"What in hell are you talking about?"

"I'm not, I'm not brave and forthright and honest."

Ben picked up the letter and read it, his eyebrows raised, one corner of his mouth tucked in.

Charlie was watching him anxiously. "What's it mean, Ben?"

"It means," Ben said, "that she wants to see you again."

"But why?"

"Because she likes you. Don't try to figure it out. Just enjoy it. She likes you, she wants to see you again. You want to see her too, don't you?"

"Yes."

"All right, then. Go and do it. Right after supper."

"I will," Charlie said. "I have to set her straight. I can't let her go on thinking all those good things about me when they aren't true."

Ben took it very quietly, without arguing or making a fuss or giving a lecture. But after supper, when the dishes were done, he changed back into the brown gabardine suit he wore to the cafeteria he managed. Then he told Charlie, "It's such a nice night I think I'll take a little walk to the library."

"It's foggy out, Ben."

"I like fog."

"It's bad for your bronchial tubes."

"I'm going with you," Ben said heavily, "because I know that if I don't, you'll louse things up for yourself. You may, anyway; in fact, you probably will. But the least I can do is try and stop you."

The rest of that night was never quite clear in Charlie's mind. He remembered the fog and Ben walking grayly beside him, in absolute silence. He remembered how, at the library, he'd stood beside the newspaper rack while Ben and Louise talked at Louise's desk. Every now and then they would glance, sympathetically and kindly, over at Charlie, and Charlie knew that between the two of them they were creating a fictional character, a person who didn't exist, called Charlie Gowen; a brave, forthright, honest man, too modest to admit his good qualities; every maiden's dream, every brother's joy.

The scene in the library had taken place a year ago. Since then Louise had become almost part of the family, but Charlie often felt that there had been no real change during the year. He was still standing apart, across a room, unrecognized, unidentified, while Ben and Louise talked, adding more touches to their creation, the Charlie doll. They were so proud of their doll that Charlie did his best to copy it.

Charlie located the package of cardboard skeletons and took them up to the front of the building. Mr. Warner's secretary hadn't returned from her lunch hour and Warner had just left for his, so the office was empty. This was the first time Charlie had been in the office when it was empty and it gave him an odd but not unpleasant feeling that he was doing something wrong. It was like entering a private bedroom while the owner slept, exposed, defenseless, and searching through the contents of pockets and purses and bureau drawers and suitcases.

To make room for the package on Mr. Warner's desk, Charlie had to move the telephone. As he touched it, an impulse seized him to call Louise. He dialed the number of the library and asked for the reference department.

"Louise? It's me, Charlie."

"Hello, Charlie." She seemed, as she always did, very happy to hear his voice. "Your timing is good. I just this minute arrived at work."

"Louise, would you do me a small favor?"

"Consider it done."

"Would you look up an address in the city directory and tell me who lives there? It's 319 Jacaranda Road. You don't have to do it immediately. Just make a note of the name and give it to me tonight when you come over."

"What's the mystery?"

"Nothing. I mean, it's not a mystery, I'll tell you about it tonight."

"Are you feeling all right, Charlie?"

"Sure I am. Why?"

"You sound kind of excited."

"No. No, I don't," Charlie said, and hung up.

She must be crazy, he thought. *Why should I be excited? What have I got to be excited about?*

(**4**)

Mary Martha Oakley was on the window seat in the front room, playing with her cat, Pudding. Her feelings toward the cat were ambivalent. Sometimes she loved him as only a solitary

child can love an animal. At other times she didn't want to see
him because he symbolized all the changes that had taken place
in her life during the last two years. Her mother had brought
the cat home from the pet shop on the same day her father
had moved out of the house.

*"See, lamb? It's a real live kitten, just what you've always
wanted."*

Where had her father gone?

*"Look at his adorable eyes and his silly little nose. Isn't he
adorable?"*

Was he coming back?

*"Let's think of a real yummy name for him. How about
Pudding?"*

After the cat there were other changes: new locks on the
doors and the downstairs windows and the garage, a private
phone with an unlisted number that Mary Martha wasn't allowed
to tell anyone, even her teachers at school or her best friend,
Jessie. Furniture began to disappear from the upstairs rooms,
silver and china from the dining room, pictures from the walls,
and all the pretty bottles from the wine cellar. The cook and
the gardener stopped coming, then the cleaning woman, the
grocery boy, the once-a-month seamstress, the milkman. Kate
managed everything herself, and did her own shopping at a
cash-and-carry supermarket.

Pudding was the only one of these changes that Mary Martha
liked. Into his furry and uncritical ear she whispered her con-
fidences and her troubled questions, and if Pudding couldn't give
her any answers or reassurance, he at least listened, blinking his
eyes and now and then twitching his tail.

"Mary Martha, I've been calling you."

The child raised her head and saw her mother standing in
the doorway looking hot and fretful as she always did when she
worked in the kitchen. "I didn't hear you."

"It's all right, it's not important. I just—" *I just wanted to
talk to somebody.* "I just wanted to tell you that dinner will be
a little late. It's taking the hamburgers longer to thaw than I

reckoned it would. . . . Stop letting the cat bite your ponytail. It's not sanitary."

"He's as clean as I am."

"No, he isn't. Besides, he should go outside now. He doesn't get enough fresh air and sunshine."

Mrs. Oakley leaned over to pick up the cat and it was then that she saw the old green coupé parked at the curb across the street. At noon when she'd unlatched the front screen door to let the girls in, she'd seen it too, but this time she knew it couldn't be a coincidence. She knew who was behind the wheel, who was staring out through the closed, dirty window and what was going on in his closed, dirty mind.

Her hands tightened around the cat's body so hard that he let out a meow of pain, but she kept her voice very casual. "Mary Martha, I've been concerned about those book reports that were assigned to you for summer work. How many do you have to write?"

"Ten. But I've got a whole month left."

"A month isn't as long as you think, lamb. I suggest you go up to your room right now and start working on one. After all, you want to make a good first impression on your new teacher."

"She already knows me. It's just Mrs. Valdez."

"Are you going to argue with me, lamb?"

"I guess not."

"That's my angel. You may take Pudding up with you if you like."

Mary Martha went toward the hallway with the cat at her heels. Though she couldn't have put her awareness into words, she realized that the more pet names her mother called her, the more remote from her she actually was. Behind every lamb and angel lurked a black sheep and a devil.

"Mother—"

"Yes, sweetikins?"

"Nothing," Mary Martha said. "Nothing."

As soon as Kate Oakley heard Mary Martha's bedroom door slam shut, she rushed out to the telephone in the front hall.

With the child out of the way she no longer had to exercise such rigid control over her body. It was almost a relief to let her hands tremble and her shoulders sag as they wanted to.

She dialed a number. It rang ten, twelve, fifteen times and no one answered. She was sure, then, that her suspicions were correct.

She dialed another number, her mouth moving in a silent prayer that Mac would still be in his office, detained by a client or finishing a brief. She thought of how many times she had been the one who detained him, and how many tears she had shed sitting across the desk from him. If they had been allowed to collect, Mac's office would be knee-deep in brine, yet they had all been in vain. She had been weeping for yesterday as though it were a person and would be moved to pity by her tears and would promise to return . . . *Don't cry, Kate. You will be loved and cherished forever, and forever young. Nothing will change for you.*

Mac's secretary answered, sounding as she always did, cool on the hottest day, dry on the wettest. "Rhodes and MacPherson. Miss Edgeworth speaking."

"This is Mrs. Oakley. Is Mr. MacPherson in?"

"He's just going out the door now, Mrs. Oakley."

"Call him back, will you? Please."

"I'll try. Hold on."

A minute later Mac came on the line, speaking in the brisk, confident voice that had been familiar to her since she was Mary Martha's age and her father had died. "Hello, Kate. Anything the matter?"

"Sheridan's here."

"In the house? That's a violation of the injunction."

"Not in the house. He's parked across the street, in an old green car he probably borrowed from one of his so-called pals. He won't use his own, naturally."

"How do you know it's Sheridan? Did you see him?"

"No, he's got the windows closed. But it couldn't be anyone else. There's nothing across the street except a vacant lot. Also,

I called his apartment and he wasn't home. When you add two and two, you get four."

"Let's just add one and one first," Mac said. "Do you see anybody in the car?"

"No. I told you, the windows are closed—"

"So you're not sure that there's even anyone in it?"

"I *am* sure. I *know*—"

"It's possible the car stalled or ran out of gas and was simply abandoned there."

"No. I saw it at noon, too." Her voice broke, and when she spoke again, it sounded as if it had been pasted together by an amateur and the pieces didn't fit. "He's spying on me again, trying to get something on me. What does he hope to gain by all this?"

"You know as well as I do," Mac said. "Mary Martha."

"He can't possibly prove I'm an unfit mother."

"I'm aware of that, but apparently he's not. Divorces can get pretty dirty, Kate, especially if there's a child involved. When money enters the picture too, even nice civilized people often forget every rule of decency they ever knew."

Kate said coldly, "You're speaking, I hope, of Sheridan."

"I'm speaking of what happens when people refuse to admit their own mistakes and take cover behind self-righteousness."

"You've never talked to me like this before."

"It's been a long day and I'm tired. Perhaps fatigue works on me like wine. You and Sheridan have been separated for two years and you're still bickering over a financial settlement, you haven't come to an agreement about Mary Martha, there have been suits, countersuits—"

"Please, Mac. Don't be unkind to me. I'm distracted, I'm truly distracted."

"Yes, I guess you truly are," Mac said slowly. "What do you want me to do about it?"

"Tell Sheridan to get out of town and I'll settle for eight hundred dollars a month."

"What about Mary Martha? He insists on seeing her."

"He'll see her over my dead body and no sooner. I won't change my mind about that."

"Look, Kate, I can't tell a man that simply because his wife no longer loves him he has to quit his job, leave the city he was born and brought up in and give up all rights to his only child."

"He's always loathed this town and said so. As for that silly little job, he only took it to get out of the house. He has enough money from his mother's trust fund. He can well afford to pay me a thousand dollars—"

"His lawyer says he can't."

"Naturally. His lawyer's on his side." She added bitterly, "I only wish to God my lawyer were on mine."

"I can be on your side without believing everything you do is right."

"You don't know, you don't *know* what I've gone through with that man. He's tried everything—hounding me, holding back on support money so I've had to sell half the things in the house to keep from starving, following me around town, standing outside the door and ringing the bell until my nerves were shattered—"

"That's all over now. He's under a court order not to harass you."

"Then what's he doing parked outside right this minute? Waiting to see one of my dozens of lovers arrive?"

"Now don't work yourself up, Kate."

"Why can't he leave us alone? He's got what he wanted, that fat old gin-swilling whore who treats him like little Jesus. Does he actually expect me to allow Mary Martha to associate with *that*?"

Lying on her stomach on the floor of the upstairs hall, Mary Martha suddenly pressed her hands against her ears. She had eavesdropped on dozens of her mother's conversations with Mac and this was no different from the others. She knew from experience that it was going to last a long time and she didn't want to hear any more.

She thought of slipping down the back stairs and going over

to Jessie's house, but the steps creaked very badly. She got to her feet and tiptoed down the hall to her mother's room.

To Mary Martha it was a beautiful room, all white and pink and frilly, with French doors opening onto a little balcony. Beside the balcony grew a sycamore tree where she had once found a hummingbird's tiny nest lined with down gathered from the underside of the leaves and filled with eggs smaller than jelly beans.

It was the cat, Pudding, who had alerted Mary Martha to the possibilities of the sycamore tree. Frightened by a stray dog, he had leaped to the first limb, climbed right up on the balcony and sat on the railing, looking smugly down on his enemy. Mary Martha wasn't as fearless and adept a climber as either Pudding or Jessie, but in emergencies she used the tree and so far her mother hadn't caught her at it.

She stepped out on the balcony and began the slow difficult descent, trying not to look at the ground. The gray mottled bark of the tree, which appeared so smooth from a distance, scratched her hands and arms like sandpaper. She passed the kitchen window. The hamburger was thawing on the sink and the sight of it made her aware of her hunger but she kept on going.

She dropped onto the grass in the backyard and crossed the dry creek bed, being careful to avoid the reddening runners of poison oak. A scrub jay squawked in protest at her intrusion. Mary Martha had learned from her father how to imitate the bird, and ordinarily she would have squawked back at him and there would have been a lively contest between the two of them. But this time she didn't even hear the jay. Her ears were still filled with her mother's voice: *"He's got what he wanted, that fat old gin-swilling whore who treats him like little Jesus."* The sentence bewildered her. Little Jesus was a baby in a manger and her father was a grown-up man with a mustache. She didn't know what a whore was, but she assumed, since her father was interested in birds, that it was an owl. Owls said, "Whoo," and were fat and lived to be quite old.

Mr. and Mrs. Brant were in the little fenced-in patio at the back of their house, preparing a barbecue. Mr. Brant was trying to get the charcoal lit and Mrs. Brant was wrapping ears of corn in aluminum foil. They both wore shorts and cotton shirts and sandals.

"Why, it's Mary Martha," Ellen Brant said, sounding pleased and surprised, as though Mary Martha lived a hundred miles away and hadn't seen her for a year. "Come in, dear. Jessie will be out in a few minutes. She's taking a bath."

"I'm glad she didn't get blood poisoning and convulsions," Mary Martha said gravely.

"So am I. Very."

"Jessie is my best friend."

"I know that, and I think it's splendid. Don't you, Dave?"

"You bet I do," Dave said, turning to give Mary Martha a slow, shy smile. He was a big man with a low-pitched, quiet voice, and a slight stoop to his shoulders that seemed like an apology for his size.

It was his size and his quietness that Mary Martha especially admired. Her own father was short in stature and short of temper. His movements were quick and impatient and no matter what he was doing he always seemed anxious to get started on the next thing. It was restful and reassuring to stand beside Mr. Brant and watch him lighting the charcoal.

He said, "Careful, Mary Martha. Don't get burned."

"I won't. I often do the cooking at home. Also, I iron."

"Do you now. In ten years or so you'll be making some young man a fine wife, won't you?"

"No."

"Why not?"

"I'm not going to get married."

"You're pretty young to reach such a drastic decision."

Mary Martha was staring into the glowing coals as if reading her future. "I'm going to be an animal doctor and adopt ten children and support them all by myself so I don't have to sit around waiting for a check in the mail."

Over her head the Brants exchanged glances, then Ellen said in a firm, decisive voice, "No loafing on the job, you two. Put the corn on and I'll get the hot dogs. Would you like to stay and eat with us, Mary Martha?"

"No, thank you. I would like to but my mother will be alone." *And she will have a headache and a rash on her face and her eyes will be swollen, and she'll call me sweetie-pie and lambikins.*

"Perhaps your mother would like to join us," Ellen said. "Why don't you call her on the phone and ask her?"

"I can't. The line's busy."

"How do you know that? You haven't tried to—"

"She wouldn't come, anyway. She has a headache and things."

"Well," Ellen said, spreading her hands helplessly. "Well, I'd better get the hot dogs."

She went inside and Dave was left alone with Mary Martha. He felt uneasy in her presence, as if, in spite of her friendliness and politeness, she was secretly accusing him of being a man and a villain and he was secretly agreeing with her. He felt heavy with guilt and he wished someone would appear to help him carry it, Jessie or Ellen from the house, Michael from the football field, Virginia and Howard Arlington from next door. But no one came. There was only Mary Martha, small and pale and mute as marble.

For a long time the only sound was an occasional drop of butter oozing from between the folds of the aluminum foil and sputtering on the coals. Then Mary Martha said, "Do you know anything about birds, Mr. Brant?"

"No, I'm afraid not. I used to keep a few homing pigeons when I was a boy but that's about all."

"You didn't keep any owls?"

"No. I don't suppose anyone does."

"My ex-father has one."

"Does he now," Dave said. "That's very interesting. What does he feed it?"

"Gin."

"Are you sure? Gin doesn't sound like a suitable diet for an owl or for anything else, for that matter. Don't owls usually eat small rodents and birds and things like that?"

"Yes, but not this one."

"Well," Dave said, with a shrug, "I don't know much either about owls or about your fath—your ex-father, so I'll just have to take your word for it. Gin it is."

Twin spots of color appeared on Mary Martha's cheeks, as if she'd been stung by bees or doubts. "I heard my mother telling Mac about it on the telephone. My ex-father has a fat old whore that drinks gin."

There was a brief silence. Then Dave said carefully, "I don't believe your mother was referring to an owl, Mary Martha. The word you used doesn't mean that."

"What does it mean?"

"It's an insulting term, and not one young ladies are supposed to repeat."

Mary Martha was aware that he had replied but hadn't answered. The word must mean something so terrible that she could never ask anyone about it. Why had her mother used it then, and what was her father doing with one? She felt a surge of anger against them all, her mother and father, the whore, David, and even Jessie who wasn't there but who had a real father.

Inside the kitchen the phone rang and through the open door and windows Ellen's voice came, clear and distinct: "Hello. Why yes, Mrs. Oakley, she's here. . . . Of course I had no idea she didn't have your permission. . . . She's perfectly all right, there's no need to become upset over it. Mary Martha isn't the kind of girl who'd be likely to get in trouble. . . . I'll have Dave bring her right home. . . . Very well, I'll tell her to wait here until you arrive. Good-bye."

Ellen came outside, carrying a tray of buttered rolls and hot dogs stuffed with cheese and wrapped in bacon. "Your mother just called, Mary Martha."

Mary Martha merely nodded. Her mother's excitement had an almost soothing effect on her. There would be a scene, naturally, but it would be like a lot of others, nothing she couldn't handle, nothing that hadn't been said a hundred times. *"If you truly love me, Mary Martha, you'll promise never to do such a thing again." "I truly love you, Mother. I never will."*

"She's driving over to get you," Ellen added. "You're to be waiting on the front porch."

"All right."

"Jessie will wait with you. She's just putting her pajamas on."

"I can wait alone."

"Of course you can, you're a responsible girl. But you came over here to see Jessie, didn't you?"

"No, ma'am."

"Why did you come, then?"

Mary Martha blinked, as if the question hurt her eyes. Then she turned and walked into the house, closing the screen door carefully and quietly behind her.

Dave Brant watched his wife as she began arranging the hot dogs on the grill. "Maybe you shouldn't question her like that, Ellen."

"Why not?"

"She might think you're prying."

"She might be right."

"I hope not."

"Oh, come on, Dave. Admit it—you're just as curious as I am about what goes on in that household."

"Perhaps. But I think I'm better off not knowing." He thought of telling Ellen about the fat old whore but he couldn't predict her reaction. She might be either quite amused by the story or else shocked into doing something tactless like repeating it to Mrs. Oakley. Although he'd been married to Ellen for eighteen years, her insensitivity to certain situations still surprised him.

"Dave—"

"Yes?"

"We'll never let it happen to our children, will we?"

"What?"

"Divorce," Ellen said, with a gesture, "and all the mess that goes with it. It would kill Michael, he's so terribly sensitive, like me."

"He's going to have plenty of reason to be sensitive if he's not home by 6:30 as he promised."

"Now, Dave, you wouldn't actually punish him simply for losing track of the time."

"He has 20-20 vision and a wrist watch," Dave said. But he wasn't even interested in Michael at the moment. He merely wanted to change the subject because he couldn't bear to talk or even think about a divorce. The idea of Jessie being in Mary Martha's place appalled him. Michael was sixteen, almost a man, but Jessie was still a child, full of trust and innocence, and the only person in the world who sincerely believed in him. She wouldn't always. Inevitably, the time would come when she'd have to question his wisdom and courage, perhaps even his love for her. But right now she was nine, her world was small, no more than a tiny moon, and he was the king of it.

The two girls sat outside the front door on the single concrete step which they called a porch. Jessie was picking at the loose skin on the palm of one hand, and Mary Martha was watching her as if she wished she had something equally interesting to do.

Jessie said, "You'll probably catch it when your mother comes."

"I don't care."

"Do you suppose you'll cry?"

"I may have to," Mary Martha said thoughtfully. "It's lucky I'm such a good crier."

Jessie agreed. "Maybe you should start in right now and be crying when she arrives. It might wring her heart."

"I don't feel like it right now."

"I could make up a real sad story for you."

"No. I know lots of real sad stories. My ex-father used to tell them to me when he was you-know-what."

"Drunk?"

"Yes."

It had been two years now since she'd heard any of these stories but she remembered them because they were all about the same little boy. He lived in a big redwood house which had an attic to play in and trees around it to climb and a creek at the back of it to hunt frogs in. At the end of every story the little boy died, sometimes heroically, while rescuing an animal or a bird, sometimes by accident or disease. These endings left Mary Martha in a state of confusion: she recognized the house the little boy lived in and she knew he must be her father, yet her father was still alive. Why had the little boy died? *"He was better off that way, shweetheart, much better off."*

"I wish you could stay at my house for a while," Jessie said. "We could look at the big new book my Aunt Virginia gave me. It's all about nature, mountains and rivers and glaciers and animals."

"We could look at it tomorrow, maybe."

"No. I have to give it back as soon as she gets home from the beach."

"Why?"

"It was too expensive, twenty dollars. My mother was so mad about it she made my father mad too, and then they both got mad at me."

Mary Martha nodded sympathetically. She knew all about such situations. "My father sends me presents at Christmas and on my birthday, but my mother won't even let me open the packages. She says he's trying to buy me. Is your Aunt Virginia trying to buy you?"

"That's silly. Nobody can buy children."

"If my mother says they can, they can." Mary Martha paused. "Haven't you even heard about nasty old men offering you money to go for a ride? Don't you even know about *them*?"

"Yes."

"Well, then."

She saw her mother's little Volkswagen rounding the corner. Running out to the curb to meet it she tried to make tears come to her eyes by thinking of the little boy who always died in her father's stories. But the tears wouldn't come. Perhaps her father was right and the little boy was better off dead.

Kate Oakley sat, pale and rigid, her hands gripping the steering wheel as if she were trying to rein in a wild horse with a will of its own. Cars passed on the road, people strolled along the sidewalk with children and dogs and packages of groceries, others watered lawns, weeded flower beds, washed off driveways and raked leaves. But to the woman and child in the car, all the moving creatures were unreal. Even the birds in the trees seemed made of plastic and suspended on strings and only pretending to fly free.

Mary Martha said in a whisper, "I'm sorry, Momma."

"Why did you do it?"

"I thought you'd be talking on the telephone for a long time and that I'd be back before you even missed me."

"You heard me talking on the telephone?"

"Yes."

"And you listened, deliberately?"

"Yes. But I couldn't help it. I wanted to know about my father, I just wanted to *know*, Momma."

Real tears came to her eyes then, she didn't have to think of the little dead boy.

"God forgive me," her mother said as if she didn't believe in God or forgiving. "I've tried, I'm still trying to protect you from all this ugliness. But how can I? It surrounds us like a lot of dirty water, we're in it right up to our necks. How can I pretend we're standing on dry land, safe and secure?"

"We could buy a boat," Mary Martha suggested, wiping her eyes.

There was a silence, then her mother said in a bright, brittle voice, "Why, lamb, that's a perfectly splendid idea. Why didn't I think of it? We'll buy a boat just big enough for the two of us, and we'll float right out of Sheridan's life. Won't that be lovely, sweetikins?"

"Yes, ma'am."

Quickly and quietly, Charlie let himself in the front door. He was late for supper by almost an hour and he knew Ben would be grumpy about it and full of questions. He had his answers ready, ones that Ben couldn't easily prove or disprove. He hated lying to Ben but the truth was so simple and innocent that Ben wouldn't believe it: he'd gone to 319 Jacaranda Road, where the child Jessie lived, to see if she was all right. She'd taken a bad fall at the playground, she could have injured herself quite seriously, her little bones were so delicate.

He knew from experience what Ben's reaction would be. Playground? What were you doing at a playground, Charlie? How did you learn the child's name? And where she lives? And that her little bones are delicate? How did she fall, Charlie? Were you chasing her and was she running away? Why do you want to chase little girls, Charlie?

Ben would misunderstand, misinterpret everything. It was better to feed him a lie he would swallow than a truth he would spit out.

Charlie took off the windbreaker he always wore no matter what the weather and hung it on the clothes rack beside the front door. Then he went down the dark narrow hall to the kitchen.

Ben was standing at the sink, rinsing a plate under the hot-water tap. He said, without turning, "You're late. I've already eaten."

"I'm sorry, Ben. I had some trouble with the car. I must have flooded it again. I had to wait half an hour before the engine would turn over."

"I've told you a dozen times, all you've got to do when the engine's flooded is press the accelerator down to the floorboard and let it up again very slowly."

"Oh, I did that, Ben. Sometimes it doesn't work."

"It does for me."

"Well, you've got a real way with cars. You command their respect."

Ben turned. He didn't look in the least flattered, as Charlie had hoped he would. "Louise called. She'll be over early. She's getting off at seven because she's taking another girl's place tomorrow night. You'd better hurry up and eat."

"Sure, Ben."

"There's a can of spaghetti in the cupboard and some fish cakes."

Charlie didn't particularly like fish cakes and spaghetti but he took the two cans out of the cupboard and opened them. Ben was in a peculiar mood, it would be better not to cross him even about so minor a thing as what to have for supper. He wanted to cross him, though; he wanted to tell him outright that he, Charlie, was a grown man of thirty-two and he didn't have to account for every minute of his time and be told what to eat and how to spend the evening. So Louise was coming. Well, suppose he wasn't there when she arrived. Suppose he walked out right now . . .

No, he couldn't do that, not tonight anyway. Tonight she was bringing him something very important, very urgent. He didn't understand why he considered it so important but it was as if she were going to hand him a key, a mysterious key which would unlock a door or a secret box.

He thought of the hidden delights behind the door, inside the box, and his hands began to tremble. When he put the fish cakes in the frying pan, the hot grease splattered his knuckles. He felt no pain, only a sense of wonder that this grease, which had no mind or will of its own, should be able to fight back and assert itself better than he could.

"For Pete's sake, watch it," Ben said. "You're getting the stove dirty."

"I didn't mean to."

"Put a lid on the frying pan. Use your head."

"My head wouldn't fit, Ben. It's too small."

Ben stared at him a moment, then he said sharply, "Stop doing that. Stop taking everything literally. You know damned well I didn't mean for you to decapitate yourself and use your head as a lid for the frying pan. Don't you know that?"

"Yes."

"Damn it all, why do you do it then?"

Charlie turned, frowning, from the stove. "But you said, put a lid on the frying pan, use your head. You *said* that, Ben."

"And you think I meant it like that?"

"I wasn't really thinking. My mind was occupied with other things. Maybe with Louise coming and all like that."

"Look, Charlie, I'm only trying to protect you. You pull something like this at work and they'll consider you a moron."

"No," Charlie said gravely. "They just laugh. They think I'm being funny. Actually, I don't have much of a sense of humor, do I?"

"No."

"Did I ever? I mean, when we were boys together, Ben, before—well, before anything had happened, did I have a sense of humor then?"

"I can't remember."

"I bet you can if you tried. You've always had a good memory, Ben."

"Now I've got a good forgetter," Ben said. "Maybe that's more essential in this life."

"No, Ben, that's wrong. It's important for you to remember how it was with us when we were kids. Mother and Dad are dead, and I can't remember, so if you don't, it's like it never happened and we were never kids together—"

"All right, all right, don't get excited. I'll remember."

"Everything?"

"I'll try."

"Did I have a sense of humor?"

"Yes. Yes, you did, Charlie. You were a funny boy, a very funny boy."

"Did we do a lot of laughing together, you and I and Mom and Dad?"

"Sure."

"Louise laughs a lot. She's very cheerful, don't you think?"

"Louise is a very cheerful girl, yes."

Slowly and thoughtfully, Charlie turned the fish cakes. They were burned but he didn't care. It would only be easier to pretend they were small round tender steaks. "Ben?"

"Yes."

"She wouldn't stay cheerful very long if she married me, would she?"

"Stop talking like—"

"I mean, you haven't leveled with her, Ben. She doesn't realize what a drag I am and how she'd have to worry about me the way you do. I would hurt her. I would be hurting her all the time without meaning to, maybe without even knowing it. Would she be cheerful then? Would she?"

Ben sat down at the table, heavily and stiffly, as if each of the past five minutes had been a crippling year.

"Well? Would she, Ben?"

"I don't know."

Charlie looked dismayed, like a child who's been used to hearing the same story with the same happy ending, and now the ending has been changed. It wasn't happy any more, it wasn't even an ending. Did the frog change into a prince? *I don't know.* Did he live happily ever after with his princess? *I don't know.*

Charlie said stubbornly, "I don't like that answer. I want the other one."

"There is no other one."

"You always used to say that marriage changed a man, that Louise could be the making of me and we could have a good life together if we tried. Tell it to me just like that all over again, Ben."

"I can't."

"All right then, give me hell. Tell me I'm downgrading myself, that I'd better look on the bright side of things, start putting on a front—that's all true, isn't it?"

"I don't know," Ben said. "Eat your supper."

"How can I eat, not knowing?"

"The rest of us eat, not knowing. And work and sleep, not knowing." He added in a gentler voice, "You're doing all right, Charlie. You're holding down a job, you've got a nice girl friend, you're keeping your nose clean—you're doing fine, just fine."

"And you're not mad at me any more for being late?"

"No."

"I flooded the engine, see. I had to wait and wait for the gas to drain out of it. I thought of calling you, but then I thought, Ben won't be worrying, he knows I'm behaving myself, keeping my nose clean. . . ." *I watched from the road. The house is a long way back among the trees but I could see the child sitting at one of the front windows. Poor Jessie, poor sweetheart, resting her little bruised body. Why don't her parents protect her? If anything happens to the girl it will be their fault, and their fault alone.*

(6)

The Arlingtons arrived home from the beach at seven o'clock and Virginia went directly to her room, without saying a word. Howard was in the kitchen unpacking the picnic basket when the dog, Chap, began barking and pawing at the back door.

Howard called out, "Who's there?"

"It's me, Uncle Howard. Jessie."

"Oh. Well, come on in."

Jessie went in, wearing a robe over her pajamas and carrying the book that weighed nearly half as much as she did. "Is Aunt Virginia here?"

"Oh, she's here all right, but she's incommunicado."

"Does that mean in the bathroom?"

Howard laughed. "No, it means she's sore at me."

"Why?"

"A dozen reasons. She's sunburned, she's got sand in her hair, she doesn't like the way she looks in a bathing suit, a bee stung her on the foot—all my fault, of course." Howard put the picnic basket, now empty, on the top shelf of the broom closet, and closed the door. "When you grow up, are you going to fuss about things like that?"

"I don't think so."

"Atta girl."

Jessie put the book on the table, then leaned over to pet the dog. Chap, smelling the butter that had dribbled down her chin from an ear of corn, began licking it off. Jessie was so flattered she stood the tickling without a giggle, though it was almost unbearable. "Do you think Chap likes me, Uncle Howard?"

"Obviously."

"Does he like everybody?"

"As a matter of fact, no," Howard said dryly. "He doesn't even like me."

"Why? Is he afraid of you?"

"Afraid of me? Why should he be? What gave you that idea?"

"I don't know."

"Well, I don't beat him, kid, if that's what you mean. He's just been spoiled rotten by women. All he has to do is roll his eyes and he gets a T-bone steak. A little more," he added, "is required of the human male though God knows what it is."

Jessie wasn't sure what he was talking about but she realized he was in a bad mood and she wished Aunt Virginia would come out of communicado.

Howard said, "Who's the book for?"

"Aunt Virginia. She gave it to me this afternoon, only when my mother saw it she told me I had to give it back."

"Why?"

"It cost twenty dollars."

"Oh?" Howard opened the book and looked at the price on the inside back jacket. "So it did. Twenty dollars."

He sounded very calm but his hands were shaking and both the child and the dog sensed trouble.

"Virginia!"

There was no response from the bedroom.

"You'd better come out here, Virginia. You have a visitor, one I'm sure you wouldn't want to miss."

Virginia's voice answered, soft and snuffly, "I'm in bed."

"Then get out of bed."

"I—I can't."

"You can and you will."

The dog, tail between his legs, crawled under the table, his eyes moving from Howard to the bedroom door and back to Howard.

The door opened and Virginia came out, clutching a long white silk robe around her. All of her skin that was visible was a fiery red and her eyes were bloodshot. "I'm not feeling very well, Howard. I have a fever."

"You also have a visitor," Howard said in the same calm voice. "Jessie has come to return the book you gave her this afternoon. It seems her mother considered it too expensive a gift for her to accept. How much did it cost, Virginia?"

"Please, Howard. Not in front of the child. It's—"

"How much?"

"Twenty dollars."

"And where did you get the twenty dollars, Virginia?"

"From my—purse."

Howard laughed.

"Where did you get the money in your purse? Perhaps you've taken a job and the twenty came out of your salary?"

"You know I haven't, it didn't. . . . Jessie, you'd better go home now. Right away, dear."

"Let her stay," Howard said.

"Please, Howard. She's only a little girl."

"Little girls can cause big troubles. And do. I want you to tell me, in front of Jessie, just where the twenty dollars came from."

"From you, Howard."

"That's right. From my pay check. So that makes me the Santa Claus of the neighborhood, not you, Virginia. Right?"

"Yes."

He picked the book up from the table and held it out toward Jessie. "Here you are, kid. Take the book, it's all yours, with love and kisses from Santa Claus."

Jessie stared at him, wide-eyed. "I can't. My mother won't let—"

"Take it. Get it out of here. I'm sick of the sight of it."

"I don't want it."

"You don't want it. I see. Maybe you'd rather have the money, eh? All right."

He reached for his wallet, pulled out two ten-dollar bills and thrust them into her hand. Behind his back she saw Virginia nod at her and smile a shaky little smile that asked her to humor Howard. Jessie looked down at the bills in her hand, then she put them in the pocket of her bathrobe, quickly, as though she didn't like the feel of them. She remembered the conversation she'd had with Mary Martha about grownups buying children and she wondered if she had been bought and what buying and selling really meant.

Sex had no particular interest or mystery for Jessie. Her mother and father had explained it to her quite carefully. But nobody had ever explained money and why people were affected by it. To Jessie it seemed like black magic, nice when it was on your side and bad when it wasn't, but you couldn't tell in advance which it would be. Money was what bought things to make people happy, like the new house, but it was also what parents quarreled about when they thought the children were sleeping; it caused Virginia to cringe in front of Howard, and lie about the patio umbrella; it made her mother irritable when the mail arrived and made her brother Michael threaten to quit school and get a job. It was as mysterious as God, who had to be thanked for blessings but couldn't be blamed for their lack.

The pocket of her bathrobe felt heavy with power and with guilt. She could buy things now, but she had also been bought.

"What are you standing around for, kid?" Howard said. "You have your money and your earful. That's about all you can expect from one visit."

Virginia walked quickly to the back door and opened it. Her

face appeared very peculiar because she was trying, with one part of it, to give Howard a dirty look, and with the other part, to smile reassuringly at Jessie. "Good night, dear. Don't worry. I'll explain things to your mother in the morning."

"I bet you will," Howard said when Jessie had gone. "The explanation should be a doozy. I wish I could stick around to hear it but I can't. I'm leaving."

"Why? Haven't you done enough damage for one night?"

"I'm afraid I might do more if I stay."

He went into the bedroom. His suitcase was lying on the floor, open but still unpacked except for his toothbrush and shaving kit. He gave it a kick and the lid fell shut.

Virginia said from the doorway, "You don't have to be childish."

"It's better than kicking you or the dog, isn't it?"

"Why do you have to kick anything?"

"Because I'm a bully, I'm the kind of guy who forces sweet little wife to go out in the nasty sun and fresh air down to the nasty beach. That's your version of this afternoon, isn't it?"

"I can't help it if I sunburn easily."

"Well, here's my version. This is my first day at home in two weeks. I wanted to be with my wife and I also wanted to get some fresh air and exercise which I happen to need. That's all. Not exactly reaching for the moon, was I, Virginia?"

"No. But—"

"Let me finish. I realized my wife had a delicate skin so I bought her a large straw hat and a beach umbrella. She decided the hat wasn't becoming enough, and after a while she got bored sitting under the umbrella so she went for a walk. The sun was strong, there was a wind and there was also, unfortunately, a half-dead bee which she stepped on. To complicate matters, she became conscious of all the young girls on the beach with young figures and by the time we were ready to eat she'd decided to go on a diet. She didn't eat anything. I did, though, the way any man would when he hasn't had a meal at home in two weeks. My wife sat and watched me. She was sunburned, hungry, nurs-

ing a sore foot and silent as a tomb. It was an interesting afternoon. I thank you for it, Virginia. It makes going back to work
a real pleasure."

"Is that where you're going now, back to work?"

"Why not?"

He picked his suitcase up off the floor and tossed it on the
bed. A sock and a drip-dry shirt fell out and Virginia went over
to pick them up. The shirt was clean but wrinkled, as if Howard
had laundered it himself and hung it up on the shower rod of
any of a dozen anonymous motor courts or hotels.

Virginia held the shirt against her breasts as if it, more than
the man who wore it, could move her to pity. "Did you wash
this yourself, Howard?"

"Yes."

"Where? I mean, what city, what hotel?"

He looked at her, puzzled. "Why do you want to know that?"

"I just do."

"It was the Hacienda Inn in Bakersfield. There was an all-
night party going on next door. Instead of taking a sleeping pill
I got up and did some laundry."

"Howard, your job isn't much fun, is it?"

"Sometimes it is, in some ways," he said brusquely. "I don't
expect to go around laughing all the time."

After a moment's hesitation Virginia went over to the bed
and started taking the things out of his suitcase and putting them
away in the clothes closet and the bureau drawers. She worked
quickly and nervously as if she wanted to get it done before he
had a chance to protest. Neither of them spoke until the suitcase
was empty and snapped shut and hidden under the bed. Then
Virginia said, "I'm sorry I was such a poor sport this afternoon."

"I knew you were a poor sport when I married you," Howard
said quietly. "I should have had more sense than to plan a beach
picnic."

"But you wanted one, you deserved one. You work hard at a
difficult job and—"

"Come on now, don't go to extremes. I do a job, like any

other man. I also get mad and lose my temper. Yes, and I guess I get jealous, too. . . . I'm sorry I made an ass of myself in front of the kid. Giving her twenty dollars like that—God, what'll Dave and Ellen think when she tells them?"

"Nothing. She won't tell them."

"Why not?"

"Because they'd make her return the money and she doesn't want to."

Howard sat down on the edge of the bed, shaking his head ruefully. "I'm sorry. I'm very sorry."

"Stop thinking about it. We were both wrong and we're both sorry." Virginia sat down beside him and put her head on his shoulder. "I'm a poor sport and you're a jealous idiot. Maybe we deserve each other."

"Your sunburn—"

"It doesn't hurt so much any more."

After a time he said, "I'll be very gentle with you, Virginia."

"I know."

"I love you."

"I know that, too."

She lay soft in his arms, her eyes closed, thinking that it had been exactly seven months and one week since she'd told Howard that she loved him.

(7)

Louise dressed carefully in a blue linen sheath with a Peter Pan collar, matching flat-heeled shoes that emphasized the smallness of her feet, and white gloves so tiny that she had to buy them in the children's department. At the last minute she pinned a bow in her short brown hair because Charlie liked girls to wear bows in their hair.

She went to the living room to say good night to her parents. Mr. Lang was doing the crossword puzzle in the evening newspaper, and Mrs. Lang was embroidering the first of a dozen pillow slips she would send to her relatives at Christmas.

"Well, I'm off," Louise said from the doorway. "I won't be late, but don't wait up."

Mrs. Lang peered at her over the top of her spectacles. "You look just lovely, dear. Doesn't she, Joe, look lovely?"

Mr. Lang put down his paper and stood up, as if Louise were a stranger he had to be polite to. Sitting, he had appeared to be of normal size, but when he stood up he wasn't much taller than Louise, though he held himself very straight. "You look very lovely indeed, my dear. Is this a special occasion?"

"No."

"Where are you going?"

"To Ben and Charlie's."

"It sounds like the name of a bar and grill on lower State Street."

"What a way to talk," Mrs. Lang said quickly. "You stop that, Joe, you just stop it. You know perfectly well who Ben and Charlie are. They're nice, respectable—"

Her husband silenced her with a gesture, then he turned his attention back to Louise. "Other girls seem to find satisfaction in dating only one gentleman at a time. They are also, I believe, called for at home by the gentleman. Are you different, Louise?"

"The situation is different."

"Exactly what is the situation?"

"One that I'm old enough to handle by myself."

"Old enough yes—at thirty-two, you should be—but are you equipped?"

"Equipped?" Louise looked down at her body as if her father had called attention to something that was missing from it, a part that had failed to grow, or one she had carelessly lost somewhere between the house and the library. She said, keeping her voice steady, "Daddy, I'm going over to play cards with two friends who happen to be male. Either one of them would be glad to pick me up here, but I have my own car and I enjoy driving it."

"Louise, honey, I'm not questioning your motives. I'm simply reminding you that you've had very little experience in—well, in keeping men in line."

"Haven't I just."

"I also remind you that appearances still count, even in this licentious world. It doesn't look right for a girl of your class and position to go sneaking off surreptitiously at night to visit two men in their house."

"Home, if you don't mind."

"Call it what you will."

"I'll call it what it is," Louise said sharply. "A *home,* where Charlie and Ben have lived since they were children. As for my sneaking off surreptitiously, that's some trick when you drive a sports car that can be heard a mile away. I must be a magician. Or are you getting deaf?"

Mrs. Lang moved her heavy body awkwardly out of her chair, grunting with the effort. She stood between her husband and daughter like a giant referee between two midget boxers who weren't obeying the rules. "Now I've heard just about enough from you two. Louise, you ought to be ashamed, talking fresh to your father like that. And you, Joe, my goodness, you've got to realize you're living in the modern world. People don't put so much stock in things like a man calling for his date at home. It's not as if Charlie was a stranger you didn't know. You've met him and talked to him. He's a nice, agreeable man."

"Agreeable, yes." Mr. Lang nodded dryly. "I said it was hot and he agreed. I said it was too bad about the stock market and he agreed. I—"

Louise interrupted. "He's shy. You embarrassed him by asking him personal questions about his background and his job."

"I don't mind people asking me about my job and my background."

"You're not shy like Charlie."

"What makes Charlie shy?"

"Sensitivity, *feeling*—"

"Which I don't have?"

Mrs. Lang put her hands, not too gently, on Louise's shoulders and pushed her out of the door into the hall. "You go along now, dear, or you'll be late. Don't pay too much attention to Dad tonight, he's having some trouble with his supervisor. Do you have your latchkey?"

"Yes."

"Enjoy yourself, dear."

"Yes." Slowly, Louise reached up and touched the bow in her hair. She could scarcely feel it through the fabric of her glove but it was still there, for Charlie. "Do I—look all right?"

"Just lovely. I told you that before, at least I think I did."

"Yes. Good night, Mother."

Mrs. Lang made sure the door was locked behind Louise, then she went back into the living room, panting audibly, as if it took more energy to be a referee than to be a contestant. She wished Joe would go to bed and leave her to dream a little: *Louise will be married in the church, of course. With a long-sleeved, floor-length bridal gown to hide her skinny arms and legs, and the right make-up to enlarge her eyes, she'll look quite presentable. She has a nice smile. Louise has a very nice smile.*

Joe was standing where she'd left him, in the middle of the room. "Sensitivity, feeling, my foot. He seemed plain ordinary stupid to me. Hardly opened his mouth."

"Oftentimes you don't bring out the best in people, Joe."

"Why shouldn't I ask him questions about his job? What's he got to hide?"

"Nothing," his wife said mildly. "Now stop carrying on, it's bad for your health. Charlie Gowen is a fine-looking young man with good manners and gainful employment. He probably has a wide choice of female companions. You should consider it a lucky thing that he picked Louise."

"Should I?"

"As for his being shy, I, for one, find it refreshing. There are so many smart-alecky young men going around tooting their own horn these days. That kind doesn't appeal to Louise. She has a spiritual nature." She added, without any change of tone, "I'm warning you, Joe. Don't ruin her chances or you'll regret it."

"Her chances for what? Becoming the talk of the town? Acquiring a bad reputation that might even cost her her job?"

"Louise and Charlie will be getting married."

For a moment Joe was stunned into silence. Then, "I see. Louise told you?"

"No."

"Charlie told you?"

"No. Nobody told me. Nobody had to. I can feel it in the air." She settled herself in the chair again and picked up her embroidery. "You may laugh at my intuition, but wasn't I right last fall when I said I could feel it in my bones that we'd have a wet winter? And about Mrs. Cudahy when I said she couldn't last more than a week and she died the next day? Wasn't I right?"

He didn't answer. It had been a wet winter, Mrs. Cudahy had died, Louise was marrying Charlie.

Ben met her at the door. He was freshly shaved—she could smell his shaving cream when they shook hands—and he had on a business suit, not the jeans and T-shirt he usually wore around the house.

"Well, you're all dressed up," Louise said, smiling. "Are we going out some place?"

Ben looked uneasy. "No. I mean, I'm going out. You and Charlie can do what you like, of course."

"But I thought we were all three of us going to play cards as usual. What made you change your mind? Has anything happened?"

"No. I just figured you and Charlie might want to be alone together for a change."

She was seized by a panic so severe that for several seconds her heart stopped. She could feel it in the middle of her chest, as heavy and silent as a stone. "If Charlie wanted to be alone with me, he'd arrange it that way, wouldn't he?"

"Not necessarily. Charlie may want something but he often doesn't know he wants it until I tell him."

"Until you tell him," she repeated. "Well, did you?"

"What?"

"Tell him he wanted to be alone with me tonight?"

"No. I just said I was going out."

"And he didn't run away," she said, "so that means he wants to be alone with me? How very romantic."

"Don't be childish, Louise. You know Charlie as well as I do. He doesn't spell romance for anyone."

A slight noise at the end of the hall made them both turn simultaneously. Charlie was standing at the door of his bedroom, coatless and with one hand on his tie as if he hadn't quite finished dressing.

"Why, I can so," he said with a frown. "I can spell *romance*. R-o-m-a-n-c-e."

Louise hesitated a moment, then gave him a quick little nod of approval. "That's very good, Charlie."

"Not really. It's an easy word. I bet I could spell it when I was nine years old."

"I bet you could."

"Maybe not, though. I can't remember much about when I was nine. Ben does my remembering for me. You know what he remembered tonight, Louise?"

"No. What?"

"That I had a nice sense of humor when I was young."

"I'm not surprised."

"I am." He turned to Ben. "I thought you were going out tonight. Didn't you tell me that?"

"Yes."

"You'd better hurry. Louise and I have something to talk about."

Louise flushed and stared down at the stained and worn carpet. One of the first things she'd do would be to replace it. She had money in the bank, she would use it to fix the place up before she invited anyone, even her parents, to visit her in her own home.

"Well, I can take a hint," Ben said, sounding very pleased. "I know when I'm not wanted. Good night, you two. Have fun."

He went outside, closing the door softly behind him, as if the slightest sound might change Charlie's mood. The night air was cool but sweat was running down behind his ears and under his collar like cold, restless worms. Before he got into his car he turned to glance back at the house. The drapes in the front room hadn't been drawn and he could see Louise sitting on the davenport and Charlie standing facing her, bending over a little, ready to whisper into her ear.

Ben let out his breath suddenly and violently, as if he'd been holding it for years. He stood on the driveway for a long time, not watching the house any more, just breathing in and out, in and out, like any free man on a summer night.

Charlie said, "Are you comfortable, Louise?"

"Yes."

"If it's too cool for you in here, I could turn on the heater."

"I'm fine, I really am."

"You don't think I hurt Ben's feelings, practically ordering him to get out of the house like that?"

"I'm sure he's not hurt. Stop worrying and sit down."

He sat beside her and she leaned toward him a little so that their shoulders touched and she could feel the smoothness of his arm and the hardness of its muscle. She wanted to tell him how strong he was and how much she admired strength when it was combined with gentleness like his. But she was afraid he would become mute with embarrassment, or else claim, quite flatly, that he wasn't the way she imagined him at all, he was weak and brutal.

"I had to get rid of him," Charlie said, "so you and I could talk. Ben doesn't have to be in on everything, does he?"

"No."

"When he's around and I make a remark or ask a question, he always has to know why. Ben always has to know the why of things. Sometimes there *is* no why. You understand that, don't you?"

"Of course," Louise said softly. "It's that way with love."

"Love?"

"Nobody can explain what it is, what makes people fall in love with each other. Do you remember that first night when you were sitting in the library and I looked over and there you were with that book on architecture? I felt so strange, Charlie, as if the world had begun to move faster and I had to cling like mad to stay on it. It hasn't slowed down even for a minute, Charlie."

He stared down at the floor, frowning, as if he were trying to see it move in space. "I don't like that idea. It makes me dizzy."

"I'm dizzy, too. So we're two dizzy people. What's the matter with that?"

"It's not scientific. Nobody can feel the world move."

"I can."

He drew away from her as if she'd confessed having a disease he didn't want to catch. Then he got up entirely and walked over to the window. He could see the dark figure of a man standing in the driveway and he knew it must be Ben. It worried him. Ben didn't stand quietly in driveways, he was always busy, always moving like the world and making people dizzy, unsure of themselves, unable to figure out the why of anything even if there was one.

He said, "Did you tell Ben what we talked about on the telephone?"

"What we talked—?"

"The information I asked you to get for me. The house, who lives in the house on Jacaranda Road. You found out for me, didn't you?"

Louise was sitting so still he thought she'd suddenly gone to sleep with her eyes open, a dreamless sleep because her face held no expression whatever. In nice dreams you smiled, in bad ones you cried and woke up screaming and Ben came in and asked *why?*

He went over and put his hand on her shoulder to wake her up. "Louise? You didn't forget about it, did you? It's important to me. You see, these people——the people who live in the house

—have a dog, a little brown dog. When I drove past there this morning on my way to work the dog chased my car and I nearly hit the poor creature. One inch closer and I would have killed it. I must tell those people they've got to take better care of their little dog unless they want it to be killed by a car or something. Isn't that the right thing for me to do?"

He knew she wasn't sleeping because she stirred and blinked her eyes, though she still didn't speak.

"Louise?"

"Is—this what you wanted to talk to me about, Charlie?"

"Why, yes. It may not seem important to you, but I love dogs. I couldn't bear to hurt one, see it all mangled and bloody."

She looked down at her blue dress. It was spotless, unwrinkled. It bore no sign that she had run out into the street after Charlie's car and been dragged under the wheels and lacerated; and Charlie, unaware that anything had happened, had driven on alone. He had seen nothing and felt little more. *Maybe I felt a slight bump but I thought it was a hole in the road, I certainly didn't know it was you, Louise. What were you doing out on the road chasing cars like a dog?*

"Oakley," she said in a high, thin voice. "Mrs. Cathryn Oakley."

"The little dog has no father?"

"I guess not."

"Do you spell her first name with a *C* or a *K*?"

"C-a-t-h-r-y-n."

"You must have looked it up in the city directory?"

"Yes. Mrs. Oakley is listed as head of the household, with one minor child."

Charlie's face was flushed, as if he'd come out of the cold into some warm place. "It's funny she'd want to live alone in that big house with just a little girl."

He knew, as soon as the words left his mouth, that he'd made a mistake. But Louise didn't seem to notice. She had stood up and was brushing off her dress with both hands. He could see the outline of her thighs, thin, delicate-boned, with hardly any solid flesh to protect them from being crushed under a man's weight. She wasn't wearing any garters and he would have liked to ask her how she kept her stockings up. It was a perfectly innocent question on his part, but he was afraid she would react the way Ben would, as if such thoughts didn't occur to normal men, only to him, Charlie. *"Why do you ask that, Charlie?" "Because I want to know." "But why do you want to know?" "Because it's interesting." "Why is it interesting?" "Because gravity is pulling her stockings down and she must be doing something to counteract it."*

Louise had taken her gloves out of her handbag and was putting them on, holding her fingers stiff and smoothing the fabric down over each one very carefully. Charlie looked away as if she were doing something private that he had no right to watch.

She said, "I'd better be going now."

"But you just got here. I thought you and I were going to have a talk."

"We already have, haven't we?"

"Not real—"

"I think we've covered the important thing, anyway—Mrs. Oakley and her dog and her child. That was the main item on tonight's agenda, wasn't it? Perhaps the only one, eh, Charlie?"

She sounded friendly and she was smiling, but he was suddenly and terribly afraid of her. He backed away from her, until his buttocks and shoulders touched the wall. It was a cool wall with hot red roses climbing all over it.

"Don't," he whispered. "Don't hurt me, Louise."

Her face didn't alter except that one end of her smile began to twitch a little.

"Louise, if I've done anything wrong, I'm sorry. I try to do what you and Ben tell me to because my own thinking isn't too good sometimes. But tonight nobody told me."

"That's right. Nobody told you."

"Then how was I to know? I saw you and Ben looking at each other in the hall and I could sense, I could feel, you were expecting me to do something, but I didn't understand what it was.

You and Ben, you're my only friends. I'd do anything for you if you'd just tell me what you want."

"I won't do that."

"Why not?"

"You must figure it out for yourself, apart from Ben and me."

"I can't. I *can't*. Help me, Louise. Hold out your hand to me."

She walked toward him, her arms outstretched stiffly like a robot obeying an order. He took both her hands and pressed them hard against his chest. She could feel the fast, fearful beating of his heart and she wished it would stop suddenly and forever, and hers would stop with it.

"Oh God, Louise, don't leave me here alone in this cold dark."

"I can't make it any lighter for you," she said quietly. "Warmer, yes, because there would be two of us. I've had foolish dreams about you, Charlie, but I've never kidded myself that I could turn on any lights for you when other people, even professionals, have failed. I can share your darkness, though, when you need me. I know what darkness is, I have some of my own."

"For me to share?"

"Yes."

"And I can help you, too?"

"You already have."

He held her body close against his own. "It's warmer already, isn't it, Louise? Don't you feel it?"

"Yes."

"Imagine me helping anybody, that's a switch. I could laugh. I could laugh out loud."

"Don't."

She put one hand gently over his mouth, staring into his eyes as she would twin pools of water. On the surface she saw her own reflection, but underneath there were live creatures of every shape and size, moving mysteriously in and out, toward and past each other; arriving, departing, colliding, unconcerned with time or joy or grief. At the bottom of the cold, dark water lay the stones of death, but small green creatures clung to them and survived, unafraid. There was enough light to live by, even down there, and they had each other for comfort.

Charlie said, "Why—are you looking at me like that?"

"Because I love you."

"That's not a reason."

"It's reason enough for anything."

"You talk sillier than I do," he said, touching her hair and the ribbon in it. "I like silly girls."

"I've never been called a silly girl before. I'm not sure I approve."

"You do, though. I can tell."

He laughed, softly and contentedly, then he swooped her up in his arms and carried her over to the davenport. She sat on his lap with her face pressed against the warm moist skin of his neck.

"Louise," he said in a whisper, "I want you and me to be married in a church and everything, like big shots."

"I want that too."

"You in a long fluffy dress, me in striped trousers and a morning coat. I can rent an outfit like that down at Cosgrave's. One of the fellows at work rented one for his sister's wedding and he said it made him feel like an ambassador. He hated to take it back because actually he's just a truck driver. I wouldn't mind feeling like an ambassador, for a few hours anyway."

"An ambassador to where?"

"Anywhere. I guess they all feel pretty much the same."

"I suppose I could stand being an ambassador's wife for a few hours," Louise said dreamily, "as long as I could have you back again exactly the way you are now."

"Exactly?"

"Yes."

"Now you're talking silly again. I mean, it's not sensible to want me just as I am, with all my—my difficulties."

"Shhh, Charlie. Don't think about the difficulties, think about us. We must start planning. First, we'll have to decide on a church and a date and make a reservation. Someone told me that autumn weddings are starting to outnumber June weddings."

"Autumn," he repeated. "It's August already."

"If that's too soon for you," she said quickly, "we'll postpone it. Is it too soon, Charlie?"

She knew the answer before she asked the question. The muscles of his arms had gone rigid and the pulse in his neck was beating fast and irregularly. It was as if he could picture her in a long fluffy dress and himself in a morning coat, looking like an ambassador, but he couldn't put the two of them together, at one time and in one place.

"Actually," she said, "when I consider it, it does seem like rushing things. There are so many plans to make, and as you said, it's August already."

"Yes."

"I've always thought Christmas would be a good time for a wedding. Things are so gay then, with all the pretty parcels and people singing carols. And the weather's usually good here at Christmas too. Sometimes it's the very best weather of the year. You wouldn't have to worry about rain getting your striped trousers wet. You couldn't very well feel like an ambassador with your trousers wet, could you?"

"I guess not."

"You like Christmas, don't you, Charlie? Opening packages and everything? Of course I don't want to rush you. If you'd rather wait until early spring or even June—"

"No," he said, touched by her desire to please him and wanting to please her in return. "I don't want to wait even until Christmas. I think we should be married right away. Maybe the first week of September, if you can be ready by then."

"I've been ready for a year."

"But we just met a year ago."

"I know."

"You mean you fell in love with me right away, just looking at me, not knowing a thing about me? That's funny."

"Not to me. Oh, Charlie, I'm so happy."

"Imagine me making anyone happy," Charlie said. "Ben will certainly be surprised."

Ben wouldn't be able to say *I don't know* any more. He'd have to admit that the frog turned into a prince and lived happily ever after with his princess.

"Louise, I just thought, what if your parents don't approve? Your father doesn't seem to like me very much."

"Yes, he *does*. He told me tonight as I was leaving that you were a fine young man."

"Did he really?"

"It wouldn't matter anyway, Charlie."

"Yes, it would. I want everything to be right, everyone to be —well, on our side."

"Everything will be right," she said. "Everyone is on our side."

She thought of the small green creatures clinging to the stones at the bottom of the cold dark water. They survived, with nothing on their side but each other.

(8)

It was the following noon that Kate Oakley received the letter. She was alone in the house; Mary Martha had gone to the playground with Jessie and Jessie's brother, Mike, who was supposed to see to it that the girls stayed off the jungle gym and kept their clothes clean. Kate had promised to drive them to the Museum of Natural History right after lunch.

She liked to take the girls places and let people assume they were both her daughters, but she was dreading this particular excursion. The museum used to be—and perhaps still was—one of Sheridan's favorite hangouts. He hadn't seen Mary Martha for four months and Kate was afraid that if he ran into her now there would be a scene in front of everybody, quiet and sarcastic if he was sober, loud and weepy if he wasn't. Still, she had to risk it. There weren't many places she could take Mary Martha without having to pay, and money was very short.

She had received no check from Sheridan for temporary support for nearly two months. She knew it was Sheridan's way of punishing her for keeping him away from Mary Martha but she was determined not to give in. She was strong—stronger than he was—and in the end she would win, she would get the money she needed to bring Mary Martha up in the manner she deserved. Things would be as they were before. She would have a woman to do the cleaning and laundering, a seamstress to make Mary Martha's school clothes, a gardener to mow the vast lawn and cut the hedges and spray the poison oak. The groceries would be delivered and she would sign the bill without bothering to check it and tip the delivery boy with real money, not a smile, the way she had to tip everyone now.

These smile tips didn't cost her anything but they were expensive. They came out of her most private account, her personal capital. Nothing had been added to this capital for a long time; she had been neither loved nor loving, she offered no mercy and accepted none; hungry, she refused to eat; weary, she couldn't rest; alone, she reached out to no one. Sometimes at night, when Mary Martha was in bed asleep and the house seemed like a huge empty cave, Kate could feel her impending bankruptcy but she didn't realize that it had very little connection with lack of money.

She was vacuuming the main living room when she saw the postman coming up the flagstone walk. She went out into the hall but she didn't open the door to exchange greetings with him. She waited until he dropped the mail in the slot, then she scooped it up greedily from the floor. There was no check from Sheridan, only a couple of bills and a white envelope with her name and address printed on it. The contents of the envelope were squeezed into one corner like a coin wrapped in paper and her first thought was that Sheridan was playing another trick on her, sending her a dime or a quarter to imply she was worth no more than that. She ripped open the envelope with her thumbnail. There was no coin inside. A piece of notepaper had simply been folded and refolded many times, the way a child might fold a note to be secretly passed during class.

The note was neatly printed in black ink:

> Your daughter takes too dangerous risks with her deli-
> cate body. Children must be guarded against the cruel haz-
> ards of life and fed good, nourishing food so their bones
> will be padded. Also clothing. You should put plenty of
> clothing on her, keep arms and legs covered, etc. In the
> name of God please take better care of your little girl.

She stood for a minute, half paralyzed with shock. Then,
when her blood began to flow again, she reread the note, more
slowly and carefully. It didn't make sense. No one—not even
Sheridan, who'd accused her of everything else—had ever accused her of neglecting Mary Martha. She was well fed, well
clothed, well supervised. She was, moreover, rather a timid child,
not given to taking dangerous risks or risks of any kind unless
challenged by Jessie.

Kate refolded the note and put it back in the envelope. She
thought, *it can't be a mistake because it's addressed to me and
my name's spelled correctly. Perhaps there's some religious
crank in the neighborhood who's prejudiced against divorced
women, but it hardly seems possible now that divorce is so
common.*

Only one thing was certain: the letter was an attack, and the
person most likely to attack her was Sheridan.

She went out into the hall and telephoned Ralph MacPherson's office. "Mac, I hate to bother you again."

"That's all right, Kate. Are you feeling better today?"

"I was, until the mail came. I just received an anonymous
letter and I think I know who—"

"Don't think about it at all, Kate. Tear it up and forget it."

"No, I want you to see it."

"I've seen quite a few of them in my day," Mac said. "They're
all the same, sick and rotten."

"I want you to see it," she repeated, "because I'm pretty sure it's from Sheridan. If it is, he's further gone than I imagined. He may even be—well, committable."

"That's a big word in these parts, Kate. Or in any parts, for that matter."

"People are committed every day."

"Not on the word of a disgruntled spouse. . . . All right. Bring the letter down to my office. I'll be here until I leave for court at 1:30."

"Thank you, Mac. Thank you very much."

She dressed hurriedly but with care, as if she were going to be put on exhibition in front of a lot of people, one of whom had written her the letter.

Before leaving the house she made sure all the windows and doors on the ground floor were locked, and when she had backed her car out of the garage she locked the garage doors behind her. She had nothing left to steal, but the locking habit had become fixed in her. She no longer thought of doors as things to open; doors were to close, to keep people out.

She usually handled her small car without thinking much about it, but now she drove as she had dressed, with great care, as though a pair of unfriendly eyes was watching her, ready to condemn her as an unfit mother if she made the slightest mistake, a hand signal executed a little too slowly, a corner turned a little too fast.

She headed for the school playground, intending to tell the girls that she would be late picking them up. She had gone about three blocks when she stopped for a red light and saw, in the rear-view mirror, an old green coupé pull up behind her. Kate paid more attention to cars than most women, especially since she'd been living alone, and she recognized it instantly as the car she'd noticed parked outside her house the previous afternoon.

She tried to keep calm, the way Mac had told her to: *Don't jump to conclusions, Kate. If you thought Sheridan was driving that car, why didn't you go out and confront him, find out why he was there? If it happens again—*

Well, it was happening again.

She opened the door and had one foot on the road when the light changed. The left lane was clear and the green coupé turned into it and shot past her with a grinding of gears. Its grimy windows were closed and she could see only that a man was behind the wheel. It was enough. Sheridan was following her. He may even have been waiting outside the house while the postman delivered his letter, eager to watch its effect on her. She thought, *Well, here it is, Sheridan, here's the effect.*

She didn't hesitate even long enough to close the door. She pressed down on the accelerator and the door slammed shut with the sudden forward thrust of her car. For the next five minutes she was not in conscious control either of herself or of the car. It was as though a devil were driving them both and he was responsible to no one and for no one; he owned the roads, let others use them at their own risk.

Up and down streets, around corners, through a parking lot, down an alley, she pursued the green coupé. Twice she was almost close enough to force it over to the curb but each time it got away. She was not even aware of cars honking at her and people yelling at her until she ran a red light. Then she heard the shrieking of her own brakes as a truck appeared suddenly in front of her. Her head snapped forward until it pressed against the steering wheel. She sat in a kind of daze while the truck driver climbed out of the cab.

"For Chrissake, you drunk or something? That was a red light."

"I didn't—see it."

"Well, keep your eyes open next time. You damn near got yourself killed. You woulda spoiled my record, I got the best record in the company. How they expect a guy to keep his record with a lot of crazy women scooting around in kiddie cars?"

"Shut up," she said. "Please shut up."

"Well, well, now you're trying to get tough with me, eh? Listen, lady, you'll be damn lucky if I don't report you for reckless driving, maybe drunk driving. You been drinking?"

"No."

"They all say that. Where's your driver's license?"

"In my purse."

"Get it out."

"Please don't—"

"Lady, a near accident like this happens and I'm supposed to check on it, see? Maybe you've got some kind of restriction on your license, like you're to wear glasses when you're driving, or a hearing aid."

She fumbled around in her purse until she found her wallet with her driver's license in it. On the license there was a little picture of her, taken the day she'd passed her test. She was smiling confidently and happily into the camera.

She saw the truck driver staring at the picture in disbelief. "This is you, lady?"

She wanted to reach out and strike him between the eyes, but instead she said, "It was taken three years ago. I've been— things have happened to me. When you lose weight, it always shows in the face, it makes you appear—well, older. I was trying to think of a nicer word for it but there isn't one, is there? More aged? That's no improvement. More ancient, decrepit? Worn out? Obsolete?"

"Lady, I didn't mean it like that," he said, looking embarrassed. "I mean—oh hell, let's get out of here."

A crowd had begun to gather. The truck driver waved them away and climbed back into his cab. The green coupé had long since disappeared.

The two girls, on Mike's orders, were sitting on a bench in an area of the playground hidden from the street by an eight-foot oleander hedge. Mike was lying face down on the grass nearby, listening to a baseball game on a transistor radio. Every now and then he raised his head, consulted his wrist watch in an authoritative manner, and gave the girls what was intended to be a hypnotic glance.

They had both been absolutely silent and motionless for seven minutes except for the occasional blink of an eye or twitch of a nose. Mike was beginning to worry about whether he actually had hypnotized them and how he was going to snap them out of it, when Jessie suddenly jumped off the bench.

"Oh, I hate this game! It's not even a *game,* seeing who can stay stillest the longest."

"You're just sore because Mary Martha won," Mike said airily. "I was betting she would. You can't keep your trap shut for two seconds."

"I can if I want to."

"Yackety yak."

"Anyhow, I know why you're making us sit here."

"O clever one, do tell."

"So none of your buddies going past will see you baby-sitting. I heard you tell Daddy you'd never be able to hold up your head in public again if they saw you playing with two little girls. But Daddy said you had to play with us anyway. Or else."

"Well, I wish I'd taken the *or else,*" Mike said in disgust. "Anything'd be better than looking after a pair of dimwitted kids who should be able to look after themselves. *I* didn't need a baby-sitter at your age."

Jessie blushed, but the only place it showed was across the bridge of her nose where repeated sunburns had peeled off layers of skin. "I don't need one either except I've got sore hands."

"You're breaking my heart with your itty bitty sore hands. Man, oh man, you get more mileage out of a couple of blisters than I could get from a broken neck."

"If I won the game," Mary Martha said wistfully, "may I move now? There's a bee on my arm and it tickles me."

"So tickle it back," Mike said and turned up the volume of the radio.

"My goodness, he's mean," Mary Martha whispered behind her hand. "Was he born that way?"

"I've only known him for nine years, but he probably was."

"Maybe some evil witch put a curse on him. Do you know any curses?"

"Just g-o-d-d-a-m, which I never say."

"No, I mean real curses." Mary Martha contorted her face until it looked reasonably witchlike. Then she spoke in a high eerie voice:

> "Abracadabra,
> Purple and green,
> This little boy
> Will grow up mean."

"Did you just make that up?" Jessie asked.

"Yes."

"It's very good."

"I think so, too," Mary Martha said modestly. "We could make up a whole bunch of them about all the people we hate. Who will we start with?"

"Uncle Howard."

"I didn't know you hated your Uncle Howard."

Jessie looked surprised, as if she hadn't known it herself until she heard her own voice say so. She stole a quick glance at Mike to see if he was listening, but he was engrossed in the ball game, his eyes closed. She said, "You won't ever tell anyone, will you?"

"Cross my heart and hope to die. Now let's start the curse. You go first."

"No, you go first."

Mary Martha assumed her witchlike face and voice:

> "Abracadabra,
> Yellow and brown,
> Uncle Howard's the nastiest
> Man in town."

"I don't like that one very much," Jessie said soberly.

"Why not?"

"Oh, I don't know. Let's play another game."

From the street a horn began to blow, repeating a pattern of three short, two long.

"That's my mother," Mary Martha said. "We'd better wake Mike up and tell him we're leaving."

"I'm awake, you numbskull," Mike said, opening his eyes and turning down the volume of the radio. Then he looked at his watch. "It's only a quarter after twelve. She's not supposed to be here until one." He rolled over on his back and got up. "Well, who am I to argue with good fortune? Come on, little darlings. Off to the launching pad."

"You don't have to come with us," Jessie said.

"No kidding? You mean you can actually walk out of here without breaking both your legs? I don't believe it. Show me."

"Oh, shut up."

"Yes, you shut up," Mary Martha added loyally.

The two girls went out through the stone arch, arm in arm, as if to show their solidarity against the enemy.

Mike waited a couple of minutes before following them. He saw Mrs. Oakley standing on the curb talking to them, then Mary Martha and her mother got into the car and Jessie turned and walked back to the playground, alone. She was holding her head high and her face was carefully and deliberately blank.

Mike said, "What's the matter?"

"We're not going to the Museum today."

"Why not?"

"Mrs. Oakley has some errands to do in town. Mary Martha didn't want to go along but she had to."

"Why?"

"Mrs. Oakley won't leave her at the playground alone any more."

"What does she mean, alone?" Mike said, scowling. *"I'm* here."

"I guess she meant without a grownup."

"For Pete's sake, what does she think I am? A two-year-old child? Man, oh man, women sure are hard to figure. . . . Well, come on, no use hanging around here any more. Let's go home."

"All right."

"Aren't you even going to argue?"

"No."

"You're sick, kid."

"I'm sorry," Kate Oakley repeated for the third or fourth time. "I hate to disappont you and Jessie but I can't help it. Something unexpected came up and I must deal with it. You understand that, don't you?"

Mary Martha nodded. "But I could have stayed at the playground with Jessie while you were dealing."

"I want you with me."

"Why? To protect you?"

"No," Kate said with a sharp little laugh. "You've got it all wrong, sweetikins. *I'm* protecting *you*. What on earth gave you the silly idea that I need your protection?"

"I don't know."

"Sometimes your mind works in a way that truly baffles me. I mean, really, angel, it doesn't make sense that I need your protection, does it? I am a grownup and you're a little girl. Isn't that right?"

"Yes, ma'am," Mary Martha said politely. She would have liked to ask what her mother was protecting her from, but she was aware that Kate was already upset. The signs were all there: some subtle, like the faint rash that was spreading across her neck; some obvious, like the oversized sunglasses she was wearing. Mary Martha didn't understand why her mother put on these sunglasses when she was under pressure, she knew only that it was a fact. Even in the house on a dark day Kate sometimes wore them and Mary Martha had come to hate the sight of them. They were like a wall or a closed door behind which untold, untellable things were happening. If you threw questions at this wall they bounced back like ping-pong balls: *what on earth do you mean, lamb?*

They had reached the center of town by this time. Kate drove into the parking lot behind the white four-story building where Mac had his office. It was the first inkling Mary Martha had of where her mother was going and she dreaded the thought of waiting in Mac's outer office, listening to the rise and fall of voices, never hearing quite enough and never understanding quite enough of what she heard. If the voices became distinct enough, Miss Edgeworth, Mac's receptionist, started talking loudly and cheerfully about the weather and how Mary Martha was doing in school and what a pretty dress she was wearing.

When her mother got out of the car Mary Martha made no move to follow her.

"Well?" Kate said. "Aren't you coming?"

"I can wait here."

"No. I don't like the look of that parking-lot attendant. You can't trust these—"

"Or I could go to the library and maybe start on one of my book reports."

"I don't think a nine-year-old should be wandering around downtown by herself."

"The library's only a block away."

Kate hesitated. "Well, all right. But you've got to promise you'll go straight there, not loiter in the stores or anything. And once you're there, you're to stay. No matter how long I am, don't come looking for me, just wait right there."

"I promise."

"You're a good girl, Mary Martha."

Mary Martha got out of the car. She was glad that her mother called her a good girl but she couldn't understand why she said it in such a strange, sad voice, as if having a good child was somehow harder to bear than having a bad one. She wondered what would happen if she turned bad. Maybe Kate would give her to Sheridan and that would be the end of the fighting over the divorce terms. Or maybe Sheridan wouldn't want her either, and she'd have to go and live with a foster family like the Brants and be Jessie's almost-sister.

Once the idea occurred to her, the temptation to try being bad was irresistible. The problem was how to begin. She thought of loitering in the stores, but she wasn't sure what loitering was or if she could do it. Then she heard her mother say, "I don't know what I'd do without you, Mary Martha," and the temptation died as suddenly as it had been born. She felt rather relieved. Loitering in stores didn't sound like much fun and probably the Brants couldn't afford to feed another mouth anyway.

Kate went in the rear entrance of the building and up the service stairs to avoid meeting anyone. After the bright light of noon the stairway seemed very dark. She stumbled once or twice but she didn't remove her sunglasses, she didn't even think of it. By the time she reached Mac's office on the third floor she was breathing hard and fast and the rash on her neck had begun to itch.

Miss Edgeworth was out to lunch. Her typewriter was covered and her desk was bare of papers, as though she'd tidied everything up in case she decided never to come back.

The door of Mac's office was open and he was sitting at his desk with his chair swiveled around to face the window. He was eating a sandwich, very slowly, as if he didn't like it or else liked it so much he didn't want to reach the end of it. Kate had known him for over twenty years and it seemed to her that he hadn't changed at all since she first met him. He was still as thin as a rake, and his hair was still brown and curly and cut very short to deny the curl. He had the reddish tan and bleached eyes of a sailor.

"Mac?"

He turned in surprise. "I didn't hear the elevator."

"I used the back steps."

"Well, come in, Kate, if you don't mind watching me eat. There's extra coffee, would you like some?"

"Yes, please."

He poured some coffee into a plastic cup. "Sit down. You look a bit under the weather, Kate. You're not dieting, I hope."

"Not by choice," she said grimly. "The support check's late again. Naturally. He's trying to make me crawl. That I'm used to, that I can stand. It's these—these awful other things, Mac."

"Have you seen him today?"

"About half an hour ago, on my way here. He was driving

that same old green car he drove yesterday when he was parked outside the house. When I saw it in the rear-view mirror, something terrible came over me, Mac. I—I just wanted to *kill* him."

"Now, now, don't talk like that."

"I mean it. All I could think of was chasing him, ramming his car, running him down, getting rid of him some way, any way."

"But you didn't."

"I tried."

"You tried," he repeated thoughtfully. "Tell me about it, Kate."

She told him. He listened, with his head cocked to one side like a dog hearing a distant sound of danger.

"You might have been killed or seriously injured," he said when she'd finished.

"I know that now. I may even have known it then, but it didn't matter. I wasn't thinking of myself, or even, God help me, of Mary Martha. Just of him, Sheridan. I wanted to—I *had* to get even with him. This time he went too far."

"This time?"

"The letter, the anonymous letter."

"Have you got it with you?"

"Yes."

"Show it to me."

She took the letter out of her handbag and put it on his desk.

He studied the envelope for a minute, then removed the wad of paper and began unfolding it. He read aloud: "Your daughter takes too dangerous risks with her delicate body. Children must be guarded against the cruel hazards of life and fed good, nourishing food so their bones will be padded. Also clothing. You should put plenty of clothing on her, keep arms and legs covered, etc. In the name of God please take better care of your little girl."

"Well?" Kate said.

He leaned back in his chair and looked up at the ceiling. "It's a curious document. The writer seems sincere and also very fond—if fond is the correct word—of children in general."

"Why in general? Why not Mary Martha in particular? Sheridan's never particularly liked children; he's crazy about Mary Martha because she's an extension of his ego, such as it is."

"This doesn't sound like Sheridan's style to me, Kate."

"Who else would accuse me of neglecting my daughter?"

"I don't read this as an accusation, exactly. It seems more like a plea or a warning, as if the writer believes he has advance knowledge that something will happen to Mary Martha unless you take preventative steps." Alarmed by her sudden pallor, he added quickly, "Notice I said he *believes* he has such knowledge. Beliefs often have little relationship to fact. My own feeling is that this is from some neighborhood nut. Have you or Mary Martha had any unpleasantness with any of your neighbors recently?"

"Of course not. We mind our own business and I expect other people to mind theirs."

"Perhaps you expect too much," Mac said with a shrug. "Well, I wouldn't worry about the letter if I were you. It's unlikely, though not impossible, that Sheridan wrote it. If he did, he's flipped faster and further than I care to contemplate."

"Will you find out the truth?"

"Naturally I'll try to contact him. If he's pulling these shenanigans he's got to be stopped, for his own sake as well as yours and Mary Martha's. Meanwhile I'll keep the letter, with your permission. I have a friend who's interested in such things. By the way, was it folded half a dozen times like this when it was delivered?"

"Yes."

"Kid stuff, I'd say. Just one more question, Kate. Did you manage to get the license number of the green car?"

"Yes. It's GVK 640."

"You're sure of that?"

"I should be," she said harshly. "I rammed his license plate."

"Kate. Kate, listen to me for a minute."

"No. I can't. I can't listen any more. I want to talk, I've got to *talk* to somebody. Don't you understand, Mac? I spend all my time with a child. She's a wonderful girl, very bright and sweet, but she's only nine years old. I can't discuss things with her, I can't burden her with my problems or ask her for help or support. I've got to put up a front, pretend that everything's all right, even when I can feel the very earth crumbling under my feet."

"You've isolated yourself, Kate," he said calmly. "You used to have friends you could talk to."

"Friends are a luxury I can't afford any more. Oh, people were very kind when Sheridan first moved out. They invited me over to cheer me up and hear all the gruesome details. One thing I learned, Mac, and learned well: the only people who really enjoy a divorce are your best friends. All that vicarious excitement and raw emotion, all the blood and guts spilled—why, it was almost as good as television."

"You're being unfair to them."

"Perhaps. Or perhaps I didn't have the right kind of friends. Anyway, I stopped accepting invitations and issuing them. I didn't want people coming over and feeling sorry for me because I was alone, and sorry for themselves because I couldn't afford to offer them drinks. You want to lose friends, Mac? Stop buying liquor. No money down, results guaranteed."

"What about Mary Martha?" Mac said.

"What about her?"

"She needs some kind of social environment."

"She has friends. One friend in particular, Jessie Brant. I don't especially care for the Brants—Ellen's one of these pushy modern types—but Jessie's an interesting child, free-wheeling and full of beans. I think she's a good influence on Mary Martha, who's inclined to be overcautious. . . . That's another thing about the letter, Mac. It was inaccurate. Mary Martha doesn't take dangerous risks, and I certainly wouldn't call her delicate. She's the same age and height as Jessie but she outweighs her by eight or ten pounds."

"Perhaps the 'risks' mentioned didn't refer to a physical activity like tree-climbing, but to something else that Mary Martha did. Say, for instance, that she was a little reckless while riding her bike and one of the neighbors had to swerve his car to avoid hitting her—"

"Mary Martha is very careful on her bicycle."

"Yes. Well, it was only a suggestion."

She was silent for a minute. Then she said in a low bitter voice, "You see? It's happened the way it always does. I was talking about myself, and now we're suddenly talking about Mary Martha again. There is no me any more. There's just the woman who lives in the big house who looks after the little girl. I've lost my personhood. I might just as well have a number instead of a name."

"Calm down now, Kate, and get hold of yourself."

"I told you, myself doesn't exist any more. There is no me, there's nothing to get hold of."

In the outer office Miss Edgeworth had come back from lunch. As soon as she'd found out that Mrs. Oakley had made an appointment with Mac, she'd gone out and bought two chocolate bars to give to Mary Martha. When she saw that Mrs. Oakley hadn't brought Mary Martha along after all, Miss Edgeworth was so relieved she ate both of the chocolate bars herself.

(9)

After the noon lunchers departed and before the one o'clock lunchers arrived there was always a short lull in the cafeteria which Ben managed for the owner. Ben used this period to stand out in the alley behind the cafeteria and soak up a little sun and smoke his only cigarette of the day. Ben didn't enjoy smoking but he became sick of food odors and he believed that smoking would dull his sense of smell.

He watched a flock of seagulls circling overhead, waiting for a handout. He thought what a fine day it was for the beginning of his new life. Charlie was engaged. Charlie and Louise were going to be married. Ben had told the good news to his employees and some of his regular customers, and though most of them didn't even know Charlie, they were pleased because Ben was. The whole place seemed livelier. A wedding was in the air, it hardly mattered whose.

Ben leaned against the sunny wall, letting the smoke curl up through his nostrils like ether. He felt a little dizzy. He wasn't sure whether it was from the cigarette or from the surges of happiness that had been sweeping over him off and on all morning. *I'll let Louise and Charlie have the house, Mother always planned it that way. I'll get a little apartment down near the beach and buy a dog. I've always wanted a dog. I could have bought one years ago—Charlie would never have mistreated an animal, he's crazy about animals—but I never got around to it. I don't know the reason. Why, Charlie would cut off his right arm before he'd hurt a dog.*

"Ben."

At the sound of his name Ben turned, although he didn't recognize the voice. It was a little boy's voice, high and thin, not like Charlie's at all. Yet it was Charlie running toward him, down the alley from the street. His clothes were disheveled and he was clutching his stomach with both hands as though he were suffering an acute attack of cramps. Ben felt the happiness draining out of him. All the pores of his skin were like invisible wounds from which his life was spurting.

"What's—the matter, Charlie?"

"Oh God, Ben. Something terrible. She tried to kill me. A woman, a woman in a little blue car. I swear to God, Ben, she meant to kill me and I don't even know her, I never saw her before."

"Sshhh." Ben looked quickly up and down the alley. "Keep your voice down. Someone might hear you."

"But it's true! I didn't imagine it. I don't imagine things like that, ever. Other things, maybe, but not—"

"Calm down and tell me about it, quietly."

"Yes. Yes, I will, Ben. Anything you say."

"Take a deep breath."

"Yes."

"Now where did this happen?"

Charlie leaned against the wooden rubbish bin. His whole body was shaking and the more he tried to control it, the more violently it shook, as though the lines of communication between his brain and his muscles had been cut. "I d-don't remember the name of the street but it was over on the north side. I'd gone to Pinewood Park to eat my lunch."

"Why?"

"Why?" Charlie repeated. "Well, for the fresh air. Sun and fresh air, they're nice, they're good for you. Didn't you tell me that, Ben?"

"Yes. *Yes.* Now go on."

"I was driving back to work and this little blue car was in front of me, with a lady at the wheel. She was going real slow like maybe she was drunk and trying to be extra careful to avoid an accident. Well, I passed her. That's all I did, Ben, I just passed her."

"You didn't honk your horn?"

"No."

"Or look at her in a way that she might have—well, mis-interpreted?"

"*No.* I swear to you, Ben, I just *passed* her. Then I heard this terrible sound of gears and I looked around and she was after me. I stepped on the gas to get away from her."

"Why?"

"What else could I have done? What would you have done?"

"Pulled over to the curb, or into a gas station, and asked the lady what the hell she thought she was doing."

"I never thought of that," Charlie said earnestly. "When someone chases me, I run."

"Yes, I guess you do." Ben wiped the sweat off his forehead with the back of his hand. Only a few minutes ago the sun had been like a warm, kindly friend. Now it was his enemy. It stabbed his eyes and temples and burned the top of his head where his hair was thinning, and the dry tender skin around his mouth. It imprisoned him in the alley with the smell of cooking food and the smell of Charlie's fear.

He lit another cigarette and blew the smoke out through his nostrils to deaden them. It was when he threw away the spent match that he noticed the little plant growing out of a crack in the concrete a yard or so from where Charlie was standing. It was about six inches high. It was covered with city dust and some of its leaves had been squashed by the wheel of a car, but it was still growing, still alive. He was filled with a sense of wonder. The little plant had nothing going for it at all: seeded by accident out of garbage, driven over, walked on, unwatered, with no rain since March, it was still alive.

He said, "Everything's going to be O.K., Charlie. Don't worry about it. Things work out one way or another."

"But what do I do now, Ben?"

"Get back on the job or you'll be late."

"I can't use my own car."

"What's the matter with it?"

"Nothing," Charlie said. "The engine's running fine, only— well, here's how I figure it, Ben. That woman, she couldn't have anything against me when I don't even know her. So it must be the car. She has a grudge against the former owner and she thought he was driving, not me. So it seems obvious what I've got to do now."

"To you, perhaps. Not to me."

"Don't you see, Ben? Everything will be solved if I buy a new car. Oh, not a brand-new one but a different one so that woman won't chase me again."

If there was a woman, Ben thought, *and if there was a chase. Maybe he invented the whole thing as an excuse to change cars again.* "You can't afford to buy a car now," he said bluntly, "with the wedding coming up so soon."

Charlie looked surprised as if he'd forgotten all about the wedding. "I have money in the bank."

"You'll be needing it to buy Louise's ring, pay for the honeymoon, buy yourself some new clothes—"

"I'm old enough to make my own decisions," Charlie said, kicking the side of the rubbish bin. "I'm an engaged man. An engaged man has to plan things for himself."

Ben looked down at the little tomato plant growing out of the crack in the concrete. "Yes. Yes, I suppose he does."

"Thank you, Ben. I really do thank you."

"What for?"

"For everything. Even just for being around."

"You're an engaged man now, Charlie. I'm not going to be around much longer. You and Louise will be making a life of your own."

One of the Mexican busboys came out into the alley and said something to Ben in Spanish. The boy spoke softly, smiled softly, moved softly. Ben gave him fifty cents and the boy went back inside.

Charlie had paid no attention to the interruption. His eyes were fixed on Ben's face and his thin silky brows were stitched together in a frown. "You talk as if everything's going to change between us. But it's not. You'll be living with Louise and me, we'll be eating our meals together and playing cards in the evening the way we used to. Why should we let things change?"

"Things change whether we let them or not. And that's good —it keeps us from getting bored with life and with each other."

"But I'm *not* bored."

"Listen to me, Charlie. I won't be living with you and Louise, first because I don't want to, and second, because Louise wouldn't want me to, and third be—"

"Louise wouldn't mind. She's crazy about you, Ben. Why, I bet when you come right down to it, she'd just as soon marry you as marry me."

Ben reached out and grabbed him by the shoulder. "Goddam it, don't you talk like that. It's not fair to Louise. Do you hear me?"

"Yes," Charlie said in a whisper. "But I was only—"

"Sure, you were *only*. You're always *only*. You know what happens when you're *only*? Things get so fouled up—"

"I'm sorry, Ben."

"Yeah. Sure. Well."

"I only meant it as a compliment, to show you how much Louise likes you and that she wouldn't mind at all if you lived with us."

Ben took a deep drag on his cigarette. "I have to go back inside."

"You're not really mad at me?"

"No."

"And it's O.K. if I buy another car, say right after work?"

"It's your money."

"Wouldn't you like to come along and give me advice on what make and model to get and things like that?"

"Not this time."

Charlie heard the finality in his voice and he knew Ben meant *not this time and not any time ever again.*

He watched Ben go back into the cafeteria kitchen and he felt like a child abandoned in the middle of a city, in a strange noisy alley filled with the clatter of dishes and the clanking of pots and pans, and voices shouting, in Spanish, words he couldn't understand.

I'm frightened. Help me, Ben!

Not this time. Not any time ever again.

The two Charlies walked, together but not quite in step, down the alley and into the street, the engaged man about to buy a new car, and the little boy looking for a little girl to play with.

(10)

Miss Albert first noticed the child because she was so neat and quiet. Most of the children who came to the library during summer vacation wore jeans or shorts with cotton T-shirts, as if they were using the place as a rest stop between beach and ball game, movie and music lesson. In groups or alone, they were always noisy and always chewing something—chocolate bars, bubble gum, peanut brittle, apples, ice cream cones, bananas, occasionally even cotton candy. Miss Albert had a recurrent nightmare in which she opened up one of the valuable art books and found all the pages glued together with cotton candy.

The little girl with the blond pontytail was not chewing anything. She wore a pink dress with large blue daisies embroidered on the patch pockets. Her shoes had the sick-white color that indicated too many applications of polish to cover too many cracks in the leather. The child's expression was blank, as if her hair was drawn back and fastened so tightly that her facial muscles couldn't function. *It must be just like having your hair pulled all the time,* Miss Albert thought. *I wouldn't like it one bit. She probably doesn't either, poor child.*

The girl picked a magazine from the rack and sat down. She opened it, turned a few pages, then closed it again and sat with it on her lap, her eyes moving from the main door to the clock on the mezzanine and back again. The obvious conclusion was that the girl was waiting for someone. But Miss Albert didn't care for the obvious; she preferred the elaborate, even the bizarre. The child's family had just arrived in town, possibly to get away from a scandal of some kind—what kind Miss Albert would decide on her lunch hour—and the girl, alone and friendless, had come to the library for the children's story hour at half past one. But Miss Albert was not satisfied with this explanation. The girl had no look of anticipation on her face, no look of anything, thanks to that silly hair-do. *She'd be cute as a bug with her hair cut just below her ears and a fluffy bang. Or maybe with an Alice-in-Wonderland style like Louise, except on Louise it looks ridiculous at her age. Imagine Louise getting married, I think it's just wonderful. It shows practically anything can happen if you wait long enough.*

Half an hour passed. Miss Albert's stomach was rumbling and her arms were tired from taking books from her metal cart and putting them back on their proper shelves. From the children's section adjoining the main reading room, she could hear a rising babble of voices and the scrape of chairs being rearranged. In ten minutes the story hour would begin and Mrs. Gambetti, with nothing to do at children's checkout, would come and relieve Miss Albert for lunch. And Miss Albert would take her sandwich and Thermos of coffee over to Encinas Park to watch the people with their sandwiches and their Thermoses of coffee.

But I really can't leave the child just sitting there, she thought. *Very likely she doesn't know where to go and she's probably too timid to ask, having been through all that scandal whatever it was but I'm sure it was quite nasty.*

Miss Albert pushed her empty cart vigorously down the aisle like a determined week-end shopper. At the sound of its squeaking wheels, Mary Martha turned her head and met Miss Albert's kindly and curious gaze.

Miss Albert said, "Hello."

Mary Martha had been instructed not to speak to strangers but she didn't think this would apply to strangers in a library, so she said, "Hello," back.

"What's your name?"

"Mary Martha Oakley."

"That's very pretty. You're new around here, aren't you, Mary?"

The child didn't answer, she just looked down at her shoes. Her toes had begun to wiggle nervously like captive fish. She didn't want the lady to notice so she attempted to hide her feet under the chair. During the maneuver, the magazine slid off her lap onto the floor.

Miss Albert picked it up, trying not to look surprised that a child so young would choose *Fortune* as reading material. "Did you move to town recently, Mary?"

"I'm not supposed to answer when people call me Mary because my name is Mary *Martha.* But I guess it's all right in a library. We didn't move to town, we've always lived here."

"Oh. I thought—well, it doesn't matter. The story hour is beginning in a minute or two. You just go through that door over there"—Miss Albert pointed—"and turn to the right and take a seat. Any seat you like."

"I already have a seat."

"But you can't hear the story from this distance."

"No, ma'am."

"You don't want to hear the story?"

"No, ma'am, I'm waiting for my mother."

Miss Albert concealed her disappointment behind a smile. "Well, perhaps you'd like something to read that would be a little more suitable for your age bracket."

Mary Martha hesitated, frowning. "Do you have books about everything?"

"Pretty nearly everything, from aardvarks to zulus. What kind of book are you interested in?"

"One about divorce."

"Divorce?" Miss Albert said with a nervous little laugh. "Goodness, I'm not sure I— Wouldn't you like a nice picture book to look at instead?"

"No, ma'am."

"Well, I'm afraid I don't—that is, perhaps we'd better ask Miss Lang in the reference department. She knows more about such situations than I do. Come on, I'll take you over and introduce you."

Behind the reference desk Louise was acting very busy but Miss Albert wasn't fooled. Checking the number of sheep in Australia or the name of the capital of Ghana hadn't put the color in her cheeks and the dreamy, slightly out-of-focus look in her eyes.

"I hope I'm not interrupting anything," Miss Albert said, knowing very well she was, but feeling that it was the kind of thing that should be interrupted, especially during working hours. "This is Mary Martha Oakley, Louise. Mary Martha, this is Miss Lang."

Louise stared at the girl and said, "Oh," in a cold way that puzzled Miss Albert because Louise was usually very good with children.

"Mary Martha," Miss Albert added, "wants a book on divorce."

"Does she, indeed," Louise said. "Am I to gather, Miss Albert, that you've encouraged the child in her request by bringing her over here?"

"Not exactly. My gosh, Louise, I thought you'd get a kick out of it, a laugh."

"You know the rules of the library as well as I do, or you should. You're excused now, Miss Albert."

"Good," Miss Albert said crisply. "It happens to be my lunch hour."

Over Mary Martha's head she gave Louise a dirty look, but Louise wasn't even watching. Her eyes were still fixed on Mary Martha, as if they were seeing much more than a little girl in a pink dress with daisies.

"Oakley," she said in a thin, dry voice. "You live at 319 Jacaranda Road?"

"Yes, ma'am."

"With your mother."

"Yes."

"And your little dog."

"I don't have a little dog," Mary Martha said uneasily. "Just a cat named Pudding."

"But there's a dog in your neighborhood, isn't there? A little brown mongrel that chases cars?"

"I never saw any."

"Never? Perhaps you don't particularly notice dogs."

"Oh yes, I do. I always notice dogs because they're my favorites even more than cats and birds."

"So if you had one, you'd certainly protect it, wouldn't you?"

"Yes, ma'am."

Louise leaned across the desk and spoke in a smiling, confidential whisper. "If I had a dog that chased cars, I wouldn't be anxious to admit it, either. So of course I can't really blame you for fibbing. Just between the two of us, though—"

But there was nothing between the two of them. The child, wary-eyed and flushed, began backing away, her hands jammed deep in her pockets as if they were seeking the roots of the embroidered daisies. Ten seconds later she had disappeared out the front door.

Louise watched the door, in the wild hope that the girl would decide to come back and change her story—yes, she had a little dog that chased cars; yes, one of the cars was an old green Ford coupé.

There was a dog, there had to be, because Charlie said so. It had chased his car and Charlie, afraid for the animal's safety, felt that he should warn the owner. That's why he wanted to find out who lived at 319 Jacaranda Road. What other reason could he possibly have had?

He's not a liar, she thought. *He's so devastatingly honest sometimes it breaks my heart.*

She rubbed her eyes. They were dry and gritty and in need of tears. It was as if dirt, blowing in from the busy street, had altered her vision and blurred the distinctions between fact and fantasy.

"Don't talk so fast, lamb," Kate Oakley said. "Now let me get this straight. She asked you if you had a little brown dog that chased cars?"

Mary Martha nodded.

"And she wouldn't believe you when you denied it?"

"No, ma'am."

"It's crazy, that's what it is. I declare, I think the whole world has gone stark staring mad except you and me." She spoke with a certain satisfaction, as if the world was getting no more than it deserved and she was glad she'd stepped out of it in time and taken Mary Martha with her. "You'd expect a librarian, of all people, to be sensible, with all those books around."

Immediately after Kate's departure, Ralph MacPherson made two telephone calls. The first was to the apartment where Sheridan Oakley claimed to be living. He let the phone ring a dozen times, but, as on the previous afternoon and evening, there was no answer.

The second call was to Lieutenant Gallantyne of the city police department. After an exchange of greetings, Mac came to the point:

"I'm in the market for a favor, Gallantyne."

"That's no switch," Gallantyne said. "What is it?"

"A client of mine claims that her husband, from whom she's separated, is harassing her and her child. She says he's driving around town in a green Ford coupé, six or seven years old, license GVK 640."

"And?"

"I want to know if he is."

"All I can do is check with Sacramento and find out who owns the car. That may take some time, unless you can come up with a more urgent reason than the one you've given me, say like murder, armed robbery—"

"Sorry, no armed robbery or murder. Just a divorce, with complications."

"I think your cases are often messier than mine are," Gallantyne said with a trace of envy.

"Could be. We'll have to get together on one sometime."

"Let's do that. Now, you want us to contact Sacramento about the green Ford?"

"Yes, but meanwhile pass the license number around to the traffic boys. If they spot the car anywhere I'd like to hear about it, any time of the day or night. I have an answering service."

"What's that license again?"

"GVK, God's Very Kind, 640."

He bought the new car right after work, a three-year-old dark, inconspicuous sedan. As soon as he got behind the wheel he felt safe and secure as though he'd acquired a whole new body and nobody would recognize the old Charlie any more. He felt quite independent, too. He had chosen the car by himself, with no help from Ben, and he had paid for it with his own money. The used-car salesman had taken his check without hesitation as if he couldn't help but trust a man with such an honest face as Charlie's. And Charlie, inspired by this trust, was absolutely convinced that the car had been driven only 10,000 cautious miles by one owner and a Detroit-trained garage mechanic at that. A man so skillful, Charlie reasoned, would have practically no spare time and that would account for the extremely low mileage on the car.

It seemed to him that the salesman, who had paid little attention to him when he first started browsing around the lot, noticed the change in him, too. He started to call him sir.

"I hope you'll be very happy with your car, sir."

"Oh, I will. I already am."

"There's no better advertising than a satisfied customer," the salesman said. "The only trouble with selling a man a good car like this is that we don't see him around for a long time. Good luck and safe driving to you, sir."

"Thank you very much."

"It was a pleasure."

Charlie eased the car out into the street. It was getting quite late and he knew Ben would be starting to worry about him, but he didn't want to go home just yet. He wanted to drive around, to get the feel of his new car and test the strength of his new body before he exposed either to Ben or Louise. They would both be suspicious, Ben of the car and the salesman and the garage mechanic, Louise of the change in him. He realized, in a vague way, that Louise didn't really want him to change, that she was dependent on his weakness though he couldn't understand why.

When he started out, he had, at the conscious level, no destination in mind. At crossroads he made choices seemingly unconnected with what he was thinking. He turned left because the car in front of him did; he turned right to watch a flock of blackbirds feeding on a lawn; he went straight because the road crossed a creek and he liked bridges; he turned left again because the setting sun hurt his eyes. The journey took on an air of adventure, as if the streets, the bridge, the blackbirds, the setting sun were all strange to him and he was a stranger to them. He wasn't lost—nobody could get lost in San Felice where the mountains were to the east and the sea to the west, with one or the other, or both, always visible—he was deliberately misplaced, as if he were playing a game of hide-and-seek with Ben and Louise. An hour must have passed since the game started. *Ready or not, you must be caught, hiding around the goal or not.*

The sun had gone down. Wisps of fog were floating in from the sea and gathering in the treetops like spiders' webs. It was time to turn on the headlights but he wasn't sure which button to press, there were so many of them on the dashboard. He pulled over to the curb and stopped the car about fifty feet from an intersection. The intersection looked familiar to him although he didn't recognize it. It wasn't until he switched on the headlights and their beam caught the street sign and held it, that he knew where he was. Jacaranda Road, 300 block.

He felt a sudden and terrible pain in his head. He heard his own voice in his ears but he couldn't tell whether it was a whisper or a scream.

"Ben! Louise! Come and find me, I'm not hiding. It's not a game any more. Help me. Come and take me home, Louise, don't leave me in this bad place. You don't know, nobody knows, how bad—dirty—dirty bad—"

At 8:30 the phone rang and Ben, who'd been sitting beside it for a long time, answered on the first ring.

"Hello."

"Ben, this is Louise. Charlie was supposed to pick me up half an hour ago. He may have forgotten, so I thought I'd call and jog his memory a bit."

"He's not here."

"Well, he's probably on his way then. I'll just go wait on the steps for him. It's a nice night."

"It's cold."

"No, it's not," Louise said, laughing. "You know how it is when you're in love, Ben. All the weather is wonderful."

"You'd better stay in the house, Louise. I don't think he's on his way over."

"Why not? Is something the matter?"

"I'm not sure," Ben said in his slow careful voice. "He came to the cafeteria at noon with some crazy—a far-fetched story about a strange woman trying to kill him with her car. I didn't know how much of it, if any, to believe. He may have invented the whole thing as an excuse to buy a new car. You know Charlie, he can't just go ahead and do something; he has to have a dozen reasons why, no matter how nutty some of them are. Anyway, he told me he was going to buy a new car after work."

"He got off work three and a half hours ago. How long does it usually take him to buy a car?"

"Judging from past performance, I'd say five minutes. He sees one he likes the look of, kicks a couple of the tires, sounds the horn, and that's it. It can be the worst old clunker in town but he buys it."

"Then he should be home by now."

"Yes."

"Ben, I'm coming over."

"What good will that do? It will simply mean two of us sitting around worrying instead of one. No, you stay where you are, Louise. Get interested in something. Read a book, wash your hair, call a girl friend, anything."

"I can't. I won't."

"Look, Louise, I don't want to be brutal about this, but waiting for Charlie is something you must learn to handle gracefully. You may be doing quite a bit of it. Ten chances to one, he's O.K., he's just gotten interested in something and—"

"I can't afford to bet on it, even at those odds," Louise said and hung up before he could argue any further.

She went down the hall toward her bedroom to pick up a coat. All the weather was wonderful, but sometimes it paid to carry a coat.

She walked quickly and quietly past the open door of the shoebox-sized dining room where her parents were still lingering over coffee and the evening paper, going line by line over the local news, the obituaries and divorces and marriages, the water connections and delinquent tax notices and building permits and real estate transfers. But she didn't move quietly enough. *No one could,* she thought bitterly. *Not even the stealthiest cat, not even if the carpet were velvet an inch thick.*

"Louise?" her father called out. "Are you still here, Louise?"

"Yes, Daddy."

"I thought you were going out tonight."

"I am. I'm just leaving now."

"Without saying good-bye to your parents? Has this great romance of yours made you forget your manners? Come in here a minute."

Louise went as far as the door. Her parents were seated side by side at the table with the newspaper spread out in front of them, like a pair of school children doing their homework together.

Mr. Lang rose to his feet and made a kind of half-bow in Louise's direction. For as long as Louise could remember he had been doing this whenever she entered a room. But his politeness was too elaborate, as if, by treating her like a princess, he was actually calling attention to her commonness.

Louise stared at him, wondering how she could ever have been impressed by his silly posturings or affected by his small, obvious cruelties. She said nothing, knowing that he hated silence because his weapon was his tongue.

"I understood," he said finally, "that this was the night your mother and I were to congratulate our prospective son-in-law. Am I to assume the happy occasion has been postponed?"

"Yes."

"What a pity. I had looked forward to some of his stimulating conversation: yes, Mr. Lang; no, Mr. Lang—"

"Good night."

"Wait a minute. I haven't finished."

"Yes, you have," Louise said and walked down the hall and out the front door. For once, she was grateful for her father's cruelty. It had saved her from trying to explain where Charlie was and why he hadn't kept their date.

Ben must have been watching for her from the front window because as soon as she pulled up to the curb in front of the house he came out on the porch and down the steps.

To the question in her eyes he shook his head. Then, "You might as well go home, Louise."

"No."

"All right. But it's silly to start driving around looking for him when I haven't the slightest idea where he is."

"I have," she said quietly. "It's just a feeling, a hunch. It may be miles off but it's worth trying. We've got to find him, Ben. He needs us."

"He needs us." Ben got in the car and slammed the door shut. "Where have I heard that before? Charlie needs this, Charlie needs that, Charlie needs, period. Some day before I die, *I'm* going to have a need. Just once somebody's going to say, *Ben* needs this or that. Just once— Oh, what the hell, forget it. I don't really need anything."

"I do."

"What?"

"I need Charlie."

"Then I'm sorry for you," Ben said, striking his thigh with his fist. "I'm so sorry for you I could burst into tears. You're a decent, intelligent young woman, you deserve a life. What you're getting is a job."

"Don't waste any pity on me. I'm happy."

"You're happy even now, with Charlie missing and maybe in the kind of trouble only Charlie can get into?"

"He's alive—you'd have been notified if he'd been killed in an accident or anything—and as long as Charlie's alive, I'm happy."

"I'm not," he said bluntly. "In fact, there have been times, dozens, maybe hundreds of times, when I've thought the only solution for Charlie would be for him to step in front of a fast-moving truck. Before this is all over, you might be thinking the same thing."

"That's a—a terrible thing to say to me."

"I'm sorry, I had to do it. I didn't want to hurt you, but—"

"Isn't it funny how many times people don't want to hurt you, *but*?"

"I suppose it's pretty funny, yes."

She was staring straight ahead of her into the darkness but her eyes were squinting as if they were exposed to too much light. "Stop worrying about Charlie and me. If you want us to get married, give us your blessing and hope we'll muddle through all right. If you don't want us to get married, say so now, tonight."

"You have my blessing and my hope. I'm not much of a hoper, or a blesser either, but—"

"Sssh, no buts. They ruin everything." She smiled and touched his arm. "You see, Ben, you've been very good to Charlie. I think, though, that I'll be better *for* him."

"I hope so."

"Thanks for talking to me, and letting me talk. I feel calmer and more sure of myself, and of Charlie, than I ever have before. Good night, Ben."

"Good night? I thought we were going out to look for Charlie."

"You're not, I am. Looking for Charlie is my job now."

"All right." He got out of the car and stood on the curb with the door open, trying to decide whether to get back in. Then he leaned down and shut the door very firmly, as if this was a door he'd had trouble with in the past and he knew it needed a good slam to stay closed. "Good night, Louise."

If she said good night to him again he didn't hear it above the roar of the engine. She was out of sight before he reached the top of the steps.

He felt no sharp, sudden pain, only a terrible sadness creeping over him like fog over the city. He thought, *she's driving blind, following a wild hunch,* and he wondered how many hunches she would have before she gave up. One in twenty might be correct and she'd bank on that one, believing that she finally understood Charlie, that she'd pressed the right button and come up with the right answer. It would take her a long time to realize that with Charlie the buttons changed position without reason, and yesterday's answer was gibberish and today's only a one-in-twenty hunch.

Ben remembered the document word by word, though it had been years since he'd seen it:

> We are recommending the release of Charles Edward Gowen into the custody and care of his brother. We feel that Gowen has gained insight and control and is no longer a menace to himself or to others. Further psychiatric treatment within the closed environment of a hospital seems futile at this time. Gainful employment, family affection and outside interests are now necessary if he is to become a useful and self-sufficient member of society.

(12)

The fog thickened as she drove. Trees lost their tops, whole sections of the city disappeared, and street lights were no more than dim and dirty halos. But inside her mind everything was becoming very clear, as if the lack of visibility around her had forced her to look inward.

What she had called a hunch to Ben was now a conclusion based on a solid set of facts. Charlie was frightened beyond the understanding of anyone like Ben or herself; he was running away from Ben, from her, from marriage, from the responsibility of growing up. He must be treated like a scared boy, shown the dark room and taught that it had no more terrors than when it was light; he must be trusted even when trust was very difficult. But first he must be found because he was trying to escape into a world that seemed safe to him, that seemed to present no challenge. Yet it was a dangerous place for Charlie, this world of children.

Her hands were gripping the steering wheel so tightly that the muscles of her forearms ached, but she felt compelled to go on thinking calmly and reasonably, like a mathematician faced with a very long and difficult equation. *If I am to deal with this thing, if I am to help Charlie deal with it, I must know what it is. I must know. . . .*

Charlie had never even mentioned children to her, he never looked at them passing on the street or watched them playing in the park. Yet somehow, somewhere, he had seen the girl, Mary Martha, and found out where she lived. Louise remembered his excitement the previous night when he was talking about 319 Jacaranda Street and the little dog that chased cars. Well, there was no little dog; there was a child, Mary Martha. Charlie had said so himself and though Louise had deafened her ears at the time, his words rang in them now like the echo of tolling bells: *"It's funny she'd want to live alone in the big house with just a little girl."*

She wondered whether it had been a slip of the tongue or whether Charlie, in some corner of his mind, wanted her to know about it and was asking for her help.

"Oh God," she said aloud, "how do you help someone like Charlie?"

She found him at the corner of Toyon Drive and Jacaranda Road. He was leaning against the hood of a dark car she didn't recognize, his hands folded across his stomach, his head sunk low on his chest. A passing stranger might think he'd had engine trouble, had lifted the hood and discovered something seriously wrong and given up in despair.

Although he must have heard her car stop and her footsteps as she approached, he didn't move or open his eyes. Jacaranda petals clung thickly to his hair and his windbreaker. They looked very pale in the fog, like snowflakes that couldn't melt because they'd fallen on something as cold as they were.

She spoke his name very softly so she wouldn't startle him.

He opened his eyes and blinked a couple of times. "Is that— is that you, Louise?"

"Yes."

"I was calling you. Did you hear me?"

"No. Not in the way you mean. I heard, though, Charlie. I'll always hear you."

"How can you do that?"

"It's a secret."

He stood up straight and looked around him, frowning. "You shouldn't be here, Louise. It's a bad place for women and children. It's—well, it's just a bad place."

"The children are all safe in bed," she said with calm deliberation. "And, as a woman, I'm not afraid because I have you to look after me. It's awfully cold, though, and I'll admit I'd feel more comfortable at home. Will you take me home, Charlie?"

He didn't answer. He was staring down at the sidewalk, mute and troubled.

"You've bought a new car, Charlie."

"Yes."

"It's very sleek and pretty. I'd like a ride in it."

"No."

"You were calling me, Charlie. Why did you call me if you didn't want to see me?"

"I did, I do want to see you."

"But you won't drive me home?"

"No," he said, shaking his head. "It would be too complicated."

"Why?"

"Well, you see, there are two cars and two people, so each of the cars has to be driven by one person. That's just plain arithmetic, Louise."

"I suppose it is."

"If I take you home, your car will be left sitting here alone, and I told you what kind of place this is."

"It looks like a perfectly nice residential neighborhood to me, Charlie."

"That's on the surface. I see what's underneath. I see things so terrible, so—" He began to grind his fists into his eyes, as though he were trying to smash the images he saw into a meaningless pulp.

She caught his wrists and held them. "Stop it. Stop it, please."

"I can't."

"All right," she said steadily. "So you see terrible things. Perhaps they exist, in this neighborhood and in yourself. But you mustn't let them blind you to the good things and there are more of them, many more. When you take a walk in the country, you can't stop and turn over every stone. If you did, you'd miss the sky and the trees and the flowers and the birds. And to miss those would be a terrible thing in itself, wouldn't it?"

He was watching her, earnest and wide-eyed, like a child listening to a story. "Are there good things in me, Louise?"

"Too many for me to tell you."

"That's funny. I wonder if Ben knows."

"Ben knows."

"Is that why he never tells me about them? Because there are too many?"

"Yes."

"That's nice, that's very nice," he said, nodding. "I like that about the stones, Louise. Ben and I used to turn over a lot of stones when we went hiking in the mountains. We used to find some very interesting things under stones. No birds, naturally, but sow bugs and lizards and Jerusalem crickets. . . . I made a crazy mistake the first time I ever saw a young Jerusalem cricket. It lay there on its back in the ground, flesh-colored and wriggling its—well, they looked like arms and legs. And I thought it was a real human baby and that that was where they came from. When I asked Ben about it he told me the truth, but I didn't like it. It didn't seem nearly so pleasant or so natural as the idea of babies growing in the ground like flowers. If I could start all over again, I'd want to start like that, growing up out of the ground like a flower. . . . You're shivering, Louise. Are you cold?"

"Yes."

"I'll take you home."

"That's a good idea," she said soberly, as if it had not occurred to her before.

He opened the door for her and she got into the car. The seat covers felt cold and damp like something Charlie had found under a stone.

He walked around the front of the car. The headlights were still on and as he passed them he shielded his entire face with his hands like a man avoiding a pair of eyes too bright and knowing. But as soon as he got behind the wheel of the car and turned on the ignition, he began to relax and she thought, *the crisis is over. At least, one part of one crisis is over. That's all I dare ask right now.*

She said, "The engine sounds very smooth, Charlie."

"It does to me, too, but of course I'm not an expert like Ben. Ben will probably find a dozen things the matter with it."

"Then we won't listen to him."

"I don't have enough courage not to listen to Ben. In fact, I just don't have enough courage, period."

"That's not true," she said, thinking, *for people with problems, like Charlie, just to go on living from day to day requires more courage than is expected of any ordinary person.* "Does the fog bother you, Charlie?"

He gave a brief, bitter laugh. "Which fog, the one out there or the one in here?"

"Out there."

"I like it. I'd like to lose myself in it forever and that'd be the end of me, and good riddance."

"It would be the end of me too, Charlie. And I don't want to end yet. I feel I only began after I met you."

"Don't say that. It scares me. It makes me feel responsible for you, for your life. I'm not fit for that. Your life's too valuable and mine's not worth a—"

"All lives are valuable."

"Oh God, I can't *explain* to you. You won't *listen*."

"That's right, I won't listen."

"You're stubborn like Ben."

"No," she said, smiling. "I'm stubborn like myself."

For the next few blocks he didn't speak. Then, stopping for a red light, he blurted out, "I didn't mean it to be like this, Louise."

"Mean what to be like what?"

"Tonight, our date, the car. I was—I was going to come to your house and surprise you with the new car. But I decided I'd better drive around a bit first and get used to the motor so I wouldn't make any mistakes in front of you. I started out, not thinking of where or why, not thinking of anything. Then I stopped, I just stopped, I don't even remember if I had a reason. And there I was, in that place I hate. I hate it, Louise, I hate that place."

"Then you mustn't go there any more," she said calmly. "That makes sense, doesn't it, Charlie? To avoid what makes you feel miserable?"

"I didn't *go* there. I was led, I was driven. Don't you understand that, Louise?"

"I'm trying."

She watched the street lights step briskly out of the fog and back into it again like sentries guarding the greatness of the night. She wondered how much she could afford to understand Charlie and whether this was the time to try. Perhaps she might never have a better opportunity than now, with Charlie in a receptive mood, humble, wanting to change himself, and grateful to her for finding him.

She bided her time, saying nothing further until they arrived at her apartment house and Charlie parked the car at the curb. He reached for her hands and held them tightly in his own, against his chest. She almost lost her nerve then, he looked so tired and defenseless. She had to remind herself that it wasn't enough just to get by, to smooth things over for one day when there were thousands of days ahead of them. *I must do it,* she thought. *I can't hurt him any more than he's already hurting himself.*

"To me," she said finally, "Jacaranda Road is like any other. Why do you hate it, Charlie? Why do you call it a bad place?"

"Because it is."

"The whole street is?"

He let go of her hands as if they'd suddenly become too personal. "I don't want to dis—"

"Or just one block? Or perhaps one house?"

"Please stop. Please don't."

"I have to," she said. "The bad part, is it the house where the little Oakley girl lives with her mother?"

He kept shaking his head back and forth as though he could shake off the pain like a dog shaking off water. "I don't—don't know any Oakley girl."

"I think you do, Charlie. It would help you, it would help us both, if you'd tell me the truth."

"I don't know her," he repeated. "I've seen her, that's all."

"You've never approached her?"

"No."

"Or talked to her?"

"No."

"Then nothing whatever has happened," she said firmly. "You have no reason to feel so bad, so guilty. Nothing's *happened,* Charlie, that's the important thing. It doesn't make sense to feel guilty about something that hasn't even happened."

"Do you think it's that simple, Louise?"

"No. But I think it's where we have to start, dividing things into what's real and what isn't. You haven't harmed anyone. The Oakley girl is safe at home, and I believe that even if I hadn't found you when I did, she'd still be safe at home."

He was watching her like a man on trial watching a judge. "You honest to God believe that, Louise?"

"Yes, I do."

"Tell it to me again. Say it all over again."

She said it over again and he listened as if he'd been waiting all of his life to hear it. It wasn't like anything he would have heard from Ben: *"Can't you use your head for a change? You've got to avoid situations like that. God knows what might have happened."*

"Nothing happened," he said. "Nothing happened at all, Louise."

"I know."

"Will you—that is, I suppose you'll be telling Ben about all this business tonight."

"Not if you don't want me to."

"He wouldn't understand. Not because he's dumb or anything, but because I've disappointed him so often, he can't help expecting the worst from me. . . . You won't tell him where you found me?"

"No."

"How did you find me, Louise? Of all the places in the city, what made you go there?"

"A lucky guess based on a lucky coincidence," she said, smiling. "The little Oakley girl was in the library this afternoon. She wanted a special book and Miss Albert brought her to my department and introduced her to me. Since I'd just looked up who lived at 319 Jacaranda Road for you, I asked her if that was her address and she said yes. It was that simple."

"No, it couldn't have been. You couldn't have even guessed anything from just that much."

"Well, we talked a little."

"Not about me. She's never even seen me."

"We talked," Louise said, "about her cat. She doesn't own a dog."

He turned away from her and looked out the window though there was nothing to see but different shades of grayness. "That wasn't a very good lie about the little dog that chased cars, I guess."

"No, it wasn't."

"It's a funny thing, her coming to the library like that. It's as if someone planned it, God or Ben or—"

"Nobody planned it. Kids go to libraries and I work in one, that's all. . . . You see lots of little girls, Charlie. What made you—well, take a fancy to that particular one?"

"I don't know."

"Was it because she reminded you of me, Charlie? She reminded me of me right away, with those solemn eyes and that long fine blond hair."

"Blond?"

"Don't sound so incredulous. I used to be a regular towhead when I was a kid."

He put his hands on the steering wheel and held on tight like a racing driver about to reach a dangerous curve. *Blond,* he thought. *That crazy mother has dyed Jessie's hair blond. No, it's impossible. Jessie's hair is short, it couldn't have grown long in a day. A wig, then. One of those new wigs the young girls are wearing now—*

"There must be trouble in the family," Louise said. "Mary Martha wanted a book on divorce."

"Who?"

"The Oakley girl, Mary Martha. . . . You look upset, Charlie. I shouldn't go on talking about her like this, and I won't. I promise not to say another word." She pressed her cheek against his shoulder. "I love you so much, Charlie. Do you love me, too?"

"Yes."

"You're tired, though, aren't you?"

"Yes."

"Do you want to go home?"

"Yes," he said. *"Yes.* I—it's late, it's cold."

"I know. You go home and get a good night's sleep and you'll feel much better in the morning."

"Will I?" He looked straight ahead of him, his eyes strained, as if he was trying to make out the outlines of the morning through the fog. But all he could see was Jessie coming out of the playground with Mary Martha. Their heads were together and they were whispering, they were planning to trick him. All the time he thought they hadn't noticed him and they'd been on to him right from the start. They'd looked at him and seen even through the dirty windows of the old green car, something different about him, something wrong. And Jessie—it must have been Jessie, she was always the leader—had said, *"Let's fool him. Let's pretend I live in your house."*

Children were subtle, they could see things grownups couldn't. Their attention wasn't divided between past and present, it was focused on the present. But what was there about him that had made Jessie notice him? How had she found out he was different?"

Louise said, "Good night, Charlie."

Although he said, "Good night," in return, he was no longer even aware of Louise except as a person who'd come to bring him bad news and was now leaving. *Good riddance, stranger.*

The car door opened and closed again. He turned on the ignition and pulled out into the street. Somewhere in the city, in some house hidden now by night and fog, a little girl knew he was different—no, she was not a little girl, she was already a woman, devious, scheming, provocative. She was probably laughing about it right at this minute, remembering how she'd tricked him. He had to find her.

Reasons why he had to find her began to multiply in his mind like germs. *I'll reprimand her, without scaring her, of course, because I'd never scare a child no matter how bad. I'll*

*ask her what there was about me she noticed, why I looked
different to her. I'll tell her it's not nice, thinking such terrible
thoughts. . . .*

(13)

Jessie called out from her bedroom, "I got up for a glass of
water and now I'm ready to be tucked in again, somebody!"

She didn't especially need tucking in for the third time but
she could hear her parents arguing and she wanted to stop the
sound which was keeping her awake. She thought the argument
was probably about money, but she couldn't distinguish any
particular words. The sound was just a fretful murmur that crept
in through the cracks of her bedroom door and made her ears
itch. It wasn't a pleasant tickle like the kind she got when she
hugged the Arlingtons' dog, Chap; it was like the itch of a flea
bite, painful, demanding to be scratched but not alleviated by
scratching.

She called again and a minute later her father appeared in
the doorway. He had on his bathrobe and he looked sleepy and
cross. "You're getting away with murder, young one. Do you
realize it's after ten?"

"I can't help it if time passes. I couldn't stop it if I wanted
to."

"No, but you might make its passing a little more peaceful
for the rest of us. Mike's asleep, and I hope to be soon."

She knew from his tone that he wasn't really angry with her.
He even sounded a little relieved that his conversation with Ellen
had been interrupted.

"You could sit on the side of my bed for a minute."

"I think I will," he said, smiling slightly. "It's the best offer
I've had today."

"Now we can talk."

"What about?"

"Oh, everything. People can always find something to talk about."

"They can if one of the people happens to be you. What's on your mind, Jess?"

She leaned against the headboard and gazed up at the ceiling. "Are Ellen and Virginia best friends?"

"If you're referring to your mother and your Aunt Virginia, yes, I suppose you'd call them best friends."

"Do they tell each other everything?"

"I don't know. I hope not."

"I mean, like Mary Martha and me, we exchange our most innermost secrets. Did you ever have a friend like that?"

"Not since I was old enough to have any secrets worth mentioning," he said dryly. "Is something worrying you, Jessie?"

She said, "No," but she couldn't prevent her eyes from wandering to the closed door of her closet. A whole night and day had passed since she'd taken back the book Virginia had given her and Howard had pressed the twenty dollars into her hand. The money was out of sight now, hidden in the toe of a shoe, but she might as well have been still carrying it around in her hand. She thought about it a good deal, and always with the same mixture of power and guilt; she had money, she could buy things now, but she had also been bought. She wondered what grownups did with children they bought. Did they keep them? Or did they sell them again, and to whom? Perhaps if she returned the twenty dollars to Howard and Virginia, they would give her back to her father and everything would be normal again. She hadn't wanted the money in the first place, Howard had forced it on her; and she had a strong feeling that he would refuse to take it back.

She said in a rather shaky voice, "Am I *your* little girl?"

"That's an odd question. Whose else would you be?"

"Howard and Virginia's."

He frowned slightly. "Where'd you pick up this idea of calling adults by their first names?"

"All the other kids do it."

"Well, you don't happen to be all the other kids. You're my special gal." He added casually, "Were you over at the Arlingtons' today?"

"No."

"You seem to be doing a lot of thinking about them."

"I was wondering why they don't have children of their own."

"I'm afraid you'll have to go on wondering," he said. "It's not the kind of question people like being asked."

"They could *buy* some of their own, couldn't they? They have lots of money. I heard Ellen say—"

"Your mother."

"—my mother say that if she had a fraction of Virginia's money, she'd join a health club and get rid of some of that fat Virginia carries around. Do you think Virginia's too fat? Howard doesn't. He likes to kiss her, he kisses her all the time when he's not mad at her. Boy, he was mad at her last night, he—"

"All right, that's enough," Dave said brusquely. "I don't want to hear any gossip about the Arlingtons from a nine-year-old."

"It's not gossip. It really happened. I wanted to tell you about the twenty dollars he—"

"I don't want to listen, is that clear? Their private life isn't my business or yours. Now you'd better settle down and go to sleep before your mother comes charging in here and shows you how mad someone can really get."

"I'm not afraid of her. She never *does* anything."

"Well, *I* might do something, kiddo, so watch it. No more drinks of water, no more tucking in, and no more gossip. Understand?"

"Yes."

"Lie down and I'll turn out your light."

"I haven't said my prayers."

"Oh, for heaven's sa— O.K. O.K., say your prayers."

She closed her eyes and folded her hands.

> "Dear Jesus up in heaven,
> Like a star so bright,

> I thank you for the lovely day,
> Please bless me for the night.

"Amen. I don't really think it's been such a lovely day," she added candidly. "But that's in the prayer so I have to say it. I hope God won't consider me a liar."

"I hope not," her father said. His hand moved toward the light switch but he didn't turn it off. Instead, "What was the matter with your day, Jessie?"

"Lots of things."

"Such as?"

"I was treated just like a child. Mike even went to the school with me and Mary Martha to make sure I didn't play on the jungle gym because of my hands. He acted real mean. I'm thinking of divorcing him."

"Then you'd better think again," Dave said. "You can't divorce a brother or any blood relative."

"Mary Martha did. She divorced Sheridan."

"That's silly."

"Well, she never ever sees him, so it's practically the same thing as divorce."

"Why doesn't she ever see him?"

Jessie looked carefully around the room as if she were checking for spies. "Can you keep a secret even from Ellen?"

Although he smiled, the question seemed to annoy him. "It may be difficult but I could try."

"Cross your heart."

"Consider it crossed."

"Sheridan went to live with another woman," Jessie whispered, "so he can't see Mary Martha ever again. Not ever in his whole life."

"That seems a little unreasonable to me."

"Oh no. She's a very bad woman, Mary Martha told me this morning. She looked up a certain word in the dictionary. It took her a long time because she didn't know how to spell it but she figured it out."

"She figured it out," Dave repeated. "Yes, that's Mary Martha all right."

"Naturally. She's the best speller in the school."

"And you, my little friend, are about to become the best gossip."

"Why is it gossip if I'm only telling the truth?"

"You don't know it's the truth, for one thing." He paused, rubbing the side of his neck as if the muscles there had stiffened and turned painful. "The woman involved might not be so bad. Certainly Mrs. Oakley's opinion of her is bound to be biased." He paused again. "How on earth I get dragged into discussions like this, I don't know. Now you settle down and close your eyes and start thinking about your own affairs for a change."

She lay back on the pillow but her eyes wouldn't close. They were fixed on Dave's face as if she were trying to memorize it. "If you and Ellen got divorced, would I ever see you again?"

"Of course you would," he said roughly and turned out the light. "I want no more nonsense out of you tonight, do you hear? And kindly refer to your mother as your mother. This first-name business is going to be nipped in the bud."

"I wish the morning would hurry up and come."

"Stop wishing and start sleeping and it will."

"I hate the night, I just hate it." She struck the side of the pillow with her fist. "Nothing to do but just lie here and sleep. When I'm sleeping I don't feel like me, myself."

"You're not supposed to feel like anything when you're sleeping."

"I mean, when I'm sleeping and wake up real suddenly, I don't feel like me. It's different with you. When you wake up and turn on the light, you see Ellen in the other bed and you think, that's Ellen over there so I must be Dave. You know right away you're Dave."

"Do I?" His voice was grave and he didn't rebuke her for using first names. "Suppose I woke up and Ellen wasn't in the other bed?"

"Then you'd know she was just in the kitchen getting a snack or making a cup of tea. Ellen's always around some place. I never worry about her."

"That sounds as if you worry about me, Jess. Do you?"

"I guess not."

"But you're not sure?"

She put one hand over her eyes to shade them from the hall light coming through the door. "Well, fathers are different. They can just move out, like Sheridan, and you never see them any more."

"That's nonsense," he said sharply. "The Oakley case is a very special one."

"Mary Martha says it always happens the same way."

"If it makes Mary Martha feel better to believe that, let her. But you don't have to." He leaned over and smoothed her hair back from her forehead. "I'll always be around, see? In fact, I'll be around for such a long time that you'll get mighty sick of me eventually."

"No, I won't."

"Wait until the young men start calling on you and you want the living room to entertain them in. You'll be wishing dear old Dad would take a one-way trip to the moon."

She let out a faint sound which he interpreted as a giggle.

"There now," he added. "You're feeling better, aren't you? No more worrying about me and no more thinking about the Oakleys. They're in a class by themselves."

"No, there are others."

"Now what do you mean by that, if anything? Or are you just trying to prolong the conversation by dreaming up—"

"*No.* I heard with my own ears."

"Heard what?"

"You might call it gossip if I tell you."

"I might. Try me."

She spoke in a whisper as if the Arlingtons might be listening at the window. "Howard is moving out, exactly the way Sheridan did. He told Virginia last night, right in front of me. 'I'm leaving,' he said, and then he stomped away."

"He didn't stomp very far," Dave said dryly. "I saw him outside helping the gardener this morning. Look, Jessie, married people often say things to each other that they don't mean. Your mother and I do it sometimes, although we shouldn't. So do you and Mike, for that matter. You get mad at each other or your feelings are hurt and you start making threats. You both know very well they won't be carried out."

"Howard *meant* it."

"Perhaps he did at the time. But he obviously changed his mind."

"He could change it back again, couldn't he?"

"It's possible." He stared down at her but he could tell nothing from her face. She had averted it from the shaft of light coming from the hall. "You sound almost as if you wanted Howard to leave, Jessie."

"I don't care."

"The Arlingtons have always been very nice to you, haven't they?"

"I guess so. Only it would be more fun if somebody else lived next door, a family with children of their own."

"What makes you think the Arlingtons are going to sell their house?"

"If Howard leaves, Virginia will have to because she'll be without money like Mrs. Oakley."

He stood up straight and crossed his arms on his chest in a gesture of suppressed anger. "I'm getting pretty damned tired of the Oakleys. Best friend or no best friend, I may have to insist that you see less of Mary Martha if you're going to let her situation dominate your thinking."

She sensed that his anger was directed not against the Oakleys, whom he didn't even know except for Mary Martha, but against the Arlingtons and perhaps even Ellen and himself. One night she had overheard him telling Ellen he wanted to move back to San Francisco and Ellen had appeared at breakfast the next morning with her eyes swollen. Nobody questioned her story about an eye allergy but nobody believed it either. For a whole week afterward Dave had acted very quiet and allowed Mike and Jessie to get away with being late for meals and fighting over television programs.

"Did you hear me, Jessie?"

"Yes. But I'm getting sleepy."

"Well, it's about time," Dave said and went out and shut the door very quickly as if he were afraid she might start getting unsleepy again.

Left alone, Jessie closed her eyes because there was nothing to see anyway. But her ears wouldn't close. She heard the Arlingtons arriving home in Howard's car—it was noisier than Virginia's—the barking of their dog Chap, the squawk of the garage door, the quick, impatient rhythm of Howard's step, the slow one of Virginia's that sounded as if she were being dragged some place she didn't want to go.

"The Brants' lights are still on," Virginia said, her voice slurred and softened by fog. "I think I'll drop over for a minute and say good night."

"No you won't," Howard said.

"Are you telling me I *can't*?"

"Try it and see."

"What would you do, Howard? Embarrass me in front of the Brants? That's old stuff, and I don't embarrass so easily any more. Or perhaps you'd try and bring Jessie into the act. It's funny you can't solve your problems without dragging in the neighbors. You're such a big, clever man. Can't you handle one wife all by yourself?"

"I could handle a wife. I can't handle an enemy."

Jessie tiptoed over to the window and looked out through the slats of the Venetian blind. The floodlight was turned on in the Arlingtons' yard and she could see Howard bending over unlocking the back door. Virginia stood behind him holding her purse high against her shoulder as if she intended to bring it down on the back of Howard's neck. For a moment everything seemed reversed to Jessie: Howard was the smaller, weaker of the two and Virginia was the powerful one, the boss. Then Howard stood up straight and things seemed normal again.

Howard opened the door and said, "Get inside," and Virginia walked in quickly, her head bowed.

The floodlight went off, leaving the yard to the fog and the darkness, and the only sound Jessie heard was the dripping of moisture among the loquat leaves.

(**14**)

The following morning Ralph MacPherson rose, as usual, at 5:30. Since his wife had died he found it possible to fill his days, but the nights were unbearably lonely. He minimized them by getting up very early and going to bed when many lawyers were just finishing dinner. His matchmaking friends disapproved of this routine but Mac thrived on it. It was a healthy life.

Before breakfast he took his two dogs for a run, worked in the garden and put out food and water for the wild birds and mammals. After breakfast he read at the dining-room window, raising his head from time to time to watch the birds swooping down from the oaks and pines, the bush bunnies darting out of poison oak thickets at the bottom of the canyon and the chipmunks scampering up the lemon tree after the peanuts he'd placed in an empty coconut shell. Helping the wild creatures survive made him feel good, like a secret conspirator against the depredations and greed of man.

He reached his office at 8:30. Miss Edgeworth was already at her desk, looking fresh and crisp in a beige silk suit. Although he'd never accused her of it—Miss Edgeworth didn't encourage personal conversation—Mac sometimes had the notion that she was making a game out of beating him to the office, no matter how early he arrived, and that winning this game was important to her; it reinforced her low opinion of the practicality and efficiency of men.

There was always a note of triumph in her "Good morning, Mr. MacPherson."

"Good morning, Miss Edgeworth."

Her name was Alethea and she had worked for him long enough to be on a first-name basis. But it seemed to him that "Good morning, Alethea" was even more formal than "Good morning, Miss Edgeworth." He was afraid the day would come when he would accidentally call her what the girls in the office called her behind her back—Edgy.

He said, "Any calls for me?"

"Lieutenant Gallantyne wants you to contact him at police headquarters. It's about a car. Shall I get him for you?"

"No. I'll do it."

"Mrs. Oakley also—"

"That can wait."

He went into his office, closed the door and dialed police headquarters.

"Gallantyne? MacPherson here."

"Hope I didn't wake you up," Gallantyne said in a tone that hoped the opposite. "You lawyers nowadays keep bankers' hours."

"Do we. Any line on the green coupé?"

"One of the traffic boys spotted it an hour ago. It's standing in Jim Baker's used-car lot on lower Bojeta Street near the wharf."

"How long has it been there?"

"Garcia didn't ask any questions. He wasn't instructed to."

"I see. Well, thanks a lot, Gallantyne. I'll check it out myself."

He hung up, leaned back in the swivel chair and frowned at the ceiling. The fact that the green car had been sold made it more likely that Kate was right in claiming that the man behind the wheel had been Sheridan. Ordinarily Mac took her accusations against Sheridan with a grain of salt. A number of them were real, a number were fantasy, but most of them fell somewhere in the middle. If she walked across a room and stubbed her toe she would blame Sheridan even if he happened to be several hundred miles away. On the other hand, Sheridan had pulled some pretty wild stuff. It was quite possible that he'd tried to frighten her into coming to terms over the divorce and had ended up being frightened himself when she pursued him with her car.

Mac thought, as he had a hundred times in the past, that they were people caught like animals in a death grip. Neither was strong enough to win and neither would let go. The grip had continued for so long that it was now a way of life. It was not the sun that brightened Kate's mornings or the sea air that freshened Sheridan's. It was the anticipation, for each of them, of a victory over the other. They could no longer live without the excitement of battle. Mac remembered two lines from the children's poem about a gingham dog and a calico cat who had disappeared simultaneously:

> "The truth about the cat and pup
> Is this: they ate each other up."

It hardly mattered now who took the first bite, Kate or Sheridan. The important thing was how to prevent the last bite, and so far Mac hadn't found any way of doing it. With the idea that perhaps someone else could, he had tried many times to persuade Kate to engage another lawyer. She always had the same answer: *"I couldn't possibly. No other lawyer would understand me." "I don't understand you either, Kate." "But you must, you've known me since I was a little girl."*

Kate's attitude toward men was one of unrealistic expectation or unjustified contempt, with nothing in between. If they behaved perfectly and lived up to the standards she set, they were god figures. When they failed as gods, they were immediately demoted to devils. Mac had avoided demotion simply by refusing either to accept her standards or to take her expectations seriously.

Sheridan's demotion had been quick and thorough, and there was no possibility of a reversal. Sheridan was aware of this. One of the main reasons why he went on fighting her was his knowledge that no matter how generous a settlement he made or how many of her demands he satisfied, he could never regain his godship.

Mac was sorry for them both and sick of them both. He almost wished they would move away or finish the job of eating each other up. Mary Martha might be better off in a foster home.

He told Miss Edgeworth he'd be back in an hour, then he drove down to the lower end of Bojeta Street near the wharf. It was an area of the city that was doomed now that newcomers from land-locked areas were moving in and discovering the sea. Real estate speculators were greedily buying up ocean-front lots and razing the old buildings, the warehouses and fish-processing plants and shacks for Mexican agricultural workers. All of these had been built in what the natives considered the damp and undesirable part of town.

Jim Baker's used-car lot was jammed between a three-story motel under construction and a new restaurant and bar called the Sea Aira Club. A number of large signs announced bargains because Baker was about to lose his lease. Baker himself looked as if he'd already lost it. He was an elderly man with skin wrinkled like an old paper bag and a thick, husky voice that sounded as if he'd swallowed too many years of fog.

He came out of his oven-sized office, chewing something that might have been gum or what was left of his breakfast, or an undigested fiber of the past. "Can I do anything for you?"

"I'm interested in the green coupé at the rear of the lot."

"Interested in what way?" Baker said with a long, deliberate look at Mac's new Buick. "Something fishy about the deal?"

"Not that I'm aware of. My name is Ralph MacPherson, by the way. I'd like to know when the car was sold to you."

"Last night about six o'clock. I didn't handle the transaction —my son, Jamie, did—but I was in the office. I'd brought Jamie's dinner to him from home. We're open fourteen hours out of the twenty-four, and Jamie and I have to spell each other. He sold the young man a nice clean late-model Pontiac that had been pampered like a baby. I hated to see it go, frankly, but the young man seemed anxious and he had the cash. Sooo——" Baker shrugged and spread his hands.

"How young a man was he?"

"Oh, about Jamie's age, thirty-two, thirty-five, maybe."

Sheridan was thirty-four. "Do you remember his name?"

"I never knew it. It's in the book but I'm not sure I ought to look it up for you. I wouldn't want to cause him any trouble."

"I'm trying to prevent trouble, Mr. Baker. A client of mine— I'm a lawyer—is convinced that the husband she's divorcing has been using the green coupé to spy on her. I've been a family friend for many years and I'm simply trying to find out the truth one way or the other. Even a description of the man would be a big help."

Baker thought about it. "Well, he was nice, clean-cut, athletic-looking. Tall, maybe six feet, with kind of sandy hair and a smile like he was apologizing for something. Would that be the husband?"

Sheridan was short and dark and wore glasses, but Mac said, "I'm not sure. Perhaps you'd better look up the name."

"I guess it'd be all right, being as it's just a divorce case and nothing criminal. I don't want to get caught up in anything criminal. It plays hell with business."

"To the best of my knowledge, nothing criminal is involved."

"O.K., wait here."

Baker went into the office and returned in a few minutes with a name and address written on an old envelope: Charles E. Gowen, 495 Miria Street.

"Is that the man?" Baker asked.

"I'm glad to say it's not." Mac returned the envelope. "This will be good news to my client."

"Women get funny ideas sometimes."

"Do they not."

If it was good news to Kate, she didn't show it. She met him at the front door, wearing a starched cotton dress and high-heeled shoes. Her face was carefully made up and her hair neat.

It seemed to Mac that she was always dressed for company but company never came. He knew of no one besides himself who any longer got past the front door.

They went into the smaller of the two living rooms and she sat on the window seat while he told her what he'd found out. With her face in shadow and the sun at her back illuminating her long, fair hair, she looked scarcely older than Mary Martha. *She's only thirty,* Mac thought. *Her life has been broken and she's too brittle to bend down and pick up the pieces.*

"You can stop worrying about the green car," he told her. "Sheridan wasn't in it."

She didn't look as if she intended or wanted to stop worrying. "That hasn't been proved."

"The car was registered to Charles Gowen. He traded it in last night."

"Funny coincidence, don't you think?"

"Yes. But coincidences happen."

"A lot of them can be explained. I told you from the beginning that Sheridan was too crafty to use his own car. Obviously, he borrowed the green coupé from this man Gowen. The kind of people Sheridan runs around with nowadays exchange cars and wives and mistresses as freely as they exchange booze. Sheridan's moved away down in the world, farther than you think."

"I haven't time to go into that now, Kate. Let's stick to the point."

"Very well. He used Gowen's car to harass me. Then when I fought back, when I chased him, he got scared and told Gowen to sell it."

"Why? Why didn't he simply return it to Gowen and let the matter drop? Selling the car was what led me to Gowen."

"Sheridan's mind is usually, I might say always, befuddled by alcohol. He probably considered the gambit quite a cunning one."

"What about Gowen?"

"I don't know about Gowen," she said impatiently. "I've never heard of him before. But if he's typical of Sheridan's current friends, he'll do anything for a few dollars or a bottle of liquor. Don't forget, Sheridan has money to fling around. It makes him pretty popular, and I suppose powerful, in certain circles." She paused, running her hand along her left cheek. The cheek was bright red as though it had been slapped. "You asked, 'What about Gowen?' Well, why don't you find out?"

"I don't think there's enough to warrant an investigation."

She looked at him bitterly. "Not *enough?* I suppose you think I've imagined the whole thing?"

"No, Kate. But—"

"I didn't imagine that car parked outside my house, watching me. I didn't imagine an anonymous letter accusing me of neglecting my daughter. I didn't imagine that chase around town yesterday. Would an innocent man have fled like that?"

"Perhaps there are no innocent men," Mac said. "Or women."

"Oh, stop talking like a wise old philosopher. You're not old, and you're not very wise either."

"Granted."

"If you had been in that car, would you have run away like that? Answer me truthfully."

"You seem concerned only with the fact that he ran away. I'm more concerned with the fact that you chased him."

"I was upset. I'd just received that letter."

"Perhaps he had had a disturbing experience, too, and was reacting in an emotional rather than a logical manner."

She let out a sound of despair. "You won't *listen* to me. You won't take me seriously."

"I do. I am."

"No. You think I'm a fool. But I feel a terrible danger, Mac, I know it's all around me. Something awful is waiting to happen, it's just around the corner, waiting. It can't be seen or heard or touched, but it's as real as this house, that chair you're sitting on, the tree outside the window."

"And you think Sheridan is behind this danger?"

"He must be," she said simply. "I have no other enemies."

Mac thought what a sad epitaph it made for a marriage: *I*

have no other enemies. "I'll try again to contact Sheridan. As you know, he hasn't been answering his telephone."

"Another sign of guilt."

"Or a sign that he's not there," Mac said dryly. "As for Charles Gowen, I can't go charging up to him with a lot of questions. I haven't the legal or moral right. All I can do is make a few discreet inquiries, find out where he lives and works, and what kind of person he is, whether he's likely to be one of Sheridan's cronies, and so on. I may as well tell you now, though: I don't expect anything to come of it. If Gowen had a guilty reason for not wanting the green coupé found, it seems to me he'd have taken a little more trouble in disposing of it. There are at least a hundred used-car dealers between here and Los Angeles, yet Gowen sold it right here, practically in the center of town."

"He may simply be stupid. Sheridan's friends nowadays are not exactly intellectual giants."

Mac's smile was more pained than amused. "One of the things a lawyer has to learn early in his career is not to assume that the other guy is stupid."

He rose. His whole body felt heavy, and stiff with tension. He always felt the same way when he was in Kate's house, that he couldn't move freely in any direction because he was under constant and judgmental surveillance. He could picture Sheridan trying, at first anyway, to conform and to please her, and making mistakes, more and more mistakes every day, until nothing was possible but mistakes.

He knew he was not being fair to her. To make amends for his thoughts, he crossed the room and leaned down and kissed her lightly on the top of her head. Her hair felt warm to his lips, and smelled faintly of soap.

She looked up at him, showing neither surprise nor displeasure, only a deep sorrow, as if the show of tenderness was too little and too late and she had forgotten how to respond. "Is that a courtesy you extend to all your clients?"

"No," he said, smiling. "Only the ones I like and have known since they were freckle-faced little brats."

"I never had freckles."

"Yes, you did. You were covered with them every summer. You probably still would be if you spent any time in the sun. Listen, Kate, I have an idea. Why don't you and Mary Martha come sailing with me one of these days?"

"No. No, thank you."

"Why not?"

"I wouldn't be very good company. I've forgotten how to enjoy myself."

"You could relearn if you wanted to. Perhaps you don't want to."

Her sorrow had crystallized into bitterness, making her eyes shine hard and bright like blue glass. "Oh, stop it, Mac. You're offering me a day of sailing the way you'd throw an old dog a bone. Well, I'm not that hungry. Besides, I can't afford to leave the house for a whole day."

"You can't afford not to."

"Sheridan might force his way in and steal something. He's done it before."

"Once."

"He might do it ag—"

"He was drunk," Mac said, "and all he took was a case of wine which belonged to him anyway."

"But he broke into the house."

"You refused to admit him. Isn't that correct?"

"Naturally I refused. He was abusive and profane, he threatened me, he—" She stopped and took a long, deep breath. "You're always making excuses for him. Why? You're supposed to be on my side."

"I'm a man. I can't help seeing things from a man's point of view occasionally."

"Then perhaps," she said, rising, "I'd better hire a woman lawyer."

"That might be a good idea."

"You'd like to get rid of me, wouldn't you?"

"Let's put it this way: I'd like for us both to be rid of your problems. My going along with you and agreeing with everything you say and do is not a solution. It gets in the way of a solution. Your difficulties can't just be dumped in a box labeled Sheridan. You had them before Sheridan, and you're having them now, after Sheridan. I'd be doing you no favor by pretending otherwise."

"I was a happy, healthy, normal young woman when I married him."

"Is that how you remember yourself?"

"Yes."

"My memory of you is different," he said calmly. "You were moody, selfish, immature. You flunked out of college, you couldn't hold on to a job, and your relationship with your mother was strained. You tried to use marriage as a way out of all these difficulties. It put a very heavy burden on Sheridan, he wasn't strong enough to carry it. Can you see any truth in what I'm saying, Kate? Or are you just standing there thinking how unfair I'm being?"

They were face to face, but she wasn't looking at him. She was staring at a piece of the wall beyond his left shoulder, as if to deny his very presence. "I no longer expect fairness, from anyone."

"You're getting it from me, Kate."

"You call that fairness—that repulsive picture of me when I was nineteen?"

"It's not repulsive, or even particularly unusual. A great many girls in the same state go into marriage for the same reason."

"And what about Sheridan's reasons for getting married?" she said shrilly. "I suppose *they* were fine, *he* was mature, *he* got along great with *his* mother, *he* was a *big* success in the world—"

He took hold of her shoulders, lightly but firmly. "Keep your voice down."

"Why should I? Nobody will hear. Nobody can. The Oakleys were very exclusive, they liked privacy. They had to build the biggest house in town on the biggest lot because they didn't want to be bothered by neighbors. I could scream for help at the top of my lungs and not a soul would hear me. I've got enough privacy to be murdered in. Sheridan knows that. He's probably dreamed about it a hundred times: *wouldn't it be nice if someone came along and murdered Kate?* He may even have made or be making some plans of his own along that line, though I don't believe he'd have enough nerve to do it himself. He'd probably hire someone, the way he hired Gowen."

Her quick changes of mood and thought were beginning to exhaust Mac. Trying to keep track of them was like following a fast rat through a tortuous maze: Sheridan had borrowed the car from Gowen, who was one of his drunken friends—Sheridan had been at the wheel—Sheridan hadn't been at the wheel—Gowen wasn't his friend, he'd been hired—Gowen had driven the car himself. At this point Mac might have dismissed her whole story as fictional if she hadn't produced the real license number of a real car. The car existed, and so did Gowen. They were about the only facts Mac had to go on.

"Now you're suggesting," he said, "that Gowen was hired by Sheridan to intimidate you."

"Yes. He's probably some penniless bum that Sheridan met in a bar."

He didn't point out that penniless bums didn't pay cash for late-model sedans. "That should be easy enough to check."

"Would you, Mac? Will you?"

"I'll try my best."

"You're a dear, you really are."

She seemed to have forgotten her ill-feeling toward him. She looked excited and flushed as if she'd just come in from an hour of tennis in the sun and fresh air. But he knew the game wasn't tennis and the sun wasn't the same one that was shining in the window. What warmed her, brightened her, made her blood flow faster, was the thought of beating Sheridan.

(**15**)

Charlie had lain awake half the night making plans for the coming day, how he would spend his free hour at noon and where he'd go right after work. But before noon Louise phoned and invited him to meet her for lunch, and at five o'clock his boss Mr. Warner asked him to take a special delivery to the Forest Service ten miles up in the mountains. He couldn't refuse either of these requests without a good reason. His only reason would have seemed sinister to Louise and peculiar to Mr. Warner, but to Charlie himself it made sense: he had to find a little girl named Jessie to warn her not to play any more tricks on him because it was very naughty.

It was six o'clock before he arrived back at the city limits. He drove to the school grounds as fast as he could without taking any chances on being stopped by the police. The mere sight of a police car might have sent him running home to Ben, but he saw none.

At the rear of the school the parking lot, usually empty at this time, contained half a dozen cars. Charlie's first thought was that an accident had happened, Jessie had taken another fall and hurt herself very seriously and would be in the hospital for a long period; she would be safe in a hospital with all the doctors and nurses around; no stranger could reach her, a stranger would be stopped at the door and sent packing. Alternate waves of relief and despair passed over him like cold winds and hot winds coming from places he had never visited.

He drove around to the side of the school and saw that no accident had happened. A group of older boys were playing baseball and a few spectators were watching the game, including a man and woman who acted like parents. There were no young children in sight.

Charlie pulled over to the curb and turned off the ignition. He had no reason to stay there, with Jessie gone, but he had no reason to go home either. He had called Ben from work and told him that he was going on an errand for the boss and not to expect him home until seven or later. Though Ben had sounded suspicious at first, the words "special delivery" and "Forest Service" seemed to convince him not only that Charlie was telling the truth but that Mr. Warner trusted him enough to send him on an important mission.

Charlie watched the game for a few minutes without interest or attention. Then one of the players he hadn't noticed before came up to bat. He was a boy about sixteen, tall and thin as a broom handle. Even from a distance his cockiness was evident in every movement he made. He tapped the dirt out of his cleats, took a called strike, swung wildly at the second pitch and connected with the third for a home run that cleared the fence. With a little bow to his teammates he began jogging nonchalantly around the bases. As he rounded second base Charlie recognized him as the boy he'd seen several times with Jessie. There was no doubt about his identity: he even looked like Jessie, dark, with thin features and bright, intense eyes.

Charlie sat motionless, hardly even breathing. This was Jessie's brother. The phrase kept running through his head like words on a cracked record: *Jessie's brother, Jessie's brother, Jessie's brother*. Jessie's brother would live in the same house as Jessie, so it was now simply a question of following him, cautiously so the boy wouldn't get suspicious, but keeping him in sight at all times until he stopped at a house and went inside. Charlie's throat felt so thick that he had to touch it with his fingers to make sure he was not swelling up like a balloon. *The house he goes into will be Jessie's house. If I'm lucky there'll be a name on the mailbox and I won't have to ask Louise to help me. I'll be on my own, I'll do it all by myself.*

The home run had broken up the game. There was a round of cheers and applause, with the man and woman deliberately abstaining. They walked onto the field and started talking to the pitcher, who turned his back on them. Players and spectators were dispersing, toward the parking lot and the side gate. Within five minutes the playground was empty of victors and vanquished alike, and a flock of blackbirds were walking around in the dust, nodding their heads as if they'd known right from the beginning how it would all end: someone would win, someone would lose. Charlie had done both.

The boys drifted off in twos and threes, wearing their uniforms but carrying their cleated shoes and bats and baseball mitts. Some of them passed Charlie's car, still discussing the game, but Jessie's brother and two of his teammates went out the gate on the other side of the school.

Charlie drove around the block, passed them, and parked in front of a white stucco house. As they went by the car Charlie pretended to be searching for something in the glove compartment in order to keep his face hidden from them. Their voices were so loud and clear that he had a moment's panic when he thought they were talking directly to him. They knew all about him, they were baiting him—

"—four o'clock in the morning, man, she'll have a fit," Jessie's brother said. "She's always grouching about me waking everybody up too early when I go fishing."

"We could all stay at my house overnight. My folks sleep like they're in a coma."

"Good thinking, man. I'll just check in at the house and check right out again."

"Maybe we should leave even earlier than four. We'll catch the fish before they've got their eyes open—"

The boys passed out of earshot. Cautiously, Charlie raised his head. The snatch of conversation he'd overheard worried him. He couldn't shake off the feeling that Jessie had told her brother about him and the brother had told his two friends and the three of them were taunting him: he was the fish who would be caught before he opened his eyes. They had found out from some secret source that he always woke up at four o'clock in the morning. Or was it five? Or six?

The ordinary facts of his existence were all crowding together in one part of his mind and trampling each other like frightened horses in the corner of a corral. Some died, some were mutilated beyond recognition, some emerged as strange, unidentifiable hybrids. Four and five and six were all squashed together; he didn't know what time it was now or what time he woke in the morning. The setting sun could have been a rising moon or the reflected glow of a fire or a lighted spaceship about to land. Jessie and her brother merged into a single figure, a half-grown boy-girl. Louise and Ben had faces but they wouldn't let him see; they kept their backs to him because he'd done something they didn't like. He couldn't remember what it was he'd done but it must have been terrible, their backs were rigid with disapproval and Louise had deliberately let her hair grow long and braided it around her head the way his mother used to. He hated it. He wanted to take a pair of scissors and cut it off. But the scissors wasn't in the kitchen drawer where it was always kept, and the drawer had lost its handle. It didn't even open like a drawer. It sprung out when he pushed a little silver button, like the glove compartment in a car.

Glove compartment. Car. He blinked his eyes painfully, as though he were emerging from a long and dreadful sleep. The sun was beginning to set. It was a quarter to seven by his watch. Three boys were walking up the street. He followed them.

Ralph MacPherson worked at the office until nearly seven o'clock. He felt too weary to contact Kate again but he could picture her waiting at the telephone for his call, getting herself more and more worked up, and he knew he couldn't postpone it any longer.

She answered before the second ring, in the guarded half-disguised voice she always used before he identified himself.

"Hello."

"Kate, this is Mac."

"Have you found anything out about Gowen?"

"Yes."

"Well? Was I right? He's some bum Sheridan picked up in a bar and hired to do his dirty work for him."

"I hardly think so," Mac said as patiently as he could. "I went over to Miria Street this afternoon and dropped in at a drugstore around the corner from Gowen's house. I pretended I'd lost the address. Not very subtle, perhaps, but it worked. The druggist knows the Gowen family, they've been his customers for years. It didn't take much to start him talking. Business was slow."

She made an impatient sound. "Well, what did he *say?*"

"Charles Gowen lives with his brother Ben. Ben manages a downtown cafeteria, Charles has a job with a paper company. They're both hard-working and clean-living. They don't smoke or drink, they pay their bills on time, they mind their own business. There's a neighborhood rumor that Charles is going to marry one of the local librarians, a very nice woman who is also hard-working and clean-living, etcetera, etcetera. In brief, Gowen's not our man."

"But he must be," she said incredulously. "He ran away from me. He acted guilty."

"It's possible that you scared the daylights out of him. He may not be used to strange women chasing him around town. Not many of us are. Make me a promise, will you, Kate?"

"What is it?"

"That you'll stop thinking about Sheridan's machinations just for tonight and get yourself a decent rest."

She didn't argue with him but she didn't promise either. She simply said she was sorry to have bothered him and hung up.

Parked half a block away, Charlie watched the three boys turn in the driveway of a house on Cielito Lane. Only a difference in planting and a ribbon of smoke rising from a backyard barbecue pit distinguished it from its neighbors, but to Charlie it was a very special house.

He drove past slowly. The mailbox had a name on it: David E. Brant.

(16)

It was Howard Arlington's last night in the city for two weeks and he and Virginia had been invited to a farewell barbecue in the Brants' patio. They didn't want to go but neither of them indicated this in any way. Ever since their unpleasant scene the previous night, they'd been excessively polite to each other, to Dave and Ellen and Jessie, even to the gardener and the cleaning woman. It was as if they were trying to convince everyone, including themselves, that they were not the kind of people who staged domestic brawls—not they.

This new formal politeness affected not only their speech and actions but their style of dress. They both knew that Ellen and Dave would be in jeans and sneakers, but Howard had put on a dark business suit, white shirt and a tie, and Virginia wore a pink-flowered silk dress with a stole and matching high-heeled sandals. They looked as though they were going out to dinner and a symphony instead of to the neighbors' backyard for hamburgers and hi-fi, both of which would be overdone.

The hi-fi was already going and so was the fire. Smoke and violins drifted into the Arlingtons' kitchen window. Normally, Howard would have slammed the window shut and made some caustic remark about tract houses. Tonight he merely said, "Dave's sending out signals. What time does Ellen want us over there?"

Virginia wasn't sure Ellen wanted them over there at all but the invitation had been extended and accepted, there was nothing to be done about it. "Seven o'clock."

"It's nearly that now. Are you ready?"

"Yes."

"Perhaps we'd better leave Chap in the house."

"Yes, perhaps we'd better." Her voice gave no hint of the amused contempt she felt. The big retriever was already asleep on the davenport and it would have taken Howard a long time to wake him up, coax, bribe, push and pull him outside. Chap would not be mean about it, simply inert, immovable. Sometimes she wondered whether the dog had learned this passive resistance from her or whether she'd learned it from him. In any case the dog seemed just as aware as Virginia that the technique was successful. Inaction made opposing action futile; Howard was given no leverage to work with.

They went out the rear door, leaving a lamp in the living room turned on for Chap, and the kitchen light for themselves. At the bottom of the stairs, Howard suddenly stopped.

"I forgot a handkerchief. You go on without me, I'll join you in a minute."

"I'd rather wait, thank you. We were invited as a couple, let's go as a couple."

"A couple of what?" he said and went back in the house.

Virginia's face was flushed with anger, and the rush of blood made her sunburn, now in the peeling stage, begin to itch painfully. She no longer blamed the sun as the real culprit, she blamed Howard. It was a Howardburn and it itched just as painfully inside as it did outside. There was a difference, though: inside, it couldn't be scratched, no relief was possible.

When Howard returned, he was holding the handkerchief to his mouth as if to prove to her that he really needed it. His voice was muffled. "Virginia, listen."

"What is it?"

"You don't suppose the kid told her parents about that twenty dollars I gave her?"

"I talked to Ellen today, nothing was mentioned about it. By the way, Jessie has a name. I wish you'd stop referring to her as 'the kid.' "

"There's only one kid in our lives. It hardly seems necessary to name her."

"I thought we'd agreed to be civil to each other for the rest of your time at home. Why do you want to start something now? We've had a pleasant day, don't ruin it."

"You think it's been a pleasant day, do you?"

"As pleasant as possible," Virginia said.

"As pleasant as possible while I'm around, is that what you mean? In other words, you don't expect much in my company."

"Perhaps I can't afford to."

"Well, tomorrow I'll be back on the road. You and the kid can have a real ball."

"Let's stop this right now, Howard, before it goes too far. We're not saying anything new anyway. It's all been said."

"And done," Howard added. "It's all said and done. Amen." He looked down at her with a smile that was half-pained, half-mocking. "The problem is, what do people do and say after everything's said and done? Where do we go from here?"

"To the Brants' for a barbecue."

"And then?"

"I can't think any further than that now, Howard. I can't think."

She leaned against the side of the house, hugging her stole around her and staring out at the horizon. Where the sea and sky should have met, there was a gray impenetrable mass of fog between them. She dreaded the time when this mass would begin to move because nothing, no one, could stop it. The sea would disappear, then the beaches, the foothills, the mountains. Streets would be separated from streets, houses from houses, people from people. Everyone would be alone except the women with a baby growing inside them. She saw them nearly every day in stores, on corners, getting into cars. She hated and envied the soft, confident glow in their eyes as if they knew no fog could ever be thick enough to make them feel alone.

Howard was watching her. "Let me get you a sweater, Virginia."

"No, thank you."

"You look cold."

"It's just nerves."

They crossed the lawn and the concrete driveway and Ellen's experimental patch of dichondra with a Keep Off sign in the middle. From the beginning, neither the dichondra nor the sign had stood much of a chance. The sign had been bumped or kicked or blown to a 45° angle, and between the dichondra plants were the marks of bicycle tires and children's sneakers. The sneaker marks were about the size that Jessie would make, and Virginia had an impulse to lean down and push some dirt over them with her hand so that Jessie wouldn't be blamed. But she realized she couldn't do such a thing in front of Howard; it would only aggravate his jealousy of the child. So, instead, she stepped off the flagstone path into the dichondra patch, putting her feet deliberately over the imprints of Jessie's.

Howard opened his mouth to say something but he didn't have time. Mike was coming out of the gate of the patio fence, carrying some fishing tackle, a windbreaker, and three hamburgers still steaming from the grill.

Mike grinned at Howard and Virginia but there was impatience behind the grin, as though he suspected they would try to keep him there talking when he had other and more interesting things to do.

Howard said formally, "Good evening, Michael."

"Oh hi, Mr. Arlington, Mrs. Arlington. If you'll excuse me now, I've got some of the gang waiting for me. We're going fishing at two o'clock in the morning."

"That's pretty early even for fish, isn't it?"

"Maybe. I'm not sure whether fish sleep or not."

"I'm not, either. Well, good luck anyway."

"Thanks, Mr. Arlington. So long."

Virginia hadn't spoken. She was still standing in the dichondra patch looking vague and a little puzzled, as if she was wondering how she got there, and whether fish slept or not. Her high heels were sinking further and further into the ground like the roots of a tree seeking nourishment and moisture. For a moment she imagined that she was a tree, growing deeper, growing taller, putting out new leaves and blossoms, dropping fertile seeds into the earth.

Then Howard grasped her by the arm and it was an arm, not a branch, and it would never grow anything but old.

"For heaven's sake, what are you doing, Virginia?"

"Would you really like to know?"

"Yes."

She let out a brief, brittle laugh. "I'm pretending to be a tree."

"You're acting very peculiar tonight."

"I'm a very peculiar woman. Hadn't you noticed that before, Howard? Surely those sharp eyes of yours couldn't miss anything so obvious. I'm not like other women, I'm a freak. There's something missing in me."

"Take my hand and I'll help you out of there."

"I don't want to get out. I *like* being a tree."

"Stop playing games. Are you going to let me help you?"

"No."

"All right." Without further argument he picked her up and lifted her out of the dichondra patch. He had to exert all his strength to do it because she'd made herself limp—arms, legs, waist, neck. "O.K., tree, you've just been uprooted."

"Damn you. *Damn* you."

"That's better. Now suppose we go inside and you can start pretending you're a person." He opened the gate for her. "Coming?"

"I have no choice."

"You'd have even less choice if you were a tree."

They went into the patio and Howard closed the gate behind them with unnecessary force. The loud bang seemed to Virginia to be a warning, like a shot fired over her head.

"Come in, come in," Dave said. "Welcome to Brants' Beanery."

He was standing at the barbecue grill wearing an apron over his Bermuda shorts and T-shirt, and drinking a can of beer. Ellen sat barefoot at the redwood picnic table, slicing an onion. Neither of them looked as though they expected company or particularly wanted any.

Even though Virginia had known this was how it was going to be, she felt a stab of resentment, aggravated by a feeling, a hangover from her childhood, that she was the one who was wrong, and no matter how hard she tried, she always would be. She had spent an hour dressing and fixing her hair but Dave didn't even look at her. He had opened a can of beer for Howard and the two men were already deep in conversation, one on each side of the barbecue pit.

Virginia sat down beside Ellen. "Anything I can do to help?"

"It's all done, thanks. I wouldn't allow you to touch a thing in that dress, anyway. I'd feel so guilty if you spilled something on it. It's simply gorgeous."

Virginia had to take it as a compliment but she knew it wasn't. Ellen's voice was too objective, as though the dress had nothing to do with Virginia personally; a gorgeous dress was a gorgeous dress and it didn't matter who wore it or who owned it.

"It's not new," Virginia said. "I mean, it's just been lying around." For a whole week it had been lying around, waiting for an occasion. Now the occasion had arrived, hamburger and onions and baked beans in the next-door neighbors' backyard. She thought wildly and irrationally, *damn you, Howard. You didn't have to bring me here.*

"I thought perhaps it was the one you bought last week at Corwin's," Ellen said. "You told me about it."

"No, no, I took that back. I've had this dress since—well, since before you even moved here. That seems ages ago, doesn't it? I feel so close to you and Dave and Mike and, of course, Jessie." She glanced hastily in Howard's direction to make sure he hadn't overheard the name. He was still engrossed in his conversation with Dave. "Where is Jessie?"

"In the front room watching television."

"I'll go in and say hello. I have a little something for her."

"Virginia, you shouldn't, you'll—"

"It's nothing at all, really, just a piece of junk jewelry. I saw it in a store window this afternoon and I thought Jessie would like it."

"She's too young to wear jewelry."

"It's only a small ring with an imitation pearl. I had one exactly like it when I was six years old. I remember it so clearly. My hands grew too fast and it had to be filed off."

"It won't have to be filed off Jessie," Ellen said dryly. "She'll lose it within a week."

"Then you don't mind if I give it to her?"

"I suppose not."

Virginia rose and crossed the patio, moving with unaccustomed agility as though she wanted to get away before she could be called back.

Jessie was curled up in a corner of the davenport, her chin resting on her knees, her arms hugging her legs. Her eyes widened a little when she saw Virginia in the doorway but it was the only sign of recognition she gave.

"Hello, Jessie." Virginia went over to the television set. "May I turn this down a minute?"

"I—yes, I guess."

"I haven't seen you for two days."

"I've been busy," Jessie said, looking down at the floor as if she were talking to it and not Virginia. "My mother took me swimming this afternoon. To see if the salt water would hurt my hands."

"And did it?"

"Not much."

Virginia sat down on the davenport beside her. "You know what I did this afternoon? I went downtown shopping."

"Did you buy something?"

"Yes."

"Was Howard with you to pay for it?"

Virginia sucked in her breath as though the question had knocked it out of her. "No, no, he wasn't. I paid for it myself."

"But the other night he said—"

"The other night he said a lot of things he didn't mean. He was tired and out of sorts. We all get like that sometimes, don't we?"

"Yes, sometimes."

"When two people are married, they share whatever money comes into the house, whether it's the man's salary or the woman's or both. If I see something I want and can afford, I buy it. I don't need Howard's permission." *But it helps,* she added bitterly to herself. *He likes to play Big Daddy, spoiling his foolish and extravagant little girl, as long as the little girl is duly appreciative.*

Jessie was considering the subject, her mouth pursed, her green eyes narrowed. "I guess Howard gives you lots of money, doesn't he?"

"Yes."

"Every month my daddy gives money to the bank for this house. In nineteen more years we're going to own it. When is Howard going to own you?"

"Never," Virginia said sharply. Then, seeing Jessie's look of bewilderment, she added in a softer voice, "Look, dear, I'm not a house. Howard isn't making payments on me."

"Then why does he give you money?"

"He doesn't exactly give it to me. We share it. If Howard didn't have me to look after the house for him, he'd have to hire someone else to perform the same services for him."

"If he hires you, that makes him the boss."

"No. I mean—how on earth did we get off on this subject? You're too young to understand."

"Will I understand when I'm older?"

"Yes," Virginia said, thinking, *I hope you never grow up to understand what I do. I hope you die before your innocence is torn away from you.*

Jessie was frowning and biting the nail of her left thumb. "I certainly have tons of stuff to learn when I grow up. I wish I could start right now."

"No. No, don't wish that. Stay the way you are, Jessie. Just stay, stay like this, like tonight."

"I can't," Jessie said in a matter-of-fact voice. "Mary Martha would get way ahead of me. She's already taller and spells better. Mary Martha knows a lot."

"Some of them are things I couldn't bear having you know, Jessie."

"Why not? They're not bad, they don't hurt her."

"They hurt. I see her hurting."

Jessie shook her head. "No. If she was hurting, she'd cry. She's an awful sissy sometimes, she can't stand the sight of blood or anything oozing."

"Do you ever see me cry, Jessie?"

"No."

"Well, I hurt. I hurt terribly."

"Because of your sunburn?"

Virginia hesitated a moment, then she laughed, the harsh, brief laugh she heard herself utter so often lately. It was like the distress signal of an animal that couldn't communicate in words. "Yes, of course. Because of my sunburn. I must be as big a sissy as Mary Martha."

"She's not a sissy about everything."

"Perhaps I'm not either, about everything. I don't know. Not everything's been tried on me yet. Not quite."

Jessie would have liked to ask what had or had not been tried, but Virginia had averted her face and was changing the subject, not very subtly or completely, by opening her purse. It was a pink silk pouch that matched her dress. Inside the pouch was a tiny box wrapped in white paper and tied with a miniature golden rope.

Jessie saw the box and immediately and deliberately turned her head away. "Your shoes are dirty."

"I stepped off the path. Jessie, I have a little pres—"

"You're not supposed to step off the path."

Virginia's face was becoming white even where she was sunburned, on her cheekbones and the bridge of her nose, as though whiteness was not a draining away of blood but a true pigmentation that could conceal other colors. "Jessie, dear, you're not paying attention to what I'm telling you. I said, I have a little present for you. It's something I'm sure you'll love."

"No, I won't. I *won't* love it."

"But you don't even know what it is yet."

"I don't care."

"You don't want it, is that it?"

"No."

"You won't—won't even open it?"

"No."

"That's too bad," Virginia said slowly. "It's very pretty. I used to have one exactly like it when I was a little girl and I was so proud of it. It made me feel grown-up."

"I don't want to feel grown-up any more."

"Oh, you're quite right, of course. You're really very sensible. If I had it to do over again, I wouldn't choose to grow up either. To live the happy years and die young—"

"I'm going to watch television." Jessie's lower lip was quivering. She had to catch it with her teeth to hold it still so that Virginia wouldn't see how frightened she was. She wasn't sure what had caused the sudden, overwhelming fear but she realized that she had to fight it, with any weapon at all that she could find. "My—my mother doesn't like you."

Virginia didn't look surprised, her eyes were merely soft and full of sadness. "I'm sorry to hear that because I like her."

"You're not supposed to like someone who doesn't like you."

"Really? Well, I guess I do a lot of things I'm not supposed to. I step off paths and get my shoes dirty, I buy presents for little girls— Perhaps some day I'll learn better."

"I'm going to watch television," Jessie repeated stubbornly. "I want to see the ending of the program."

"Go ahead."

"You turned it off. When company turns it off my mother makes me keep it that way."

"Turn it on again. I'm not company."

Awkwardly, Jessie unfolded her arms and legs and went over to the television set. Her head felt heavy with what she didn't yet recognize as grief: something was lost, a time had passed, a loved one was gone. "You—you could watch the ending with me, Aunt Virginia."

"Perhaps I will. That's the nice part about television programs, they start with a beginning and end with an ending. Other things don't. You find yourself in the middle and you don't know how you got there or how to get out. It's like waking up in the middle of a water tank with steep, slippery sides. You just keep swimming around and around, there's no ladder to climb out, nobody flings you a rope, and you can't stop swimming because you have this animal urge to survive. . . . No television program is ever like that, is it, Jessie?"

"No, because it has to end to make room for another program. Nobody can be left just swimming around."

"How would it end on television, Jessie?"

Jessie hesitated only long enough to take a deep breath. "A dog would find you and start barking and attract a lot of people. They'd tie all their jackets and sweaters and things together to make a rope and they'd throw it to you and lift you out. Then you'd hug the dog and he'd lick your face."

"Thanks for nothing, dog," Virginia said and got up and went over to the doorway. "I'll see you later."

"Aren't you going to stay for the ending?"

"You've already told me the ending."

"That's not *this* program. *This* is about a horse and there's no water tank in it, just a creek like the one behind Mary Martha's house."

But Virginia had already gone. Jessie turned up the sound on the television set. Horses were thudding furiously across the desert as if they were trying to get away from the loud music that pursued them. Above the horses' hoofs and trumpets, Jessie could hear Virginia laughing out on the patio. She sounded very gay.

(17)

The pain began, as it usually did, when Charlie was a couple of blocks away from his house. It started in his left shoulder and every heartbeat pushed it along, down his arm and up his neck into his head until he was on fire. Alone in his room with no one to bother him, he could endure the pain and even derive some satisfaction from not taking anything to relieve it. But tonight Ben was waiting for him. Questions would be asked—some trivial, some innocent, some loaded—and answers to them would be expected. It would be at least an hour before he was allowed to go into his room and be by himself to plan what he would say to Jessie.

He stopped for a red light and was reaching into the glove compartment for the bottle of aspirin he kept there when he remembered that he wasn't driving the green coupé any more. There was no bottle of aspirin in this one, only a map of Los Angeles, unfolded and torn, as if someone had crammed it into the glove compartment in a fit of impatience.

The light turned green. He drove past the house. Ben's car was parked in the driveway, looking, to Charlie, exactly like its owner, not new any more but sturdy and clean and well taken care of, with no secret trouble in the engine.

The drug store was around the corner, one block down. There was no one in the store but Mr. Forster, the owner, who was behind the prescription counter reading the evening newspaper.

"Well, it's you, Charlie." Mr. Forster took off his spectacles and tucked them in the pocket of his white jacket. "Long time no see. How are you?"

"Not so good, Mr. Forster."

"Yes, I see that. Yes, indeed." Mr. Forster was the chief diagnostician of the neighborhood, even for people who had their own doctors. Out of respect for his position his customers always addressed him as Mr. Forster and so did his wife. He took his responsibilities very seriously, subscribing to the A.M.A. journal and *Lancet,* and reading with great care the advertising material that accompanied each new drug sample.

"A bit feverish, aren't you, Charlie?"

"I don't think so. I have a headache. I'd like some aspirin."

"Any nausea or vomiting?"

"No."

"What about your eyes? Are they all right?"

"Yes."

"Had your blood pressure checked recently?"

"No. I just want some——"

"It sounds like a vascular headache to me," Forster said, nodding wisely. "Maybe you should try one of the new reserpine compounds. By the way, did the man find your house?"

"What—what man?"

"Oh, he was in here a while ago, nice-looking gray-haired fellow around fifty. Said he'd lost your address."

"I haven't been home yet tonight."

"Well, he may be there right now, waiting for you."

"Not for me," Charlie said anxiously. "For Ben. People come to the house to see Ben, not me."

"Isn't your name Charles Gowen?"

"You know it is, Mr. Forster."

"Well, Charles Gowen is who he wanted to see." Forster took a bottle of aspirin off a shelf. "Shall I put this in a bag for you?"

"No. No, I'll take one right away." Charlie reached for the bottle. His hands were shaking, a fact that didn't escape Forster's attention.

"Yes, sir, if I were you, Charlie, I'd have my blood pressure checked. A niece of mine had a vascular headache and reserpine fixed her up just like magic. She's a different woman."

Charlie unscrewed the cap of the bottle, removed the cotton plug and put two aspirins in his mouth. The strong bitter taste spread from his tongue all the way to his ears and his forehead. His eyes began to water so that Mr. Forster's face looked distorted, like a face in a fun-house mirror.

"Let me get you a glass of milk," Forster said kindly. "You should always take a little milk with aspirin, it neutralizes the stomach acids."

"No, thank you."

"I insist."

Forster went into the back room and came out carrying a paper cup full of milk. He stood and watched Charlie drink it as though he were watching a stomach fighting a winning battle over its acids.

"I can understand your being nervous," Forster said, "at this stage of the game."

"What game?"

"The marriage game, of course. The word's gotten out how you're engaged to a nice little woman that works in the library. Marriage is a great thing for a man, believe me. You might have a few qualms about it now but in a few years you'll be glad you took the big step. A man stays single just so long, then people begin to talk." Forster took the empty paper cup from Charlie's hand and squeezed it into a ball. "Mind if I say something personal to you, Charlie?"

Charlie didn't speak. The milk seemed to have clotted in his throat like blood.

Forster mistook silence for assent. "That old trouble of yours, you mustn't let it interfere with your happiness. It's all over and done with, people have forgotten it. Why, it was so long ago you were hardly more than a boy. Now you're living a clean, decent life, you're just as good as the next man and don't you be thinking otherwise."

Please stop, Charlie thought. *Please stop him, God, somebody, anybody, make him be quiet. It's worse than listening to Ben. They don't know, neither of them, they don't know—*

"Maybe it's not in such good taste, dragging it up like this, but I want you to understand how I feel. You're going to do fine, Charlie. You deserve a little happiness. Living with a brother is all right when it's necessary, but what the heck, a man needs a wife and family of his own. When's the big day?"

"I don't know. Louise—it's her decision."

"Don't leave all the deciding to the lady, Charlie. They like to be told once in a while, makes them feel feminine. You want me to charge the aspirin?"

"Yes."

"Right. Well, all the best to you and the little lady, Charlie."

"Thank you, Mr. Forster."

"And bear in mind what I said. The town's getting so filled up with strangers that only a few old-timers like myself know you ever had any trouble. You just forget it, Charlie. It's water under the bridge, it's spilled milk. You ever tried to follow a drop of water down to the sea? Or pour spilled milk back into the bottle?"

"No. I—"

"Can't be done. Put that whole nasty business out of your head, Charlie. It's a dead horse, bury it."

"Yes. Good-bye, Mr. Forster."

Charlie began moving toward the door but Forster moved right along beside him. He seemed reluctant to let Charlie go, as if Charlie was a link with the past, which for all its cruelties was kinder than this day of strangers and freeways and super drugstores in every shopping center.

"I've got to go now, Mr. Forster. Ben's waiting for me."

"A good man, that Ben. He was a tower of strength to you in your time of need, always remember that, Charlie. He's probably quite proud of you now, eh? Considering how you've changed and everything?"

Charlie was staring down at the door handle as though he wished it would turn of its own accord and the door would open and he could escape. *Ben's not proud of me. I haven't changed. The horse isn't dead, the milk is still spilling, the same drop of water keeps passing under the bridge.*

Forster opened the door and the old-fashioned bell at the top tinkled its cheerful warning. "Well, it's been nice talking to you, Charlie. Come in again soon for another little chat. And say hello to Ben for me."

"Yes."

"By the way, that man who was in here asking for your address, he had an official bearing like he was used to ordering people around. But don't worry, Charlie. I didn't tell him a thing about that old trouble of yours. I figured it was none of his business if he wasn't an official, and if he was he'd know about it anyway. It's all on the record."

The same drop of water was passing under the bridge, only it was dirtier this time, it smelled worse, it carried more germs. Charlie leaned forward as if he meant to scoop it up with his hand and throw it away, so far away it would disintegrate, and all the dirt and smell and germs with it. But Mr. Forster was watching him, and though his smile was benevolent his eyes were wary. *You can never tell what these nuts are going to do, no matter how hard you try to be kind to them.*

"You," Charlie said, "you look like Ben, Mr. Forster."

"What?"

"You look exactly like Ben. It shows up real clear to me."

"It does, eh? You'd better go home and get some sleep. You're tired."

He was tired but he couldn't go home. The man might be there waiting for him, ready to ask him questions. He had done nothing wrong, yet he knew he wouldn't be believed. He couldn't say it with absolute conviction, the way Louise had the night she found him on Jacaranda Road: *"Nothing's happened, Charlie . . . You haven't harmed anyone. The Oakley girl is safe at home, and I believe that even if I hadn't found you when I did, she'd still be safe at home."*

The Oakley girl was safe at home. So was the Brant girl, Jessie. Or was she? He hadn't seen her at the playground, or outside her house when he drove past. Perhaps something had happened to her and that was why the man wanted to question him. He might even have to take a lie-detector test. He had heard once that real guilt and feelings of guilt showed up almost the same on a lie-detector test. If he were asked whether he knew Jessie Brant he would say no because this was the truth. But his heart would leap, his blood pressure would rise, his voice would choke up, he would start sweating, and all these things would be recorded on the chart and brand him a liar. Even Ben would think he was lying. Only Louise would believe him, only Louise. He felt a terrible need to hear her say: *"Nothing happened, Charlie. The Oakley girl is safe at home,*

*and the Brant girl and the other little girls, all safe at home,
all snug in their beds, nothing to fear from you, Charlie. I love
you, Charlie. . . ."*

He left his car in the parking lot behind the library. The
lot was almost filled, mainly with cars bearing high school and
city college stickers. The back door of the library was marked
Employees Only, but he used it anyway because it was the
shortest way to Louise.

He found himself in the filing and catalogue room, lined with
steel drawers and smelling of floor wax. An old man with a
push broom looked at him curiously but offered no challenge;
libraries were for everybody.

"Could you," Charlie said and stopped because his voice
sounded peculiar. He cleared his throat, swallowing the last of
the clotted milk. "Could you tell me if Miss Lang is here?"

"I don't know one from the other," the old man answered
with a shrug. "I only been on the job three nights now."

Nodding his thanks, Charlie walked the length of the room
and through a corridor with an open door at the end of it.
From here he could see Louise's desk behind the reference
counter but Louise wasn't there. A woman about thirty was
sitting in her chair. She looked familiar to Charlie though he
wasn't sure he'd ever met her.

A sixth sense seemed to warn her she was being watched. She
turned her head and spotted Charlie standing in the doorway.
She got up immediately, as though she was expecting his arrival
and had planned a welcome for him. She came toward him,
smiling.

"Mr. Gowen?"

"Yes, I—yes."

"I'm Betty Albert. Louise introduced us a couple of weeks
ago. Are you looking for her?"

"Yes. I thought she was working tonight."

"She was," Miss Albert said in a confidential whisper, "but
some teen-agers gave her a bad time. Oh, she handled it beauti-
fully, it was as quiet as church within ten minutes, but the strain

upset her. She went home. The public doesn't realize yet that we have quite a policing problem in the library, especially on Friday nights when school's not in session and the kids don't have a football or basketball game to go to. I claim the schools should be open all year, it would give the little darlings something to do. Bored teen-agers running around loose act worse than maniacs, don't you think? . . . Mr. Gowen, wait. You're really not supposed to use that back exit. It's just for employees. Mr. Gowen—?"

Miss Albert returned to her desk, her step light, her eyes dreamy. *He must be madly in love with her,* she thought as she lowered herself into the chair, lifting her skirt a few inches at the back to prevent seat-sag. *Why, the instant he heard she'd had a bad time and gone home, he looked sick with worry, then off he tore out the wrong exit. He's probably speeding to her side right now. Louise doesn't realize how lucky she is to have a man speeding to her side. When there isn't a thing the matter with her except nerves.*

Miss Albert sat for a while, her emotions swinging between wonder and envy. When the pendulum stopped, she found herself thinking in a more practiced and realistic manner. Louise was her superior in the library, it wouldn't hurt to do her a favor and warn her that Charlie was coming. It would give her a chance to pretty up, she'd looked awfully ratty when she left.

Louise's number was listed on a staff card beside the telephone. Miss Albert dialed, humming softly as if inspired by the sound of the dial tone.

Louise herself answered. "Yes?"

"This is Betty Albert."

"Oh. Is anything wrong?"

"No. Mr. Gowen was just here asking for you. When I told him you'd gone home he rushed right out. He should be there any minute. I thought—"

"Did he tell you he was coming here?"

"Why, no. But—well, it seemed obvious from the way he tore out and used the wrong exit and everything. I thought I'd tell you so you'd have a chance to pretty up before he arrived."

"Thanks, I'll do that," Louise said. "Good night, Miss Albert."

She hung up and went back down the hall toward her bedroom. Through the open door of the kitchen she could see her parents, her father watching something boiling on the stove, her mother getting the company dinnerware out of the top cupboard. She remembered that it was her father's birthday, and to celebrate the occasion he was preparing a special potato dish his grandmother used to cook for him in Germany when he was a boy. The thought of having to eat and pretend to enjoy the thick gray gluey balls nauseated Louise.

She spoke from the doorway. "I'm going out for a drive, if you don't mind."

He father turned around, scowling. "But I do mind. The *kloessen* are almost done and I've gone to a great deal of trouble over them."

"Yes, I know."

"You know but you don't care. Well, that's typical of the younger generation, lots of knowledge, no appreciation. When my grandmother was making *kloessen* you couldn't have dragged any of us away from the house with wild horses. I don't understand you, Louise. One minute you're lying down half-dead and the next minute you're going out. You're not consistent this last while."

"I guess I'm not."

"It's that man who's responsible. He's no good for you. He's blinded you to—"

"A lot of blind people do very well," Louise said. "With luck, so will I."

"So now the man isn't enough. You're demanding luck too, are you?"

"No, I'm praying for it."

"Well, I hope you get it."

"Then *sound* as if you hope it, will you? Just for once, *sound* as if you believed in me, as if you wanted me to have a life of my own, independent of you, unprotected by you."

"Oh, do hush up, both of you," Mrs. Lang said, brushing some dust off a plate with her apron. "It's hot in here. Open another window, will you, Joe? And Louise, don't forget to take a coat. You never can tell when the fog might come in."

The sun had gone down and stars were bursting out all over the sky like fireworks that would burn themselves out by morning and begin their infinite fall.

Charlie leaned against the side of the building. Of all the things Miss Albert had said to him, only one had registered in his mind: Louise had gone home. When he desperately needed her reassurance, she had gone where he was afraid to follow.

Home was where people went who had never done anything wrong—like Ben and Louise. For the others—the ones like him, Charlie—there wasn't any room, no matter how large the world. There wasn't any time to rest, no matter how long the night. Whatever their course of action or inaction they were always wrong. If they called out for help they were cowards, if they didn't call they were fools. If they stayed in one place they were loitering; if they moved they were running away. *"We, the jury, find the defendant guilty of everything and sentence him to a life of nothing—"* And all the people in the crowded courtroom, all the people in the world, broke into applause.

He knew it hadn't really occurred like that. No jury would say such a thing even though it might be what they meant. Besides, there'd been no jury, only a judge who kept leaning his head first on one hand and then on the other, as if it were too heavy for his neck. And the courtroom wasn't crowded. There were just the lawyers and bailiffs and reporter and Ben and his mother sitting near Charlie, and on the other side of the room, the child's parents, who didn't even glance at him. The girl herself wasn't brought in. Charlie never saw her again. When it was all over, Charlie rode in the back of the Sheriff's car to the hospital with two other men, and Ben took his savings and his mother's, and borrowed money from the bank, and gave it to the girl's parents, who'd sued for damages. They left town and Charlie never saw them again either.

That time it had happened. Even Louise couldn't have said it didn't, that it wasn't real, that the girl was at home safe in her bed. Perhaps she would have said it anyway, knowing it wasn't true. He couldn't afford to believe her ever again. He had to find out for himself what was real and what wasn't and which children were safe at home in their beds.

(18)

Ellen had expected a dull evening because the Arlingtons were usually tense and quiet the night before Howard was to leave on another business trip. She was pleasantly surprised by Virginia's show of vivacity and by the sudden interest Howard was taking in Jessie.

While the others ate at the redwood picnic table, Howard sat with Jessie on the lawn swing, asking her all about school and what she was doing during the holidays. Jessie, who'd been taught to answer adults' questions but not to speak with her mouth full, compromised by keeping her answers as brief as possible. School was O.K. Natural history was best. During the holidays she played. With Mary Martha. On the jungle gym. Also climbing trees. Sometimes they went swimming.

"Oh, come now," Howard said. "Aren't you forgetting Aunt Virginia? You visit her every day, don't you?"

"I guess."

"Do you like to visit her?"

"Yes."

"You go downtown shopping with her and to the movies and things like that, eh?"

"Not often."

"Once or twice a week?"

"Maybe."

Howard took a bite of hamburger and chewed it as if his teeth hurt. Then he put his plate down on the grass, shoving it almost out of sight under the swing. "Does anyone else go along on these excursions of yours?"

"No."

"Just the two of you, eh?"

Jessie nodded uncomfortably. She didn't know why Howard was asking so many questions. They made her feel peculiar, as if she and Virginia had been doing wrong things.

"It's nice of you to keep Virginia company," Howard said pleasantly. "She's a very lonely woman. You eat quite a few meals with her, don't you?"

"Not so many."

"When you've finished eating, what then? She reads to you, perhaps, or tells you stories?"

"Yes."

"She tells me some, too. Do you believe her stories?"

"Yes, unless they're fairy tales."

"How can you be sure when they're fairy tales?"

"They begin 'Once upon a time.' "

"Always?"

"They have to. It's a rule."

"Is it now," Howard said with a dry little laugh. "I'll remember that. The ones that begin 'Once upon a time,' I won't believe. Do I have to believe all the others?"

"You should. Otherwise—"

"Otherwise, she'd be telling fibs, eh?"

"I don't think so. Grownups aren't supposed to tell fibs."

"Some of them do, though. It's as natural to them as breathing."

Although Virginia was talking to Dave and Ellen and hadn't even glanced in Howard's direction, she seemed to be aware of trouble. She rose and came toward the swing, her stole trailing behind her like some pink wisp of the past.

"Have you finished eating, Jessie?"

"Yes."

"It's getting close to your bedtime, isn't it?"

"The kid has parents," Howard said. "Let them tell her when to go to bed. It's none of your business."

"I don't *have* to be told," Jessie said with dignity, and slid off the swing, glad for once to be getting away from the company of adults. She wished Michael were at home so she could ask him why Howard and Virginia were acting so peculiar lately.

"Well," Howard said, "I suppose now the party's over for you, Virginia. Not much use sticking around after the kid goes to bed. Shall we leave?"

"I'm warning you. Don't make a scene or you'll regret it."

"Your threats are as empty as your promises. Try another approach."

"Such as begging? You'd like that, wouldn't you? The only time you ever feel good any more is when I come crawling to you for something. Well, you're going to have to think of other ways to feel good because from now on I'm not crawling and I'm not begging."

"Three days," Howard said bitterly, "I've been home three days and not for one minute have I felt welcome. I'm just a nuisance who appears every two or three weeks and disrupts your real life. The hell of it is that I don't understand what your real life is, so I can't try to fit into it or go along with it. I can only fight it because it doesn't include me. I want, I need, a place in it. I used to have one. What went wrong, Virginia?"

Dave and Ellen exchanged embarrassed glances like two characters in a play who found themselves on stage at the wrong time. Then Ellen put some dishes on a tray and started toward the house and after a second's hesitation Dave followed her. Their leaving made no more difference to the Arlingtons than their presence had.

"What's the matter, Virginia? If it's my job, I can change it. If it's the fact that we have no family, we can change that, too."

"No," she said sharply. "I no longer want a family."

"Why not? You've wept for one often enough."

"We no longer have anything to offer a child." She stared out beyond the patio walls to the horizon. The wall of fog had begun to expand. Pretty soon the city would disappear, streets would be separated from streets and people from people and everyone would be alone. "Yes, Howard, I wept, I wept buckets. I was young then. I didn't realize how cruel it would be to pass along such an ugly thing as life. Poor Jessie."

He frowned. "Why? Why poor Jessie?"

"She's only nine, she's still full of innocence and high hopes and dreams. She will lose her innocence and high hopes and dreams; she will lose them all. By the time she's my age she will have wished a thousand times that she were dead."

Twice Louise covered the entire length of Jacaranda Road, driving in second gear, looking at every parked car and every person walking along the street or waiting at bus stops. There was no sign of Charlie or his car, and the Oakley house at 319 was dark as if no one lived in it any more. She was encouraged by the dark house. If anything had happened, there would be light and noise and excitement. *Nothing's happened. Nothing whatever—*

She drove to Miria Street. Ben let her in the front door. "Hello, Louise. I thought you were working tonight."

"I was."

"Charlie's not here but come in anyway. I'm making a fresh pot of coffee. Would you like some?"

"Please." She followed him down the hall to the kitchen. He walked slowly as though his back ached, and for the first time she thought of him not as one of the Gowen brothers but as a middle-aged man.

She accepted the cup of coffee he poured her and sat down at the table. "Are you tired, Ben?"

"A little. It was Dollar Day in most of the stores downtown. What the ladies saved on hats and dresses they came in and spent on food." He sat down opposite her. "I think I've found the right place."

"Place?"

"The apartment I wanted down near the breakwater. It's furnished, so I wouldn't have to take a thing out of the house here, and the landlord told me I could keep a dog if it wasn't too big. I'll sign the lease as soon as you and Charlie name the wedding day. . . . You don't look very pleased. What's the matter?"

"I was trying to imagine this house without you in it. It's very—difficult."

"This house has seen enough of me. And vice versa."

"Charlie would like you to stay with us."

"He'd soon get over that idea. He's nervous, that's all. He's like a kid, dreading any change even if it's a good one."

"Maybe I'm a little like that, too."

"Come off it, Louise. Why, I'll bet after you've been married a few weeks you'll meet me on the street and think, *that guy looks familiar, I must have seen him before some place.*"

"That could never happen."

"A lot of things are going to happen. Good things, I mean, the kind you and Charlie deserve."

She took a sip of coffee. It was so strong and bitter she could hardly swallow it. "Did—did Charlie come home after work?"

"No. But don't worry about it. He had to go on an errand for the boss. It was an important errand, too—making a delivery to the Forest Service up the mountain. It shows the boss is beginning to trust him with bigger things. Charlie told me on the phone not to expect him before seven o'clock."

"It's nearly nine."

"He may have had some trouble with his car. I've had trouble up there myself on hot days. The engine started to boil—"

"He was at the library about an hour ago."

"There's more to this, I suppose?"

"Yes."

Ben's face didn't change expression but suddenly he pushed his chair away from the table with such violence that his coffee cup fell into the saucer. Brown fluid oozed across the green plastic cloth like a muddy stream through a meadow. "Well, don't bother telling me. I won't listen. I want one night, just this one night, to think about my own future, maybe even dream a little. Or don't I deserve a dream because I happen to be Charlie's older brother?"

"I'm sorry, Ben. I guess I shouldn't have come running to you." She rose, pulling her coat tightly around her body as if the room had turned cold. "I must learn to deal with situations like this on my own. Don't come with me, Ben. I can let myself out."

"Situations like what?"

"You don't want to hear."

"No, but you'd better tell me."

"I think I can handle it myself."

"By crying?"

"I'm not crying. My eyes always water when—when I'm under a strain. There's a certain nerve that runs from the back of the ear to the tear ducts and—"

"We'll discuss the structure of the nervous system some other time. Where is Charlie?"

"I don't know," she said, wiping her eyes with the back of one hand. "I've been looking for him ever since Miss Albert called to tell me he'd been at the library."

"You've been looking where?"

"Up and down Jacaranda Road."

"Why Jacaranda Road? You must have had a reason. What is it?"

She took a step back, as if dodging a blow.

"You've got to answer me, Louise."

"Yes. I'm trying—trying to say it in the right way."

"If it's a wrong thing, there's no right way to say it."

"I'm not sure that it's wrong. There may be nothing to it except in Charlie's imagination and now mine. I mean, he gets so full of worry that I start to worry, too."

"What about?"

She hesitated for a long time, then she spoke quickly, slurring her words as if to make them less real. "There's a child liv-

ing at 319 Jacaranda Road, a little girl named Mary Martha
Oakley. Charlie swears he's never even talked to her and I
believe him, but he's afraid. So am I. I think he's been watching
her and—well, fantasying about her. I know this isn't good because a fantasy that gets out of control can become a fact."

"How long have you known about the girl?"

"Two days."

"And you didn't level with me."

"Charlie asked me not to."

"But you're leveling now, in spite of that. Why?"

"I want you to tell me how it was the—the other time. I've
got to know all about it, how he acted beforehand, if he was
quiet or moody or restless, if he stayed away from the house on
nights like this without telling anyone. Did he talk about the
girl a lot, or didn't he mention her? How old was she? What did
she look like? How did Charlie meet her?"

Ben went over to the sink and tore off a couple of sheets of
paper toweling. Then he wiped the coffee off the table, slowly
and methodically. His face was blank, as if he hadn't heard a
word she'd said.

"Aren't you listening, Ben?"

"Yes. But I won't do what you're asking me to. It would
serve no purpose."

"It might. Everybody has a pattern, Ben. Even strange and
difficult people have one if you can find it. Suppose I learned
Charlie's pattern so I could be alert to the danger signals—"

"It happened a long time ago. I don't remember the details,
the fine points." Ben threw the used towel in the wastebasket
and sat down again, his hands pressed out flat on the table in
front of him, palms down. "If there were danger signals, I
didn't see them. Charlie was just a nice, quiet young man, easy
to have around, never asking much or getting much. He'd had
two years of college. The first year he did well; the second, he
had trouble concentrating—my mother suspected a love affair
but it turned out she was wrong. He didn't go back for the
third year because my father died. At least that was the ac-

cepted reason. After that he went to work. He held a succession of unimportant jobs. One of them was at a veterinary hospital and boarding kennels on Quila Street near the railroad tracks. Every day the girl walked along the tracks on her way to and from school. Charlie used to chase her away because he was afraid she'd get hurt by a train or by one of the winos who hung around the area. That's how it began, with Charlie trying to protect her."

Louise listened, remembering the reason Charlie had given her for wanting to find out the name of the people who lived at 319 Jacaranda Road: *"I must tell those people they've got to take better care of their little dog unless they want it to be killed by a car or something."*

She said, "How old was the girl?"

"Ten. But she looked younger because she was so small and skinny."

"Was she pretty?"

"No."

"What color was her hair, and was it short or long?"

"Dark and short, I think. I only saw her once, but I remember one of her front teeth was chipped from a fall."

"Though it may seem like a terrible thing to say, Ben, all this sounds very promising."

"Promising?"

"Yes. You see, I've met Mary Martha. She's a plump, pretty child with a long blond ponytail, quite mature-looking for her age. She's not a bit like that other girl. Isn't that a good sign? She doesn't fit the pattern at all, Ben." Louise's pale cheeks had taken on a flush of excitement. "Now tell me about Charlie, how he acted beforehand, everything you can think of."

"I saw no difference in him," Ben said heavily. "But then I wasn't looking very hard, I'd just gotten married to Ann. Charlie could have grown another head and I might not have noticed."

"You'd just gotten married," Louise repeated. "Now Charlie's about to get married. Is this just a coincidence or is it part of the pattern?"

"Stop thinking about patterns, Louise. A whole battery of experts tried to figure out Charlie's and got nowhere."

"Then it's my turn to try. Where did you live after the wedding?"

"Here in this house. It was only supposed to be a temporary arrangement, we were going to buy a place of our own. Then Charlie was arrested and everything blew up in our faces. I didn't have enough money left to buy a tent, but by that time it didn't matter because I had no wife either."

"And now Charlie and I will be living in this house, too." Louise was looking around the room as if she were seeing it for the first time as a place she would have to call her home. "You still don't notice any pattern, Ben?"

"What if I say yes? What do I do then?"

"You mean, what do *we* do? I'm in it with you this time."

"Don't say this time. There isn't going to be a this time. It happened once, and it's not going to happen again, by God, if I have to keep him in sight twenty-four hours a day, if I have to handcuff him to me."

"That won't be much of a life for Charlie. He'd be better off dead."

"Do you suppose I haven't thought of that?" he said roughly. "A hundred times, five hundred, I've looked at him and seen him suffering, and I've thought, this is my kid brother. I love him, I'd cut off an arm for him, but maybe the best thing I could do for him is to end it all."

"You mean, kill him."

"Yes, kill him. And don't look at me with such horror. You may be thinking the same thing yourself before long."

"If you feel like that, your problems may be worse than Charlie's." She looked a little surprised at her own words as if they had come out unplanned. "Perhaps yours are much worse because you're not aware of them. When something happens to you, or inside yourself, you've always had Charlie to blame.

It's made you look pretty good in the eyes of the world but it hasn't helped Charlie. He's already had more blame than he can handle. What he needs now is confidence in himself, a feeling that he'll do the right thing on his own and not because you'll force him to. You spoke a minute ago of handcuffing him to you. That might work, up to a point. Perhaps it would prevent him from doing the wrong thing but it wouldn't help him to do the right one."

"Well, that was quite a speech, Louise."

"There's more."

"I'm not sure I want to hear it."

"Listen anyway, will you, Ben?"

"Since when have you become an authority on the Gowen brothers?"

She ignored the sarcasm. "I've been trying to do some figuring. out, that's all."

"And you've decided what?"

"Charlie's problem wasn't born inside him. It doesn't belong only to him, it's a family affair. Some event, some relationship, or several of both, made him not want to grow up. He let you assume the grown-up role. He remained a child, the kid brother, the baby of the family. He merely went through the motions of manhood by imitating you and doing what you told him to."

She lapsed into silence, and Ben said, "I hope you've finished."

"Almost. Did you and Ann go on a honeymoon?"

"We went to San Francisco for a week. I can't see what that—"

"How soon after you got back did the trouble happen between Charlie and the girl?"

"A few days. Why?"

"Perhaps," she said slowly, "Charlie was only trying, in his mixed-up way, to imitate you by 'marrying' the girl."

Jessie had turned off her light and closed her door tightly to give her parents the impression that she'd gone to sleep. But both her side and back windows were wide open and she missed very little of what was going on.

She heard Virginia and Howard quarreling in the patio, and later, the gate opening and slamming shut again, and Howard's car racing out of the driveway and down the street. Virginia started to cry and Dave took her home and then set out in his car to look for Howard. Jessie lay in the darkness, staring up at the ceiling and wondering how adults could get away with doing such puzzling things without any reason. She herself had to have at least one good reason, and sometimes two, for everything she did.

Shortly before ten o'clock Ellen paused outside Jessie's door for a few seconds, then continued on down the hall.

Jessie called out, "I'm thirsty."

"All right, get up and pour yourself a glass of water."

"I'd rather you brought me one."

"All *right*." Ellen's voice was cross, and when she came into the bedroom with the glass of water she looked tired and tense. "Why aren't you ever thirsty during the day?"

"I don't have time then to think about it."

"Well, drink up. And if you need anything else get it *now*. I have a headache, I'm going to take a sleeping capsule and go to bed."

"May I take one, too?"

"Of course not. Little girls don't need sleeping capsules."

"Mrs. Oakley gives Mary Martha one sometimes."

"Mrs. Oakley is a— Well, anyway, you close your eyes and think pleasant thoughts."

"Why did Howard and Virginia have a fight?"

"That's a good question," Ellen said dryly. "If, within the next fifty years, I come up with a good answer, I'll tell it to you. Have you finished with the water?"

"Yes."

Ellen reached for the glass, still nearly full. "Now this is the final good night, Jessie. You understand that? Absolutely *final*." When she went out she shut the door in a way that indicated she meant business.

Jessie closed her eyes and thought of butterscotch sundaes and Christmas morning and flying the box kite with her name printed in big letters on all sides. Her name was away up in the air and she was flying up in the air to join it, carried effortlessly by the wind, higher and higher. She had almost reached her name when she heard a car in the driveway. She came to earth with a bang. The descent was so real and sudden and shocking that her arms and legs ached and she lay huddled in her bed like the survivor of a plane wreck.

She heard a man's footsteps across the driveway, then Virginia's voice, sounding so cold and hard that Jessie wouldn't have recognized it if it hadn't been coming from Virginia's back porch.

"You didn't find him, I suppose."

"No," Dave said.

"Well, that suits me. Good riddance to bad rubbish, as we used to say in my youth, long since gone, long since wasted on a—"

"Talk like that will get you nowhere. Be practical. You need Howard, you can't support yourself."

"That's a wonderful attitude to take."

"It's a fact, not an attitude," Dave said. "You seem ready to quarrel with anyone tonight. I'd better go home."

"Do that."

"Virginia, listen to me—"

The voices stopped abruptly. Jessie went over to the window and peered out through the slats of the Venetian blinds. The Arlingtons' porch was empty and the door into the house was closed.

Jessie returned to bed. Lying on her back with her hands clasped behind her head, she thought about Virginia and how she needed Howard because she couldn't support herself. She wondered how much money Virginia would require if Howard never came back. Virginia had a car and a house with furniture and enough clothes to last for years and years. All she'd really have to buy would be food.

Without moving her head Jessie could see the half-open door

of her clothes closet. In the closet, in the toe of one of her party shoes, were the two ten-dollar bills Howard had pressed into her hand. Although she would miss the money if she gave it back to Virginia, it would be a kind of relief to get rid of it and to be doing Virginia a favor at the same time. Twenty dollars would buy tons of food, even the butterscotch sundaes Virginia liked so much.

Once the decision was made, Jessie wasted no time. She put on a bathrobe and slippers, fished the two bills from the toe of her party shoe and tiptoed down the hall, through the kitchen and out the back door.

Moving through the darkness in her long white flowing robe, she looked like the ghost of a bride.

(19)

The illuminated dial on his bedside clock indicated a few minutes past midnight when Ralph MacPherson was awakened by the phone ringing. He picked up the receiver, opening his eyes only the merest slit to glance at the clock.

"Yes?"

"It's Kate, Mac. Thank heaven you're there. I need your help."

"My dear girl, do you realize what time it is?"

"Yes, of course I realize. I should, I was asleep too when the pounding woke me up."

"All right, I'm hooked," Mac said impatiently. "What pounding?"

"At the front door. There's a man out there."

"What man?"

"I don't know. I came downstairs without turning on any lights. I thought that it was Sheridan, and I was going to pretend I wasn't home."

"You're sure it's not Sheridan?"

"Yes. I can see his shadow. He's too big to be Sheridan. What will I do, Mac?"

"That will depend on what the man's doing."

"He's just sitting out there on the top step of the porch making funny sounds. I think—I think he's crying. Oh God, Mac, so many crazy things have happened lately. I feel I'm lost in the middle of a nightmare. Why should a strange man come up on my front porch to cry?"

"Because he's troubled."

"Yes, but why my porch? Why here? Why *me?*"

"It's probably just some drunk on a crying jag who picked your house by accident," Mac said. "If you want to get rid of him, I suggest you call the police."

"I won't do that." There was a silence. "It gives a place a bad reputation to have police arriving with their sirens going full blast and all."

"They don't usually— Never mind. What do you want me to do, Kate?"

"If you could just come over and talk to him, Mac. Ask him why he came here, tell him to leave. He'd listen to you. You sound so authoritative."

"Well, I don't feel very authoritative at this hour of the night but I'll try my best. I'll be there in about ten minutes. Keep the doors locked and don't turn on any lights. Where's Mary Martha?"

"Asleep in her room."

"See that she stays that way," he said and hung up. One Oakley female was enough to cope with at one time.

In the older sections of town the street lights were placed only at intersections, as if what went on at night between corners was not the business of strangers or casual passers-by. The Oakley house was invisible from the road. Mac couldn't even see the trees that surrounded it but he could hear them. The wind was moving through the leaves and bough rubbed against bough in false affection.

From the back seat Mac took the heavy flash-and-blinker light he'd kept there for years in case of emergency. A lot of emergencies had occurred since then but none in which a flashlight was any use. He switched it on. Although the beam wasn't as powerful as it had been, it was enough to illumine the flagstone path to the house.

The steps of the front porch were empty and for one very bad moment he thought Kate had imagined the whole thing. Then he saw the man leaning over the porch railing. His head was bent as though his neck had been broken. He turned toward the beam of the flashlight, his face showing no reaction either to the light or to Mac's presence. He was a tall, heavily built man about forty. He wore blue jeans and a sweatshirt, both stained with blood, and he kept one hand pressed against his chest as if to staunch a wound.

Mac said, "Are you hurt?"

The man's mouth moved but no sound came out of it.

Mac tried again. "I'm Ralph MacPherson. Mrs. Oakley, who lives in this house, called me a few minutes ago to report a man pounding on her door. That was you?"

The man nodded slightly though he looked too dazed to understand the question.

"What are you doing here?"

"My dau—dau—"

"Your dog? You've lost your dog, is that it?"

"Dog?" He covered his face with his hands and Mac saw that it was his right hand that was bleeding. "Not dog. Daughter. *Daughter.*"

"You're looking for your daughter?"

"Yes."

"What makes you think she might be here?"

"Her best—best friend lives here."

"Mary Martha?"

"Yes."

Mac remembered his office conversation with Kate about Mary Martha's best friend. "You're Jessie Brant's father?"

"Yes. She's gone. Jessie's gone."

"Take it easy now, Brant. How did you hurt yourself?"

"Don't bother about me. Jessie—"

"You're bleeding."

"I was running and I fell. I don't care about me. Don't you understand? My daughter is missing. *She is missing from her bed.*"

"All right, don't get excited. We'll find her."

Mac crossed the porch and rapped lightly on the front door. "Kate, turn on the light and open the door."

The porch light went on and the door opened almost instantly as if Kate had been standing in the hall waiting for someone to tell her what to do. She had on fresh make-up that seemed to have been applied hastily and in the dark. It didn't cover the harsh lines that scarred her face or the anxiety that distorted her eyes.

"Mac?"

"Kate, you remember Mr. Brant, don't you?"

She glanced briefly at Dave and away again. "We're acquainted. That hardly gives him the right to come pounding at—"

"Be quiet and pay attention, Kate. Mr. Brant is here looking for Jessie. Have you seen her?"

"Why no, of course not. It's after midnight. What would Jessie be doing out at a time like this? He has blood on him," she added, staring up into Mac's face. "Tell him to go away. I hate the sight of blood. I won't allow him inside my house."

Dave pressed his hands together tightly to prevent them from reaching out and striking her. His voice was very quiet. "I won't come inside your house, Mrs. Oakley. I wouldn't be here at all if I could have gotten you on the phone."

"I have an unlisted number."

"Yes. I tried to call you."

"People have no right to call others at midnight," she said, as if she herself wouldn't dream of doing such a thing. "Mary Martha and I keep early hours. She was asleep by 8:30 and I shortly afterward."

"Your daughter is in bed asleep, Mrs. Oakley?"

'Why yes, of course."

"Well, *mine isn't*."

"What do you mean?" She turned to Mac, touching his coat sleeve with her hand like a child pleading for a favor. "What does he mean, Mac? All little girls ought to be in bed at this time of night."

"Jessie is missing," Mac said.

"I'm sure she won't be missing for long. She's probably just playing a trick on her parents. Jessie's full of ideas and she truly loves to be the center of attention. She'll turn up any minute with one of her preposterous stories and everything will be fine. Won't it? Won't it, Mac?"

"I don't know. When did you see her last?"

"This afternoon. She dropped in to invite Mary Martha to go swimming with her. I didn't allow Mary Martha to go. I've been supervising her extra carefully ever since I received that anonymous letter."

Mac had forgotten the letter. He put his hand in the left pocket of his coat. There were other papers in the pocket but the letter was unmistakable to the touch. One corner of the envelope bulged where the paper had been folded and refolded until it was no more than an inch square. Mac remembered enough of the contents of the letter to make him regret not taking it immediately to his friend, Lieutenant Gallantyne. Gallantyne had a collection of anonymous letters that spanned thirty years of police work.

Mac said, "Will you describe Jessie to me, Mr. Brant?"

"I have pictures of her at home." He almost broke down at the word *home*. His face started to come apart and he turned it toward the darkness beyond the porch railing. "I must get back to my wife. She's expecting me to—to bring Jessie home with me. She was so sure Jessie would be here."

Kate was clutching her long wool bathrobe around her as though somebody had just threatened to tear it off. "I don't know why she was sure Jessie would come here. I'm the last person in the world who'd be taken in by one of Jessie's fancy schemes. I would have telephoned Mrs. Brant immediately. Wouldn't I, Mac?"

"Of course you would, Kate," Mac said. "You'd better go back in the house now and see if you can get some sleep."

"I won't be able to close my eyes. There may be some monster loose in the neighborhood and no child is safe. He won't stop with just Jessie. Mary Martha might be next."

"Shut up, Kate."

"Oh, Mac, please don't go. Don't leave me alone."

"I have to. I'm driving Mr. Brant home."

"Everybody leaves me alone. I can't stand—"

"I'll talk to you in the morning."

The door closed, the porch light went off. The two men began walking in slow, silent unison down the flagstone path, following the beam of Mac's flashlight as if it were a dim ray of hope.

Inside the car Mac said, "Where do you live, Brant?"

"Cielito Lane."

"That's in the Peppertree tract, isn't it?"

"Yes."

The car pulled away from the curb.

"Have you called the police?"

"Virginia—Mrs. Arlington did. She lives next door. She and Jessie are very good friends. My wife thought that if Jessie were in any kind of trouble or even just playing a trick on us, she'd go to the Arlingtons' house first. We searched all through it and the garage twice. Jessie wasn't there. Virginia called the police and I set out for Mrs. Oakley's. I couldn't think of any other place Jessie would go late at night. We haven't lived in town long and we have no relatives here."

"You'll forgive me for asking this," Mac said, "but is Jessie a girl who often gets into trouble?"

"No. She never does. Leaving her bicycle in the middle of the sidewalk, coming home late for meals, things like that, yes, but nothing more serious."

"Has she ever run away from home?"

"Of course not."

"Runaways are picked up by the police every day, Brant."

"She didn't run away," Dave said hoarsely. "I wish to God I could believe she had."

"Why can't you?"

"She had no money, and the only clothes missing from her closet are the pajamas she wore to bed and a bathrobe and a pair of slippers. Jessie's a sensible girl, she'd know better than to try and run away without any money and wearing an outfit that would immediately attract everybody's attention."

That might be the whole point, Mac thought, but all he said was, "Can you think of any recent family scene or event that might make her want to run away?"

"No."

"Has she been upset about something lately?"

Dave turned and looked out the window. The night seemed darker than any he could ever remember. It wasn't the ordinary darkness, an absence of light; it was a thick, soft, suffocating thing that covered the whole world. No morning could ever penetrate it.

"Has something upset her?" Mac repeated.

"I'm trying to answer. I—she's been talking a lot about divorce, fathers deserting their families like Sheridan Oakley. Obviously Mary Martha's fed her a lot of stuff and Jessie's taken it perhaps more seriously than it deserves. She's a funny kid, Jessie. She puts on a big front about not caring but she feels everything deeply, especially where Mary Martha is concerned. The two girls have been very close for almost a year now, in fact almost inseparable."

Mac remembered the opening sentence of the letter he was carrying in his pocket: *Your daughter takes too dangerous risks with her delicate body.* He said, "Do you consider Jessie a frail child, that is, delicate in build?"

"That's an odd question."

"I have good reasons for asking it which I can't divulge right now."

"Well, Jessie might look delicate to some people. Actually, she's thin and wiry like her mother, and extremely healthy. The only times she's ever needed a doctor were when she's had accidents."

"Accidents such as?"

"Falls, stings, bites. The normal things that happen to kids plus a few extra. Right now her hands are badly blistered from overuse of the jungle gym at the school playground."

"Does she often play at the school playground?"

"I don't know. I'm at work all day."

"Would you say she goes there twice a week? Five times? Seven?"

"All the neighborhood kids go there. Why shouldn't they?" Dave added defensively, "It's well supervised, there are organized games and puppet shows and things not available in the ordinary backyard. Just what were you implying?"

"Nothing. I was merely—"

"No. I think you know something that you're not telling me. You're holding out on me. Why?"

"I have no knowledge at present," Mac said, "that would be of any value or comfort to you."

"That's only a fancy way of saying you won't tell me." There was a silence, filled with sudden distrust and uneasiness. "Who are you, anyway? What are you? How did you get into this?"

"I gave you my name, Ralph MacPherson. I'm a lawyer and an old friend of Mrs. Oakley's."

"She didn't waste much time contacting a lawyer. Why?"

"She called me as a friend, not a lawyer. I've known her since she was Jessie's age. . . . Let's see, I take the next turn, don't I?"

"Yes."

All the houses in the block were dark except for two. In the driveway that separated the two, a black Chrysler sedan was parked. Mac recognized it as one of the unmarked police cars used for assignments requiring special precautions.

Except for the number of lights burning in the two houses, there was no sign that anything had happened. The streets were deserted, and if the immediate neighbors were curious, they were keeping their curiosity behind closed drapes in dark rooms.

Mac braked the car, leaving the engine running. "I'd be a

damned fool if I said I'm glad to have met you, Brant. So I'll just say I hope we meet again under more pleasant circumstances."

"Aren't you coming inside?"

"It didn't occur to me that you might want me to."

"I can't face Ellen alone."

"I don't see that I'll be of much help. Besides, you won't be alone with her, the police are there."

"I won't—I can't walk into that house and tell her I didn't find Jessie. She was so full of hope. How can I go in there and take it all away from her?"

"She has to be told the truth, Brant. Come on, I'll go with you."

The two men got out of the car and began walking toward the house. Mac had no thought of involving himself in the situation. He felt that he was merely doing his duty, helping a person in trouble, and that the whole thing—or at least his part in it— would be over in a few minutes. He could afford a few minutes, some kind words.

Suddenly the front door opened and a woman rushed out. It was as if a violent explosion had taken place inside the house and blown the door open and tossed the woman out.

She said, "Jessie?" Then she stopped dead in her tracks, staring at Mac. "Where's Jessie?"

"Mrs. Brant, I—"

"I know. You must be the doctor. It happened the way I thought. Jessie was on her way to Mary Martha's by the short cut and she fell crossing the creek. And she's in the hospital and you've come to tell me she'll be all right, it's nothing serious, she'll be home in a—"

"Stop it, Mrs. Brant. I'm a lawyer, not a doctor."

"Where is Jessie?"

"I'm sorry, I don't know."

Dave said, "She didn't go to Mary Martha's, Ellen. I haven't found her."

"Oh God. Please, God, help her. Help my baby."

Dave took her in his arms. To Mac it was not so much an embrace as a case of each of them holding the other up. He felt a deep pity but he realized there was nothing further he could do for them now. He started back to his car. The letter in his pocket seemed to be getting heavier, like a stone to which things had begun to cling and grow and multiply.

He had almost reached the curb when a voice behind him said, "Just a minute, sir."

Mac turned and saw a young man in a dark gray suit and matching fedora. The fedora made him look like an undergraduate dressed up for a role in a play. "Yes, what is it?"

"May I ask your name, sir?"

"MacPherson."

"Do you have business here at this time of night, Mr. MacPherson?"

"I drove Mr. Brant home."

"I'm sure you won't mind repeating that to the lieutenant, will you?"

"Not," Mac said dryly, "if the lieutenant wants to hear it."

"Oh, he will. Come this way, please."

As they walked down the driveway Mac saw that there was another police car parked outside the garage. Its searchlight had been angled to shine on the window of a rear bedroom. A policeman was examining the window; a second one stood just outside the periphery of the light. All Mac could see of him was his gray hair, which was cut short and stood up straight on his head like the bristles of a brush. It was enough.

"Hello, Gallantyne."

Gallantyne stepped forward, squinting against the light. He was of medium height with broad, heavy shoulders, slightly stooped. His posture and his movements all indicated a vast impatience just barely kept under control. He always gave Mac the impression of a well-trained and very powerful stallion with one invisible saddle sore which mustn't be touched. No one knew where this sore was but they knew it was there and it paid to be careful.

"What are you doing here, Mac?" Gallantyne said.

"I was invited. It seems I come under the heading of suspicious characters seen lurking in the neighborhood."

"Well, were you?"

"I was seen, I don't believe I was lurking," Mac said. "Unless perhaps I have a natural lurk that I'm not aware of. May I return the question? What are you doing here, Gallantyne? I thought you were tied to a desk."

"They untie me once in a while. Salvadore's on vacation and Weber has bursitis. Come inside. I want to talk to you."

For reasons he didn't yet understand, Mac felt a great reluctance to enter the house. He didn't want the missing child to seem any more real to him than she did now; he didn't want to see the yard where she played, the table she ate at, the room she slept in. He wanted her to remain merely a name and a number, Jessie Brant, aged nine. He said, "I'd prefer to stay out here."

"Well, I prefer different."

Gallantyne turned and walked through an open gate into a patio. He didn't bother looking back to see if he was being followed. It was taken for granted that he would be, and he was.

The back door of the house had been propped open with a flowerpot filled with earth containing a dried-out azalea. A policeman in uniform was dusting the door and its brass knob for fingerprints. There was no sign that the door had been forced or the lock tampered with.

The kitchen contained mute evidence of a family going through a crisis: cups of half-consumed coffee, overflowing ashtrays, a bottle of aspirin with the top off, a wastebasket filled with used pieces of tissue and the empty box they'd come in.

Gallantyne said, "Sit down, Mac. You look nervous. Are you the family lawyer?"

"No."

"An old friend, then?"

"I've known Brant about an hour, his wife for five minutes." He explained briefly about responding to Kate's phone call and meeting Brant on the porch of her house.

"It sounds crazy," Gallantyne said.

"Anything involving Mrs. Oakley has a certain amount of il-logic in it. She's a nervous woman and she's been under a great strain, especially for the past few days."

"Why the past few days?"

"Two reasons that I know of, though there may be more. She thinks the husband she's divorcing has hired someone to spy on her. And this week she received an anonymous letter warning her to take better care of her daughter."

Gallantyne's thick gray eyebrows leaped up his forehead. "Have you read it?"

"Yes. Mrs. Oakley brought it to my office right away. She'd pretty well convinced herself that Mr. Oakley had written it to harass her. I didn't believe it. In fact, I didn't really take the whole thing seriously. Now I'm afraid, I'm very much afraid, that I made a bad mistake."

"Why?"

"Here, see for yourself." Mac took the envelope out of his pocket. He was appalled at the severe trembling of his hands. It was as if his body had acknowledged his feelings of guilt before his mind was conscious of them. "I realize now that I should have shown this to you right away. Oh, I have the customary excuses: I was busy, I was fed up with Kate Oakley's shenani-gans, and so on. But excuses aren't good enough. If I—"

"You're too old for the if-game," Gallantyne said and took the letter out of the envelope. "Was it folded like this when Mrs. Oakley received it?"

"Yes."

"Well, that's a switch anyway." He read the letter through, half aloud. " 'Your daughter takes too dangerous risks with her delicate body. Children must be guarded against the cruel haz-ards of life and fed good, nourishing food so their bones will be padded. Also clothing. You should put plenty of clothing on her, keep arms and legs covered, etc. In the name of God please take better care of your little girl.' "

Gallantyne reread the letter, this time silently, then he tossed it on the table as though he wanted to get rid of it as quickly as possible. The grooves in his face had deepened and drops of sweat appeared on his forehead, growing larger and larger until they fell of their own weight and were lost in his eyebrows. "All I can say is, I'm damn glad this wasn't sent to the Brants. As it is, I figure the kid decided to throw a scare into her parents by running away. Probably one of the patrol cars has picked her up by now. . . . Why the hell are you staring at me like that?"

"I think the letter was intended for Mrs. Brant."

"You said it was addressed to Mrs. Oakley."

"Jessie Brant and the Oakley girl, Mary Martha, are best friends. According to Brant, they're inseparable, which no doubt involves a lot of visiting back and forth in each other's houses. Mary Martha's a tall girl for her age, a trifle overweight, and inclined to be cautious. The writer of the letter wasn't describing Mary Martha. He, or she, was describing Jessie."

"You can't be sure of that."

"I can be sure of two things. Mary Martha's at home with her mother and Jessie isn't."

Gallantyne stood in silence for a minute. Then he picked up the letter, refolded it and put it in his pocket. "We won't tell anybody about this right now, not the parents or the press or anyone else."

(20)

Howard Arlington woke up at dawn in a motel room. Seen through half-closed eyes the place looked the same as a hundred others he'd stayed in, but gradually differences began to show up: the briefcase Virginia had given him years ago was not on the bureau where he always kept it, and the luggage rack at the foot of the bed was empty. When he turned his head his starched collar jabbed him in the neck and he realized he was still fully dressed. Even his tie was knotted. He loosened it but the tightness in his throat didn't go away. It was as if, during the night, he'd tried to swallow something too large and too fibrous to be swallowed.

He got up and opened the drapes. Fog pressed against the window like the ectoplasm of lost spirits seeking shelter and a home. He closed the drapes again and turned on a lamp. Except for the outline of his body on the chenille bedspread, the room looked as though it hadn't been occupied. The clothes closet was empty, the ashtrays unused, the drinking glasses on the bureau still wrapped in wax paper.

He couldn't remember checking into the motel; yet he knew he must have registered, given his name and address and car license number, and paid in advance because he had no luggage. His last clear recollection was of Virginia standing in the Brants' patio saying she didn't want a child any more: *"We no longer have anything to offer a child. . . . How cruel it would be to pass along such an ugly thing as life. Poor Jessie. . . . She will lose her innocence and high hopes and dreams; she will lose them all. By the time she's my age she will have wished a thousand times that she were dead."*

He'd quarreled with Virginia and he was in a motel. These were the only facts he was sure of. Where the motel was, in what city, how he'd reached it and why, he didn't know. He spent so much of his life driving from one city to another and checking in and out of motels that he must have acted automatically.

He left the room key on top of the bureau and went out to his car. On the front seat there was an empty pint bottle of whiskey and a hole half an inch wide burned in the upholstery by a cigarette. *Fact three,* he thought grimly, *I was drunk.* He put the bottle in the glove compartment and drove off.

The first street sign he came to gave him another fact: he was still in San Felice, down near the breakwater, no more than four miles from his own house.

The lights in the kitchen were on when he arrived. It was too early for Virginia to be awake and he wondered whether she'd left them on, expecting him home, or whether she'd forgotten to turn them off. She often forgot, or claimed to have forgotten. Sometimes he thought she kept them on deliberately because she was afraid of the dark but didn't want to admit it. He parked his car beside hers in the garage, then crossed the driveway and walked up the steps of the back porch. The door was unlocked.

Virginia was sitting at the kitchen table with the big retriever lying beside her chair. Neither of them moved.

Howard said, "Virginia?"

The dog opened his eyes, wagged his tail briefly and perfunctorily, and went back to sleep.

"At least the dog usually barks when I get home," he said. "Don't I even rate that much any more?"

Virginia turned. Her eyes were bloodshot, the lids blistered by the heat of her tears and surrounded by a network of lines Howard had never seen before. She spoke in a low, dull voice.

"The police are looking for you."

"The police? Why in heaven's name did you call them in? You knew I'd be back."

"I didn't. Didn't know, didn't call them."

"What's going on around here anyway? What have the police got to do with my getting drunk and spending the night in a motel?"

"Is that what you did, Howard?"

"Yes."

"Can you prove it?"

"Why should I have to prove it?"

She covered her face with her hands and started to weep again, deep, bitter sobs that shook her whole body. The dog rose to a sitting position and put his head on her lap, watching Howard out of the corner of his eye, as if he considered Howard responsible for the troubled sounds.

He blames me for everything, Howard thought, *just the way she does. Only this time I don't even know what I'm being blamed for. Did I do something while I was drunk that I don't remember? I couldn't have been in a fight. There are no marks on me and my clothes aren't torn.*

"Virginia, tell me what happened."

"Jessie—Jessie's gone."

"Gone where?"

"Nobody knows. She—she just disappeared. Ellen took her a glass of water about ten o'clock and that's the last anyone saw of her except—" She stopped, pressing the back of her hand against her trembling mouth.

"Except who?" Howard said.

"Whoever made her disappear."

Howard stared at her, confused and helpless. He wasn't sure whether she was telling the truth or whether she'd imagined the whole thing. She'd been acting and talking peculiarly last night, standing in the dichondra patch saying she was a tree.

She saw his incredulity and guessed the reason for it. "You think I've lost my mind. Well, I wish I had. It would be easier to bear than this, this terrible thing." She began to sob again, repeating Jessie's name over and over as if Jessie might be somewhere listening and might respond.

Howard did what he could, brought her two tranquilizer pills and poured her some ice water from the pitcher in the refrigerator. She choked on the pills and the water spilled down the front of her old wool bathrobe. Its coldness was stinging and shocking against the warm skin between her breasts. She let out a gasp and clutched the bathrobe tightly around her neck. Her eyes were resentful but they were no longer wild or weeping.

"So the police are looking for me," Howard said. "Why?"

"They're questioning everyone, friends, neighbors, anyone who knew—who knows her. They said in cases like this it's often a relative or a trusted friend of the family."

"Cases like what?"

She didn't answer.

"When did she disappear, Virginia?"

"Between ten and eleven. Ellen tucked her in bed at ten o'clock, then she took a sleeping capsule and went to bed herself. Dave was out looking for you. Ellen said she'd locked the back door but when Dave came back it was unlocked. He checked Jessie's bedroom to see if she was sleeping. She was gone. He searched the house, calling for her, then he woke Ellen up. They came here to our house. We looked all over but we couldn't find Jessie. I called the police and Dave set out for Mary Martha's house, using the path along the creek that the girls always took."

"Kids have run away before."

"The only clothes missing are the pajamas she was wearing, a bathrobe and a pair of slippers. Besides, she had no motive and no money."

"She had the twenty dollars I gave her the other night."

"Why, of course." Virginia's face came alive with sudden hope. "Why, that would seem like a fortune to Jessie. We've got to tell—"

"We tell no one, Virginia."

"But we must. It might throw a whole new light on everything."

"Including me," Howard said sharply. "The police will ask me why I gave the kid twenty dollars. I'll tell them because I was sore at you and wanted to get back at you. But will they believe it?"

"It's the truth."

"It might not strike them that way."

She didn't seem to understand what he was talking about. When he spelled it out for her, she looked appalled. "They couldn't possibly think anything like that about you, Howard."

"Why not?"

"You're a respectable married man."

"Coraznada State Hospital is full of so-called respectable married men." He took out a handkerchief and wiped his neck. "Did the police question you?"

"Yes. A Lieutenant Gallantyne did most of the talking. I don't like him. Even when I was telling the truth he made me feel that I was lying. There was another man with him, a Mr. Mac-Pherson. Every once in a while they'd put their heads together and whisper. It made me nervous."

"Who's MacPherson?"

"Dave said he's a lawyer."

"Whose lawyer?"

"Mrs. Oakley's."

"How did Mrs. Oakley get into this?"

"I don't *know*. Stop bullying me, I can't stand it."

She seemed on the verge of breaking up again. Howard got up, put some water and coffee in the percolator and plugged it in. After a time he said, "I'm not trying to bully you, Virginia. I simply want to find out what you told the police about last night so I can corroborate it. It wouldn't be so good—for either of us—if we contradicted each other."

She was looking at him, her eyes cold under their blistered lids. "You don't care that Jessie has disappeared, do you? All you care about is saving your own skin."

"And yours."

"Don't worry about mine. Everybody knows how I love the child."

"That's not quite accurate, Virginia," he said quietly. "Everybody knows that you love her, but not how you love her."

The coffee had begun to percolate, bubbling merrily in the cheerless room. Virginia turned and looked at the percolator as if she hoped it would do something unexpected and interesting like explode.

She said, "Where did you go after you left the Brants' last night?"

"To a liquor store and then down to the beach. I ended up at a motel."

"You were alone, of course?"

"Yes, I was alone."

"What motel?"

"I don't remember, I wasn't paying much attention. But I could find it again if I had to."

"Ellen told the police," she said, turning to face him, "that you were jealous of my relationship with Jessie."

"That was neighborly of her."

"She had to tell the truth. Under the circumstances you could hardly expect her to lie to spare your feelings."

"It's not my feelings I'm worried about. It is, as you pointed out, my skin. What else was said about last night?"

"Everything that happened, how we quarreled, and the funny way you talked to Jessie as if you were half-drunk when you only had two beers; how you tore off in the car and Dave tried to find you and couldn't."

"I didn't realize what loyal friends I had. It moves me," he added dryly. "It may move me right into a cell. Or was that the real objective?"

"You don't understand. We were forced to tell the whole truth, all of us. A child's life might be at stake. Gallantyne said every little detail could be vitally important. He made us go over and over it. I couldn't have lied to protect you even if I'd wanted to."

"And the implication is, you didn't particularly want to?"

She was staring at him in incredulity, her mouth partly open. "It still hasn't come through to you yet, has it? A child is missing, a nine-year-old girl has disappeared. She may be dead, and you don't seem to care. Don't you feel *anything?*"

"Yes. I feel somebody's trying to make me the goat."

Between four and seven in the morning Ellen Brant slept fitfully on the living-room couch beside the telephone. She'd dreamed half a dozen times that the phone was ringing and had wakened up to find herself reaching for it. She finally got up, washed her face and ran a comb through her hair, and put on a heavy wool coat over her jeans and T-shirt. Then she went into the bedroom to see if Dave was awake and could hear the telephone if it rang.

He was lying on his back, peering up at the ceiling. He turned and looked at her, the question in his eyes dying before it had a chance to be born. "There's been no news, of course."

"No. I'm going over to the Oakleys'. I want to ask Mary Martha some questions."

"The lieutenant will do that."

"She might talk to me more easily. She and her mother freeze up in front of strangers."

"What's it like outside?"

"Cold and foggy."

She knew he was thinking the same thing she was, that somewhere in that cold fog Jessie might be wandering, wearing only her cotton pajamas and light bathrobe. Biting her underlip hard to keep from breaking into tears again, she went out to the garage and got into the old Dodge station wagon. The floorboard of the front seat was covered with sand from yesterday's trip to the beach. It seemed to have happened a long time ago and in a different city, where the sun had been shining and the surf was gentle and the sand soft and warm. She had a feeling that she would never see that city again.

She backed out of the driveway, tears streaming down her face, warm where they touched her cheeks, already cold when they reached the sides of her neck. She brushed them angrily away with the sleeve of her coat. She couldn't afford to cry in front of Mary Martha, it might frighten her into silence, or worse still, into lying. She had seen Mary Martha many times after an emotional scene at home. The effect on her was always the same—blank eyes, expressionless voice: no, nothing was the matter, nothing had happened.

Mary Martha answered the door herself, first opening it only as far as the chain would allow. Then, recognizing Ellen, she unfastened the chain and opened the door wide. In spite of the earliness of the hour she was dressed as if for a visit to town in pink embroidered cotton and newly whitened sandals. Her ponytail was neat and so tightly fastened it raised her eyebrows slightly. She looked a little surprised to see Ellen, as though she might have been expecting someone else.

She said, "If you want my mother, she's in the kitchen making breakfast."

"I prefer to talk to you alone, Mary Martha."

"I'd better get my mother's permission. She's kind of nervous this morning, I don't know why. But I have to be careful."

"She hasn't told you anything?"

"Just that Mac was coming over with a soldier and we were all going to have a chat."

"A soldier?"

"He's a lieutenant. I'm supposed to remember to call him that so I'll make a good impression." Mary Martha looked down at her dress as if to reassure herself that it was still clean enough to make a good impression. "Do you want to come in?"

"Yes."

"I guess it'll be all right."

She was just closing the door when Kate Oakley's voice called out from the kitchen, "Mary Martha, tell Mac I'll be there in a minute."

"It's not Mac," the child said. "It's Jessie's mother."

"Jessie's—?" Kate Oakley appeared at the far end of the hall. She began walking toward them very rapidly, her high heels ticking on the linoleum like clocks working on different time schedules, each trying to catch up with the other. Her face was heavily made up to look pink and white but the gray of trouble showed through. She placed one arm protectively around Mary Martha's shoulders. "You'd better go and put the bacon in the warming oven, dear."

"I don't care if it gets cold," Mary Martha said. "It tastes the same."

"You mustn't be rude in front of company, lamb. That's understood between us, isn't it?"

"Yes, ma'am."

"Off you go."

Mary Martha started down the hall.

"But I want to talk to her," Ellen said desperately. "I've got to. She might know something."

"She knows nothing. She's only a child."

"Jessie's only a child, too."

"I'm sorry. I really am sorry, Mrs. Brant. But Mary Martha isn't supposed to talk to anyone until our lawyer arrives."

"You haven't even told her about Jessie, have you?"

"I didn't want to upset her."

"She's got to be told. She may be able to help. She might have seen someone, heard something. How can we know unless we ask her?"

"Mac will ask her. He can handle these—these situations better than you or I could."

"Is that all it is to you, a situation to be handled?"

Kate shook her head helplessly. "No matter what I said to you now, it would seem wrong because you're distraught. Further conversation is pointless. I must ask you to leave." She opened the heavy oak door. "I'm truly sorry, Mrs. Brant, but I think I'm doing the right thing. Mac will talk to Mary Martha. She feels freer with him than she would with you or me."

"Even though he has a policeman with him?"

"Did she tell you that?"

"I figured it out."

"Well, it won't make any difference. Mary Martha adores Mac and she's not afraid of policemen."

But the last word curled upward into a question mark, and when Ellen looked back from the bottom of the porch steps, Kate was hanging on to the oak door as if for support.

When breakfast was over, Mary Martha sat on the window seat in the front room with the cat, Pudding, on her lap. She wasn't supposed to get her hands dirty or her dress wrinkled but she needed the comfort of the cat, his warm body and soft fur, his bright eyes that seemed to be aware of so many things and not to care about any of them very much.

In a little while she saw Mac and the lieutenant emerge from the fog and come up the front steps. She heard her mother talking to them in the hall, at first in the low, careful voice she used when meeting strangers, later in a higher, less restrained and more natural voice. She sounded as if she was protesting, then arguing, and finally, losing. After a time the two men came into the front room alone, and Mac closed the door.

"Hello, Mary Martha," Mac said. "This is Lieutenant Gallantyne."

Still holding the cat, Mary Martha got up and executed a brief, formal curtsy.

Gallantyne bowed gravely in return. "That's a pretty cat you have there, Mary Martha. What's his name?"

"Pudding. He has other names too, though."

"Really? Such as?"

"Geronimo, sometimes. Also King Arthur. But when he's bad and catches a bird, I call him Sheridan." She switched the cat from her left shoulder to her right. It stopped purring and made a swift jab at her ponytail. "Do you have any medals?"

Gallantyne raised his bushy eyebrows. "Well now, I believe I won a few swimming races when I was a kid."

"I mean real medals like for killing a hundred enemies."

The men exchanged glances. It was as if they were both thinking the same thing, that it seemed a long and insane time ago that men were given medals for killing.

"Lieutenant Gallantyne is not in the army," Mac said. "He's a policeman. He's also a good friend of mine, so you needn't be afraid of him."

"I'm not. But why does he want to see me instead of my mother?"

"He'll talk to your mother later. Right now you're more important."

She seemed pleased but at the same time suspicious. "Why am I?"

"We hope," Gallantyne said, "that you'll be able to help us find your friend, Jessie."

"Is she hiding?"

"We're not sure."

"She's an awfully good hider. Being so skinny she can squeeze behind things and under things and between."

"You and Jessie play together a lot, do you?"

"All the time except when one of us is being punished."

"And you tell each other secrets, I suppose?"

"Yes, sir."

"Do you promise each other never to reveal these secrets to anyone else?"

Mary Martha nodded and said firmly, "And I'm not going to, either, because I crossed my heart and hoped to die."

"Oh, I'm sure you can keep a secret very well," Gallantyne said. "But I want you to imagine something now. Suppose you, Mary Martha, were in a dangerous situation in a place nobody knew about except you and Jessie. You're frightened and hungry and in pain and you want desperately to be rescued. Under those circumstances, wouldn't you release Jessie from her promise to keep the name of that place a secret?"

"I guess so, only there isn't any place like that."

"But you have other secrets."

"Yes."

Gallantyne was watching her gravely. "I believe that if Jessie could communicate with you right now, she'd release you from all your promises."

"Why can't she comm—communicate?"

"Nobody's seen her since last night at ten o'clock. We don't know where she is or why she left or if she left by herself or with someone else."

In a spasm of fear Mary Martha clutched the cat too tightly. He let out a yowl, unsheathed his claws and fought his way out of her grasp, onto the floor. She stood, very pale and still, one hand pressed to her scratched shoulder. "He hurt me," she said in a shocked voice. "Sheridan hurt me."

"I'm sure he didn't mean to."

"He always means to. I hate him."

"You can cry if you like," Gallantyne said. "That might help."

"No."

"All right, then, we'll go on. Is that O.K.?"

"I guess so."

"Did you and Jessie ever talk about running away together? Perhaps just in fun, like, *let's run away and join the circus.*"

"That would be plain silly," she said in a contemptuous voice. "Circuses don't even come here."

"Times have changed since I was a boy. The only thing that made life bearable when I was mad at my family was the thought of running away and joining the circus. Did Jessie often get mad at her family?"

"Sometimes. Mostly at Mike, her older brother. He bosses her around, he's awfully mean. We think a bad witch put a curse on him when he was born."

"Really? What kind of curse?"

"I'm not sure. But I made one up that sounds as if it might work."

"Tell it to me."

> " 'Abracadabra,
> Purple and green,
> This little boy
> Will grow up mean.'

"It should be said in a more eerie-like voice, only I don't feel like it right now."

Gallantyne pursed his lips and nodded. "Sounds pretty authentic to me just the way it is. Do you know any more?"

> " 'Abracadabra,
> Yellow and brown,
> Uncle Howard's the nastiest
> Man in town.'

"That one," she added anxiously, "isn't so good, is it?"

"Well, it's not so much a curse as a statement. Uncle Howard's the nastiest man in town, period. By the way, who's Uncle Howard?"

"Mr. Arlington."

"Why do you think he's so nasty, Mary Martha?"

"I don't. I only talked to him once and he was real nice. He gave me fifty cents."

"Then why did you make up the curse about him?"

"Jessie asked me to. We were going to make up curses about all the people we hate and she wanted to start with Uncle—with Mr. Arlington."

"Who was next on the list?"

"Nobody. We got tired of the game, and anyway my mother came to pick me up."

"I wonder," Gallantyne said softly, "why Jessie felt that way about Mr. Arlington. Do you have any idea?"

"No, sir. That was the first day she ever told me, when we were at the playground with Mike."

"What day was that?"

"The day my mother and I went downtown to Mac's office."

"Thursday," Mac said.

Gallantyne thanked him with a nod and turned his attention back to Mary Martha. "Previous to Thursday, you thought Jessie and the Arlingtons were good friends?"

"Yes, on account of the Arlingtons were always giving her presents and making a big fuss over her."

"Both of the Arlingtons?"

"Well—" Mary Martha studied the toes of her shoes. "Well, I guess it was mostly Aunt Virginia, him being away so much on the road. But Jessie never said anything against him until Thursday."

"Let's assume that something happened, on Wednesday perhaps, that changed her opinion of him. Did you see Jessie on Wednesday?"

"Yes, I went over to her house and we sat on the porch steps and talked."

"What about?"

"Lots of things."

"Name one."

"The book Aunt Virginia gave her. It was all about glaciers and mountains and rivers and wild things. It sounded real interesting. Only Jessie had to give it back because it cost too much money and her parents wouldn't let her keep it. *My* mother," she added virtuously, "won't let me accept anything. When Sheridan sends me parcels, I'm not even allowed to peek inside. She sends them right back or throws them away, bang, into the garbage can."

Gallantyne looked at the cat. "I gather you're referring to another Sheridan, not this one."

"Cats can't send parcels," Mary Martha said with a faint giggle. "That's silly. They don't have any money and they can't wrap things or write any name and address on the outside."

Gallantyne thought, wearily, of the anonymous letter. He'd been up all night, first with the Brants and Mrs. Arlington, and later in the police lab examining the letter. He was sure now that it had been written by a man, young, literate, and in good physical health. The description fitted hundreds of men in town. The fact that Howard Arlington was one of them meant nothing in itself.

He said, "Mary Martha, you and Jessie spend quite a lot of time at the school grounds, I'm told."

"Yes. Because of the games and swings and jungle gym."

"Have you ever noticed anyone watching you?"

"The coach. That's his job."

"Aside from the coach, have you seen any man hanging around the place, or perhaps the same car parked at the curb several days in a row?"

"No." Mary Martha gave him a knowing look. "My mother told me all about men like that. They're real nasty and I'm supposed to run home right away when I see one of them. Jessie is, too. She's a very good runner."

Perhaps not quite good enough, Gallantyne thought grimly. "How are you going to recognize these men when you see them?"

"Well, they offer you things like gum or candy or even a doll. Also, a ride in their car."

"And nothing like this ever happened to you and Jessie?"

"No. We saw a mean-looking man at the playground once, but it was only Timmy's father, who was mad because Timmy missed his appointment at the dentist. Timmy wears braces."

One corner of Gallantyne's mouth twitched impatiently. *So Timmy wears braces, and he has a mean-looking father and I am getting exactly nowhere.* "Do you know the story of Tom Sawyer, Mary Martha?"

"Our teacher told us some of it in school."

"Perhaps you remember the cave that was the secret hide-out. Do you and Jessie have somewhere like that? Not a cave, particularly, but a special private place where you can meet or leave notes for each other and things like that?"

"No."

"Think carefully now. You see, I and a great many other people have been searching for Jessie all night."

"She wouldn't hide all night," Mary Martha said thoughtfully. "Not unless she took lots of sandwiches and potato chips along."

"There's no evidence that she did."

"Then she's not hiding. She'd be too hungry. Her father says he should get a double tax exemption for her because she eats so much. What's a tax exemption?"

"You'll find out soon enough." Gallantyne turned to Mac, who was still standing beside the door as if on guard against a sudden intrusion by Kate Oakley. "Have you any questions you'd like to ask her?"

"One or two," Mac said. "What time did you go to bed last night, Mary Martha?"

"About eight o'clock."

"That's pretty early for vacation time and daylight saving."

"My mother and I like to go to bed early and get up early. She doesn't—we don't like the nights."

"Did you go to sleep right away?"

"I must have. I don't remember doing anything else."

"That seems like logical reasoning," Mac said with a wry smile. "Did you get up during the night?"

"No."

"Not even to go to the bathroom?"

"No, but you're not supposed to talk about things like that in front of strangers," Mary Martha said severely.

"Lieutenant Gallantyne is a friend of mine."

"Well, he's not mine or my mother's."

"Let's see if we can change that," Gallantyne said. "Ask your mother to come in here, will you?"

"Yes, sir. Only—well, you better not keep her very long."

"Why not?"

"She might cry, and crying gives her a headache."

"We mustn't let that happen, must we?"

"No, sir." Mary Martha executed another of her stiff little curtsies, picked up the cat and departed.

"She's a funny kid," Gallantyne said. "Is she always like that?"

"With adults. I've never seen her in the company of other children."

"That's odd. I understand you're the old family friend."

"I'm the old family friend when things go wrong," Mac said dryly. "When things are going right, I think I must be the old family enemy."

"Exactly why did you invite yourself to come with me this morning, Mac?"

"Oh, let's just say I'm curious."

"Let's not."

"All right. The truth is that Kate Oakley's a very difficult and very vulnerable woman. Because she is difficult, she can't ask for or accept help the way an ordinary vulnerable person might. So I'm here to lend her moral support. I may criticize her and give her hell occasionally but she knows I'm fond of her."

"How fond?"

"She's twenty years younger than I am. Does that answer your question?"

"Not quite."

"Then I'll lay it on the line. There's no secret romance going on between Kate Oakley and myself. I was her father's lawyer when he was alive, and when he died I handled his estate, or rather the lack of it. I am officially Mary Martha's godfather, and unofficially I'm probably Kate's, too. That's the whole story."

"The story hasn't ended yet," Gallantyne said carefully. "Surely you're not naïve enough to believe we can write our own endings in this world."

"We can do a little editing."

"Don't kid yourself."

Mac wanted to argue with him but he heard Kate's footsteps in the hall. He wondered what her reaction would have been to Gallantyne's insinuations: shock, displeasure, perhaps even amusement. He could never tell what she was actually thinking. When she was at her gayest, he could feel the sadness in her, and when she was in despair he sensed that it, too, was not real. Everything about her seemed to be hidden, as if at a certain period in her life she had decided to go underground where she would be safe.

He thought about the wild creatures in the canyon behind his house. The foxes, the raccoons, the possums, the chipmunks, they could all be lured out of their winter refuge by the promise of food and the warmth of a spring sun. There was no spring sun for Kate, no hunger that could be satisfied by food. He watched her as she came in, thinking, *what do you want, Kate? Tell me what you want and I'll give it to you if I can.*

She hesitated in the doorway, looking as though she were trying to decide how to act.

Before she had a chance to decide, Gallantyne spoke to her in a quiet, confident manner, "Please sit down, Mrs. Oakley. We're hoping you'll be able to help us."

"I hope so, too. I was—I'm very fond of Jessie. If anything's happened to her, it will be a terrible blow to Mary Martha. Do you suppose it could have been a kidnaping?"

"There's no evidence of it. The Brants are barely getting by financially, and they've received no ransom demand. We're pretty well convinced that Jessie walked out of the house voluntarily."

"How can you know that for sure?"

"There were no signs of a struggle in Jessie's bedroom, the Arlington's dog didn't bark as he certainly would have if he'd heard a stranger, and the back door was unlocked. It's one of the new kinds of lock built into the knob—push the knob and it locks, pull and it unlocks. We think Jessie unlocked the door, accidentally or on purpose, when she went out. I'm inclined to

believe that she unlocked it deliberately with the intention of re-
turning to the house. Someone, or something, interfered with
that intention."

He paused to light a cigarette, cupping his hands around the
match as though he were outside on a windy day. "We'll assume, then, that she left the house under her own power and for
a reason we don't know yet. The two likeliest places she might
have gone are the Arlingtons' next door, or this house. Mrs.
Arlington claims she didn't see her and you claim you didn't."

"Of course I didn't," she said stiffly. "I would have phoned
her mother immediately."

"What I want you to consider now is the possibility that she
might somehow have gotten into the house without your seeing
her, that she might have hidden some place and fallen asleep."

"There's no such possibility."

"You seem very sure."

"I am. This house is Sheridan-proof. My ex-husband acquired
the cunning habit of breaking in during my absences and helping
himself to whatever he fancied—liquor, furniture, silver, and
more liquor. I had a special lock put on every door and window.
When I go out or retire for the night, I check them all. It would
be as much as my life is worth to miss any of them."

"Jessie knew about these locks, of course?"

"Yes. She asked me about them. It puzzled her that a house
should have to be secured against a husband and father. . . . No,
Lieutenant, Jessie could never have entered this house without
my letting her in."

That leaves the Arlingtons, he thought, *or someone on the
street between here and the Arlingtons' house.* "Would you call
Jessie a shy child, Mrs. Oakley?"

"No. She has—had quite a free and easy manner with people."

"Does that include strangers?"

"It included everyone."

"Have you had any strangers hanging around here recently?"

She gave Mac a quick, questioning look. He responded with a

nod that indicated he'd already told Gallantyne about the man in the green coupé.

"Yes," she said, "but I never connected him with Jessie or Mary Martha."

"Do you now?"

"I don't know. It seems odd that he'd show himself so openly if he were planning anything against Jessie or Mary Martha."

"Perhaps he wasn't actually planning anything, he was merely waiting. And when Jessie walked out of that house by herself, she provided what he was waiting for, an opportunity."

A spot of color, dime-sized, appeared suddenly on her throat and began expanding, up to her ear tips, down into the neckline of her dress. The full realization of Jessie's fate seemed to be spreading throughout her system like poison dye. "It could just as easily have been Mary Martha instead of Jessie. Is that what you're telling me?"

"Think about it."

"I won't. It's unthinkable. Mary Martha wouldn't leave the house without my permission, and she'd certainly never enter the car of a strange man."

"Some pretty powerful inducements can be offered a child her age who's lonely and has affection going to waste. A puppy, for instance, or a kitten—"

"No, no!" But even the sound of her own voice shouting denials could not convince her. She knew the lieutenant was right. She knew that Mary Martha had left the house without permission just a few nights before. She'd run over to Jessie's using the short cut across the creek. Suppose she'd gone out the front, the way she often did. The man had been parked across the street at that very moment. "No, no," she repeated. "I've taught Mary Martha what it took me years of torment to learn, that you can't trust men, you can't believe them. They're liars, cheats, bullies. Mary Martha already knows that. She won't have to find it out the hard way as I did, as Jessie—"

"Be quiet, Kate," Mac said in a warning tone. "The lieutenant is too busy to listen to your theories this morning."

She didn't even glance in his direction. "Poor Jessie, poor misguided child with all her prattle about her wonderful father. She believed it, and that fool mother of hers actually encouraged her to believe it even though she must have been aware what was going on."

Gallantyne raised his brows. "And what was going on, Mrs. Oakley?"

"Plenty."

"Who was involved?"

"I must caution you, Kate," Mac said, "not to make any statements you're not able and willing to substantiate."

"In other words, I'm to shut up?"

"Until you've consulted your attorney."

"All my attorney ever does for me is tell me to shut up."

"Rumors and gossip are not going to solve this case."

"No, but they might help," Gallantyne said mildly. "Now, you were going to give me some new information about Jessie's father."

Kate looked from Gallantyne to Mac, then back to Gallantyne, as if she were trying to decide which one of them was the lesser evil. "It can hardly be called new. It goes back to Adam. Brant's a man and he's been availing himself of the privilege, deceiving his wife, cheating his children out of their birthright. Oh, he puts on a good front, almost as good as Sheridan when he's protesting his great love for Mary Martha."

"You're implying that Brant is having an affair with another woman?"

"Yes."

"Who is she?"

"Virginia Arlington."

Both men were watching her, Mac painfully, Gallantyne with cool suspicion.

"It's true," she added, clenching her fists. "I can't prove it, I don't have pictures of them in bed together. But I know it's a fact."

"Facts, Mrs. Oakley, are often what we choose to believe."

"I have nothing against Mrs. Arlington, I have no reason for wanting to believe bad things about her. She's probably just a victim like me, hoodwinked by a man, taken in by his promises. Oh, you should have heard Sheridan in the heyday of his promises. . . . But then you very likely know all about promises, Lieutenant. I bet you've made lots of them."

"A few."

"And they weren't kept?"

"Some weren't."

"That makes you a liar, doesn't it, Lieutenant? No better than the rest of them—"

"Please be quiet, Kate," Mac said. "You're not doing yourself any good or Jessie any good."

He touched Gallantyne lightly on the arm and the two men walked over to the far corner of the room and began talking in whispers. Though she couldn't distinguish any words, she was sure they were talking about her until Gallantyne finally raised his voice and said, "I must ask you not to mention Charlie Gowen to anyone, Mrs. Oakley."

"Charlie Gowen? I don't even know who—"

"The man in the green coupé. Don't tell anyone about him, not your friends or relatives or reporters or any other policeman. As far as you're concerned, Charlie Gowen doesn't even exist."

(21)

When Charlie arrived home at 5:30, he was so tired he could hardly get out of his car and cross the patch of lawn that separated the driveway from the house. He had worked very hard all day in the hope that his boss, Mr. Warner, would notice, and approve of him. He especially needed Mr. Warner's approval because Ben was angry with him for staying out too late the previous night. Although he knew Mr. Warner and Ben were entirely different people, and pleasing one didn't necessarily mean placating the other, he couldn't keep from trying. In his thoughts they weighed the same, and in his dreams they often showed up wearing each other's faces.

At the bottom of the porch steps he stooped to pick up the evening *Journal*. It lay under the hibiscus bush, fastened with an elastic band and folded so he could see only the middle third of the oversized headline: U SEEN TH

Usually, Charlie waited for the *Journal* until after Ben had finished with it because Ben liked to be the first to discover interesting bits of news and pass them along. But tonight he didn't hesitate. He tore off the elastic band and unfolded the paper. Jessie's face was smiling up at him. It didn't look the way it had the last time he'd seen her, shocked and frightened, but she was wearing the same clothes, a white bathrobe over pajamas.

The headline said HAVE YOU SEEN THIS GIRL?—and underneath the picture was an explanation of it: "This is a composite picture made from a snapshot of Jessie Brant's face superimposed on one of a child of similar height and build wearing clothes similar to those missing from Jessie's wardrobe. The *Journal* is offering $1,000 reward for information leading to the discovery of Jessie Brant's whereabouts."

For a long time Charlie stood looking at the girl who was half-Jessie, half-stranger. Then he turned and stumbled up the porch steps and into the house, clutching the newspaper against his chest as though to hide from the neighbors an old wound that had reopened and started to bleed again. In his room, with the door locked and the blinds drawn, he read the account of Jessie's disappearance. It began with a description of Jessie herself; of her father, a technician with an electronics firm; her brother, Michael, who hadn't learned the news until he'd been picked off a fishing boat by the Coast Guard cutter; her mother, the last member of her family to see Jessie alive at ten o'clock.

The official police announcement was issued by Lieutenant D. W. Gallantyne: "The evidence now in our possession indicates that Jessie departed from her house voluntarily, using the back door and leaving it unlocked so she would be able to return. What person, or set of circumstances, prevented her return? We are asking the public to help us answer that question. There is a strong possibility that someone noticed her leaving the house or walking along the street, and that that person can give us further information, such as what direction she was going and whether she was alone. Anyone who saw her is urged to contact us immediately. Jessie's grief-stricken parents join us in this appeal."

The light in the room was very dim. Narrowing his eyes to keep them in focus, Charlie reread the statement by Gallantyne. It was wrong, he knew it was wrong. It hadn't happened like that. Somebody should tell the lieutenant and set him straight.

He lay down on the bed, still holding the newspaper against his chest. The ticking of his alarm clock sounded extraordinarily loud and clear. He'd had the clock since his college days. It was like an old friend, the last voice he heard at night, the first voice in the morning: *tick it, tick it, tick it.* But now the voice began to sound different, not friendly, not comforting.

Wicked wicked, wicked sicked, wicked sicked.

"I'm not," he whispered. "I'm not. I didn't touch her."

Wicked sicked, pick a ticket, try and kick it, wicked wicked, buy a ticket, buy a ticket, buy a ticket.

Ben called out, "Charlie? You in there?" When he didn't get an answer he tried the door and found it locked. "Listen, Charlie, I'm not mad at you any more. I realize you're a grown man now and if you want to stay out late, well, what the heck, that's your business. Right?"

"Yes, Ben."

"I've got to stop treating you like a kid brother who's still wet behind the ears. That's what Louise says and by golly, it makes sense, doesn't it?"

"I guess so."

"She'll be over pretty soon. You don't want her to catch you sulk—unprepared."

"I'm preparing, Ben."

"Good. I couldn't find the *Journal,* by the way. Have you got it in there?"

"No."

"The delivery boy must have missed us. Well, I hate to report him so I think I'll go pick one up over at the drug store. I'll be back in a few minutes."

"All right."

"Charlie, listen, you're O.K., aren't you? I mean, everything's fine?"

"I am not sicked."

"What? I didn't hear what you—"

"I am not sicked."

The unfamiliar word worried Ben. As the worry became larger and larger, chunks of it began dropping off and changing into something he could more easily handle—anger. By the time he reached the drug store he'd convinced himself that Charlie had used the word deliberately to annoy him.

Mr. Forster was standing outside his drug store. Though his face looked grave, there was a glint of excitement in his eyes as though he'd just found out that one of his customers had contracted a nonfatal illness which would require years of prescriptions.

"Well, well, it's Benny Gowen. How's the world treating you, Benny?"

"Fine. Nobody calls me Benny any more, Mr. Forster."

"Don't they now. Well, that puts me in a class by myself. What can I do for you?"

"I'd like a *Journal.*"

"Sorry, I'm all sold out." Mr. Forster was watching Ben carefully over the top of his spectacles. "Soon as I put them out here on the stand this afternoon people began picking them up like they were ten-dollar bills. Nothing sells papers like a real nasty case of murder or whatever it was. But I guess you know all about it, being you work downtown in the hub of things."

"I don't have a chance to read when I'm on the job," Ben said. "Who was murdered?"

"The police don't claim it was murder. But I figure it must have been. The kid's gone, nobody's seen hide nor hair of her since last night."

"Kid?"

"A nine-year-old girl named Jessie Brant. Disappeared right from in front of her own house or thereabouts. Now, nobody can tell me a nine-year-old kid wearing nightclothes wouldn't have been spotted by this time if she were still alive. It's not reasonable. Mark my words, she's lying dead some place and the most they can hope for is to find the body and catch the man responsible for the crime. You agree, Benny?"

"I know nothing about it."

Mr. Forster took off his spectacles and began cleaning them with a handkerchief that was dirtier than they were. "How's Charlie, by the way?"

He is not sicked. "He's all right. He's been all right for a long time now, Mr. Forster."

"Reason I asked is, he came in here yesterday with a bad headache. He bought some aspirin, but shucks, taking aspirin isn't getting to the root of anything. A funny thing about headaches, some doctors think they're mostly psychological, you know, caused by emotional problems. In Charlie's case I'm inclined to agree. Look at the record, all that trouble he's had and—"

"That's in the past."

"Being in the past and being over aren't necessarily the same thing." Mr. Forster replaced his spectacles with the air of a man who confidently expected new knowledge from increased vision. "Now don't get me wrong. *I* think Charlie's O.K. But I'm a friend of his, I'm not the average person reading about the kid and remembering back. There's bound to be talk."

"I'm sure you'll do your share of it." Ben turned to walk away but Mr. Forster's hand on his arm was like an anchor. "Let go of me."

"You must have misunderstood me, Ben. I *like* Charlie, I'm on his side. But I can't help feeling there's something wrong again. It probably doesn't involve the kid at all because it started yesterday afternoon before anything happened to her. Are you going to be reasonable and listen to me, Ben?"

"I'll listen if you have anything constructive to say."

"Maybe it's constructive, I don't know. Anyhow, a man came in here yesterday asking where Charlie lived. He gave me a pretty thin story about forgetting to look up the house number. I pretended to go along with it but I knew damned well he was trying to pump me."

"About Charlie?"

"Yes."

"What'd you tell him?"

"All the right things. Don't worry about that part of it, I gave Charlie a clean bill of health, 100 percent. Only—well, it's been on my mind ever since. The man looked like an official of some kind, why was he interested in Charlie?"

"Why didn't you ask him?"

"Heck, it would have spoiled the game. I was supposed to be taken in, see. I was playing the part of—"

"Playing games isn't going to help Charlie."

Mr. Forster's eyes glistened with excitement. "So now you're leveling with me, eh, Ben? There *is* something wrong, Charlie needs help again. Is that it?"

"We all need help, Mr. Forster," Ben said and walked away, this time without interference. He knew Mr. Forster would be watching him and he tried to move naturally and easily as though he couldn't feel the leaden chains attached to his limbs. He had felt these chains for almost his entire life; attached to the other end of them was Charlie.

He stopped at the corner, aware of the traffic going by, the people moving up and down and across the streets, the clock in the courthouse tower chiming six. He wanted to quiet the clock so he would lose consciousness of time; he wanted to join one of the streams of strangers, anonymous people going to unnamed places. Whoever, wherever, whenever, was better than being Ben on his way home to Charlie to ask him about a dead child.

Louise's little sports car was parked at the curb in front of the house. Ben found her in the living room, leafing through the pages of a magazine. She smiled when she looked up and saw him in the doorway, but he could tell from the uneasiness in her eyes that she'd read about the child and had been silently asking the same questions that Mr. Forster was asking out loud.

He said, trying to sound cheerful and unafraid, "Hello, Louise. When did you arrive?"

"About ten minutes ago."

"Where's Charlie?"

"In his room getting dressed."

"Oh. Are you going out some place? I thought—well, it's turning kind of cold out, it might be a nice night to build a fire and all three of us sit around and talk."

Louise smiled again with weary patience as if she was sick of talk and especially the talk of children, young or old. "I don't know what Charlie has in mind. When he answered the door he simply told me he was getting dressed. I'm not even sure he wanted me to wait for him. But I'm waiting, anyway. It's becoming a habit." She added, without any change in tone, "What time did he come home last night?"

"It must have been pretty late. I was asleep."

"You went to *sleep* with Charlie still out wandering around by himself? How could you have?"

"I was tired."

"You led me to understand that you'd go on looking for him. You said if I went home for some rest that you'd take over. And you didn't."

"No."

"Why not?"

"Because I started thinking about the conversation we had

earlier," Ben said with deliberation. "You gave me the business about how I should trust Charlie, let him have a chance to grow up, allow him to reach his own decisions. You can't have it both ways, Louise. You can't tell me one minute to treat him like a responsible adult and the next minute send me out chasing after him as if he was a three-year-old. You can't accuse me of making mistakes in dealing with him and then an hour later beg me to make the same mistakes. Be honest, Louise. Where do you stand? What do you really think of Charlie?"

"Keep your voice down, Ben. He might hear you."

"Is that how you treat a responsible adult, you don't let him overhear anything?"

"I meant—"

"You meant what you said. The three-year-old shut up in the bedroom isn't supposed to hear what Mom and Pop are talking about in the living room."

"I wouldn't want Charlie to think we're quarreling, that's all."

"But we *are* quarreling. Why shouldn't he think so? If he's a responsible adult—"

"Stop repeating that phrase."

"Why? Because it doesn't fit him, and you can't bear listening to the truth?"

"Stop it, Ben, please. This isn't the time."

"This is the very time," he said soberly. "Right now, this minute, you've got to figure out how you really feel about Charlie. Sure, you love him, we both do. But you're not committed to him the way I am, or to put it bluntly, you're not stuck with him. You still have a chance to change your mind, to get away. Do it, Louise."

"I can't."

"For your own sake, you'd better try. Walk out of here now and don't look back. For nearly a year you've been dreaming, and I've been letting you. Now the alarm's ringing, it's time to wake up and start moving. Beat it, Louise."

"You don't know what you're asking."

"I'm asking," he said, "that one out of this trio gets a chance to survive. It won't be Charlie and it can't be me. That leaves you, Louise. Use your chance, for my sake if not your own. I'd like to think of you as being happy in the future, leading a nice, uncomplicated life."

"There's no such thing."

"You won't leave?"

"No."

"Then God help you." He went over to the window and stood with his back to Louise so she wouldn't see the tears welling in his eyes. "A little girl disappeared last night. One person in this neighborhood has already mentioned Charlie in connection with the crime. There'll be others, not just common gossips like Forster, but men with authority. Whatever Charlie has or hasn't done, it's going to be rough on him, and on you, too, if you stick around."

"I'm sticking."

"Yes, I was afraid you would. Why? Do you want to be a martyr?"

"I want to be Charlie's wife."

"It's the same thing."

"Don't try to destroy my confidence completely, Ben," she said. "It would be easy, I don't have very much. But what I have may help Charlie and perhaps you, too, in the days to come."

"Days? You're thinking in terms of *days*? What about the months, years—"

"They're composed of days. I choose to think of them in that way. Now," she added in a gentler voice, "do I get your blessing, Ben?"

"You get everything I have to offer."

"Thank you."

She turned toward the doorway, hearing Charlie's step in the hall. It sounded brisk and lively as if he'd had an abrupt change of mood in the past ten minutes. When he came in she noticed that he was freshly shaved and wearing his good suit and the tie she'd given him for his birthday. He looked surprised when he saw that she was still there, and she wondered whether he'd expected her to leave, and if so, why he'd taken the trouble to get all dressed up. He was carrying the evening newspaper. It was crumpled and torn as though it had been used to swat flies.

He put it down carefully on the coffee table, his eyes fixed on Ben. "I found it after all, Ben. Right after you left to buy one I decided to go out and search for it again, and sure enough there it was, hidden behind that shrub with the pink flowers. Remember what we used to call it when we were kids, Ben? High biscuits. I used to think that it actually had biscuits on it but they were up so high I couldn't see them."

"I looked under the hibiscus," Ben said.

"You must have missed it. It was there."

"It wasn't there."

"You—you could have made a mistake, Ben. You were complaining about your eyes last week. Anyway, it's such a small thing, we shouldn't be raising all this fuss about it in front of Louise."

"Louise better get used to it. And if it's such a small thing, why are you lying about it?"

"Well, I—well, maybe it didn't happen *exactly* like that." The muscles of Charlie's throat were working, as if he was trying to swallow or unswallow something large and painful and immovable. "When I got home I picked up the paper and took it into my room to read."

"Why? You're not usually interested."

"I saw the headline about the little girl, and the picture. I wanted to study it, to make sure before—before going to the police."

Ben stared at him in silence for a moment, then he repeated, "Before going to the police. Is that what you said?"

"Yes. I'm sure now—the face, the clothes, her name and address. I'm very sure. That's why I got dressed up, so I'll make a good impression at headquarters. You've always told me how necessary a good impression is. Do I look O.K.?"

"You look dandy. You'll make a dandy impression. . . . Jesus Godalmighty, what are you trying to do to me, to yourself? It isn't enough that—"

"But I'm only doing what I have to, Ben. The paper said any witnesses should come forward and tell what they know. And I'm a witness. That's funny, isn't it? I always wanted to be somebody and now I finally am. I'm a witness. That's pretty important, according to the paper. I may even be the only one in the whole city, can you beat that?"

"No. I don't think anyone can. This time you've really done it, you've set a new high."

Charlie's smile was strained, a mixture of pride and anxiety.

"Well, I didn't actually *do* anything, I just happened to be there when she came out of the house. The police are wrong about which house she came out of. It wasn't her own, the way the paper said. It was the one—"

"You just happened to be there, eh, Charlie?"

"Yes."

"In your car?"

"Yes."

"Was the car parked?"

"I—I'm not sure but I think I may have been only passing by, very slowly."

"Very, *very* slowly?"

"I think so. I may have stopped for a minute when I saw her on account of I was surprised. It was so late and she shouldn't have been out. Her parents should have taken better care of her, not letting her run wild on the streets past ten o'clock, no one to protect her."

"Did you offer to protect her, Charlie?"

"Oh no."

"Did you talk to her at all?"

"No. I may have sort of spoken her name out loud because I was so surprised to see her, it being late and cold and lonely." He broke off suddenly, frowning. "You're mixing me up with your questions. You're getting me off the subject. That's not the important part, how I happened to be there and what I did.

The important thing is, she didn't come out of her own house. The police think she did, so it's my duty to straighten them out. I bet they'll be very glad to have some new evidence."

"I just bet they will," Ben said. "Go to your room, Charlie."

"What?"

"You heard me. Go to your room."

"I can't do that. I'm a witness, they need me. They *need* me, Ben."

"Then they'll have to come and get you."

"You're interfering with justice. That's a very wrong thing to do."

"Justice? What kind of justice do you think is in store for you, when you can't even tell them what you were doing outside the girl's house, or whether you were parked there or just passing by?"

"You've got it all wrong, Ben. They're not after me, I didn't do anything."

Ben turned away. He wanted to hit Charlie with his fist, he wanted to weep or to run shrieking out into the street. But all he could do was stand with his face to the wall, wishing he were back on the street corner where he could pretend he was anyone, going any place, at any hour of the day or night.

The only sound in the room was Charlie's breathing. It was ordinary breathing, in and out, in and out, but to Ben it was the sound of doom. "Maybe I ought to go ahead and let you ruin yourself," he said finally. "I can't do that, though. Not yet, anyway. So I'm asking you to stay in your room for tonight and we'll discuss this in the morning."

"Ben may be right, Charlie," Louise said. It was the first time she'd spoken since Charlie came into the room. She used her library voice, very quiet but authoritative. "You need time to get your story straight."

Charlie shook his head stubbornly. "It's not a story."

"All right then, you need time to remember the facts. You can't claim to have been at the scene without giving some plausible reason why you were there and what you were doing."

"I wanted some fresh air."

"Other streets, other neighborhoods, have fresh air. The police will ask you why you picked that one."

"I didn't. I was driving around everywhere, just driving around, breathing the free—the fresh air."

"The way you did the other night?"

"Other night?"

"When I found you on Jacaranda Road."

"Why do you bring that up?" he said violently. "You know nothing happened that night. You told me, you were the one who convinced me. You said, *nothing's happened, Charlie. Nothing whatever has happened, it's all in your mind.* Why aren't you saying that now, Louise?"

"I will, if you want me to."

"Not because you believe it?"

"I—believe it." She clung to his arm, half-protectively, half-helplessly.

He looked down at her as if she were a stranger making an intimate demand. "Don't touch me, woman."

"Please, Charlie, you mustn't talk to me like that. I love you."

"No. You spoil things for me. You spoiled my being a witness."

He jerked his arm out of her grasp and ran toward the hall. A few seconds later she heard the slam of his bedroom door. There was a finality about it like the closing of the last page of a book.

It's over, she thought. *I had a dream, the alarm rang, I woke up and it's over.*

She could still hear the alarm ringing in her ears, and above it, the sound of Ben's voice. It sounded very calm but it was the calmness of defeat.

"I should have forced you to leave. I would have, if I'd known what was going on in his mind. But this witness bit, how could I have called that?" He looked out the window. It was getting dark and foggy. The broad, leathery leaves of the loquat tree were already dripping and the street lights had appeared wearing their gauzy gray nightgowns. "Either the whole thing's a fantasy, or he's telling the truth but not all of it."

"All of it?"

"That he attacked the child and killed her."

"Stop it. I'll never believe that, never."

"You half believed it when you walked in this door. You came here for reassurance. You wanted to be told that Charlie arrived home early last night, that he and I had a talk and then he went to bed. Well, he didn't, we didn't. This isn't a very good place to come for reassurance, Louise. It's a luxury we don't keep in stock."

"I didn't come here for reassurance. I wanted to see Charlie, to tell him that I love him and I trust him."

"You trust him, do you?"

"Yes."

"How far? Far enough to allow him to go to the police with his story?"

"Naturally I'd like him to get the details straight first, before he exposes himself to—to their questions."

"You make it sound very simple, as if Charlie's mind is a reference book he can open at will and look up the answers. Maybe you're right, in a way. Maybe his mind is a book, but it's written in a language you and I can't understand, and the pages aren't in order and some of them are glued together and some are missing entirely. Not exactly a perfect place to find answers, is it, Louise?"

"Stop badgering me like this," she said. "It's not fair."

"If you don't like it, you can leave."

"Is that all I ever get from you any more, an invitation to leave, walk away, don't come back?"

"That's it."

"Why?"

"I told you before, one of the three of us should have a chance, just a chance." He was still watching the fog pressing at the window like the gray facelessness of despair. "Charlie's my problem, now more than ever. I'll look after him. He won't go to the police tonight or any other night. He'll do what I tell him to do. I'll see that he gets to work in the morning and that he gets home safely after work. I'll stay with him, talk to him, listen to him, play the remember-game with him. He likes that— *remember when we were kids, Ben?*—he can play it for hours. It won't be a happy life or a productive one, but the most I can hope for Charlie right now is that he's allowed to survive at all. He's a registered sex offender. Sooner or later he's bound to be questioned about the child's disappearance. I only hope it's later so I can try and push this witness idea out of his head."

"How will you do that?"

"I'll convince him that he wasn't near the house, he didn't see the child, he didn't see anything. He was at home with me, he dozed off in an armchair, he had a nightmare."

"Don't do it, Ben. It's too risky, tampering with a mind that's already confused about what's real and what isn't."

"If he doesn't know what's real," Ben said, "I'll have to tell him. And he'll believe me. It will be like playing the remember-game. *Remember last night, Charlie, when you were sitting in the armchair? And you suddenly dozed off, you cried out in your sleep, you were having a nightmare about a house, a child coming out of a house. . . ."*

He had to write the letter very quickly because he knew Ben would be coming in soon to talk to him. He folded the letter six times, slipped it into an envelope, addressed the envelope to Police Headquarters and put it in the zippered inside pocket of his windbreaker. Then he returned to his desk. The desk had been given to him when he was twelve and it was too small for him. He had to hunch way down in order to work at it but he didn't mind this. It made him feel big, a giant of a man; a kindly giant, though, who used his strength only to protect, never to bully, so everyone respected him.

When Ben came in, Charlie pretended to be studying an advertisement in the back pages of a magazine.

"Dinner's ready," Ben said. "I brought home some chicken pies from the cafeteria and heated them up."

"I'll eat one if you want me to, Ben, but I'd just as soon not."

"Aren't you hungry?"

"Not very. I had chicken pie last night."

"We had ravioli last night. Don't you remember? I cut myself opening the can. Look, here's the cut on my finger."

Charlie looked at the cut with polite interest. "That's too bad. You must be more careful. I wasn't here last night for dinner."

"Yes, you were. You ate too much and later you dozed off in Father's armchair in the front room."

"No, Ben, that was a lot of other nights. Last night was different, it was very different. First I took that delivery to the Forest Service. All that heat and dust up in the mountains gave me a headache so I went to the drug store for some aspirin."

"The aspirin made you sleepy. That's why you dozed—"

"I wasn't a bit sleepy, I was hungry. I was going to take Louise some place to eat—I don't mean eat *her*," he added earnestly. "I mean, where we could both eat some food. Only she wasn't at the library so I went by myself and had a chicken pie."

"Where?"

"The cafeteria you manage. It wouldn't be loyal to go anywhere else."

"You picked a hell of a time to be loyal," Ben said. "Did anyone see you?"

"They must have. There I was."

"Did you speak to anyone?"

"The cashier. I said hello."

"Did she recognize you?"

"Oh yes. She made a joke about how everyone had to pay around that joint, even the boss's brother."

That fixes it, Ben thought. *If he'd planned every detail in advance he couldn't have done a better job of lousing things up.* "What time were you there?"

"I don't know. I hate watching the clock, it watches me back."

"What did you do after you finished eating?"

"Drove around, I told you that. I wanted some fresh air to clear the dust out of my sinuses."

"You were home by ten o'clock."

"No, I couldn't have been. It was after ten when I saw—"

"You saw nothing," Ben said harshly. "You were home with me by ten o'clock."

"I don't remember seeing you when I came in."

"You didn't. I was in bed. But I knew what time it was because I'd just turned out the light."

"You couldn't be mistaken, like about the ravioli?"

"The ravioli business was simply a device to get at the truth. I knew you'd been to the drug store and the library but I wanted you to recall those things for yourself. You did."

"Not this other, though."

"You were home by ten. I wasn't asleep yet, I heard you come in. If anyone asks you, that's what you're to say. Say it now."

"Please leave—leave me alone, Ben."

"I can't." Ben leaned over the desk, his face white and contorted. "You're in danger and I'm trying to save you. I'm going to save you in spite of yourself. Now say it. Say you were home by ten o'clock."

"Will you leave me alone, then?"

"Yes."

"You promise?"

"*Yes.*"

"I was home by ten o'clock," Charlie repeated, blinking. "You cut yourself opening a can of ravioli. You were bleeding, you were bleeding all over the bloody kitchen. Let me see your cut again. Does it still hurt, Ben?"

"No."

"Then what are you crying for?"

"I have a—a pain."

"You shouldn't eat highly spiced foods like ravioli."

"No, that was a mistake." Ben's voice was a rag of a whisper torn off a scream. "I'll try to make it up to you, Charlie."

"To me? But it's your pain."

"We share it. Just like in the old days, Charlie, when we shared everything. Remember how my friends used to kid me about my little brother always tagging along? I never minded, I liked having you tag along. Well, it will be like that again, Charlie. I'll drive you to work in the morning, you can walk over to the cafeteria and have lunch with me at noon—"

"I have my own car," Charlie said. "And sometimes Louise and I prefer to have lunch together."

"Louise's lunch hour is going to be changed. It probably won't jibe with yours any more."

"She didn't tell me that."

"She will. As for the car, it seems wasteful to keep two of them running when I can just as easily drive you wherever you want to go. Let's try it for a while and see how it works out. Maybe we can save enough money to take a trip somewhere."

"Louise and I are going to take a trip on our honeymoon."

"That might not be for some time."

"Louise said September, next month."

"Well, things are a little hectic at the library right now, Charlie. There's a chance she might not—she might not be able to get away."

"Why does Louise tell you stuff before she tells me? Explain it to me, Ben."

"Not tonight."

"Because of your pain?"

"Yes, my pain," Ben said. "I want you to give me your car keys now, Charlie."

Charlie put his left hand in the pocket of his trousers. He could feel the outline of the keys, the round one for the trunk, the pointed one for the ignition. "I must have left them in the car."

"I've warned you a dozen times about that."

"I'm sorry, Ben. I'll go and get them."

"*No*. I will."

Charlie watched him leave. He hadn't planned it like this, in fact he had planned nothing beyond the writing of the letter. But now that he saw his opportunity he couldn't resist it any more than a caged animal could resist an open gate. He picked up his windbreaker and went quietly through the kitchen and out of the back door.

(22)

Ralph MacPherson was preparing for an early bedtime when the telephone rang. He reached for it quickly, afraid that it would be Kate calling and afraid that it wouldn't. He hadn't heard from her all day and her parting words that morning had been hostile as if she hadn't forgiven him for doubting her story about Brant and Mrs. Arlington.

"Hello."

"This is Gallantyne, Mac."

"Don't you ever sleep?"

"I had a couple of hours this afternoon. Don't worry about me."

"I'm worried about me, not you. I was just going to bed. What's up?"

"I'm calling to return a favor," Gallantyne said. "You let me read the anonymous letter Kate Oakley received, so I'll let you read one that was brought to me tonight if you'll come down to my office."

"I've had more tempting offers."

"Don't bet on it. The two letters were written by the same man."

"I'll be right down," Mac said and hung up.

Gallantyne was alone in the cubicle he called an office. He showed no signs of the fatigue that Mac felt weighing down his limbs and dulling his eyes.

The letter was spread out on the desk with a goosenecked

lamp turned on it. It was printed, like the one Kate Oakley had received, and it had been folded in the same way, many times, as though the writer was unconsciously ashamed of it and had compressed it into as small a package as possible. An envelope lay beside it, with the words Police Department printed on it. It bore no stamp.

Mac said, "How did you get hold of this?"

"It was dropped in the mail slot beside the front door of headquarters about two hours ago. The head janitor was just coming in to adjust the hot-water heater and he saw the man who put the letter in the slot. He gave me a good description."

"Who was it?"

"Charles Gowen," Gallantyne said. "Surprised?"

"I'm surprised at the crazy chances he took, delivering the letter himself, making no effort to alter his printing or the way he folded the paper."

"What kind of people take chances like that, Mac?"

"The ones who want to be caught."

Gallantyne leaned back in his chair and looked up at the ceiling. In the center of it, the shadow of the lampshade was like a black moon in a white sky. "I checked his record. It goes back a long way and he's been treated since then, both at Coraznada State Hospital and privately. But a record's a record. When a man's had cancer, the doctors can't ignore his medical history. Well, this is cancer, maybe worse. Gowen's had it, and I think he has it again. Read the letter."

It was briefer than the first one.

To the Police:

I was driving along Cielito Lane last night at 10:30 and I know you are Bad about which house Jessie came out of. It was the house next door on the west side. They will keep me a prisoner now so I can never tell you this in person but it is True.

A Witness

P.S. Jessie is my fiend.

Mac read it again, wondering who "they" were; the brother, probably, and the woman Mr. Forster the druggist had mentioned, Gowen's fiancée.

Gallantyne was watching him with eyes as hard and bright as mica.

"Interesting document, wouldn't you say? Notice the capitalizations, Bad and True. And the postscript."

"I suppose he intended to write 'friend' and omitted the 'r.' "

"I think so."

"And by 'Bad' I gather he means wrong."

"Yes. The house next door on the west side belongs to the Arlingtons." Gallantyne leaned forward and moved the lamp to one side, twisting the shade. The black moon slid down the white sky and disappeared. "As soon as the letter came, I sent Corcoran over to Gowen's house. The brother was there, Ben, and Gowen's girl friend, Louise Lang. Gowen was missing. The brother and girl friend claimed they didn't know where he'd gone, but according to Corocoran, they were extremely nervous and what they weren't saying, they were thinking. Anyway, I gave the word for Gowen to be picked up for questioning."

"Do you believe what he said in his letter about Jessie coming out of the Arlingtons' house?"

"Well, it seems to fit in with Mrs. Oakley's story that Mrs. Arlington and Brant were something more than neighbors."

"I've told you before, you can't afford to take Kate too seriously. She frequently thinks the worst of people, especially if they have any connection in her mind with Sheridan."

"The letter tends to support her statement."

"I don't see it."

"Then you're not looking. And the reason you're not looking is obvious—Kate Oakley. You're doing your best, in a quiet way, to keep her out of this case."

"That's a false conclusion," Mac said. "When a statement in a letter showing certain signs of disturbance is supported by the word of a woman who shows similar signs, it doesn't mean both are right because they agree. It could mean that neither is right."

"You want more evidence? O.K., let's gather some." Gallantyne got up, the swivel chair squawking in protest at the sudden, violent movement. "I'm going to talk to Brant. Coming with me?"

"No. I prefer to get some sleep."

"Sleep is for babies."

"Look, I don't want to be dragged into this thing any further."

"You dragged yourself in, Mac. You didn't come here tonight out of idle curiosity or because anyone forced you. You're here on the chance that you might be able to help Kate Oakley. Why don't you admit it? Every time you mention her name, I see it in your face and hear it in your voice, that anxious, protective—"

"It's none of your business."

"Maybe not, but when I'm working with somebody I want to be sure he's working with me and not against me on behalf of a woman he's in love with."

"Now you're telling me I'm in love with her."

"I figure somebody should. You're a little slow about some things, Mac. No hard feelings, I hope?"

"Oh no, nothing like that."

"Then let's go."

The Brant house was all dark except for a light above the front door and a lamp burning behind the heavily draped windows of the living room.

Gallantyne pressed the door chime and waited. For the first time since Mac had known him, he looked doubtful, as if he'd just realized that he was about to do something he wouldn't approve of anyone else doing, dealing another blow to a man already reeling.

"Sure, it's a dirty business," he said, as much to himself as to Mac. "But it's got to be done. It's my job to save the kid, not spare the feelings of the family and the neighbors. And by

God, I think the whole damn bunch of them have been holding out on me."

"If the only way you can handle this situation is to get mad," Mac said, "all right, get mad. But watch your step. The fact that Brant's daughter is missing doesn't deprive him of his rights, both legal and human."

"How I feel now is nobody has any rights until that kid is found alive and kicking."

"That's dangerous talk coming from a policeman. If you ignore Brant's rights, or Gowen's, you're giving people an invitation to ignore yours."

Gallantyne pressed the door chime again, harder and longer this time, although the answering tinkle was no louder and no faster. "I'm sick of a little lie here and a little lie there. Gowen's in the picture all right, but he's only part of it. I want the rest, the whole works in living color. Why did Mrs. Arlington claim the kid didn't go to her house?"

"Gowen might be the one who's lying, or mistaken."

"I repeat, his statement jibes with Kate Oakley's."

"It's not necessary to drag Kate into—"

"Mrs. Oakley dragged herself in, the same way you did. She volunteered that information about Brant. Nobody asked her, nobody had to pump it out of her. She's in, Mac, and she's in because she wanted to be in."

"Why?"

"Who knows? Maybe she needs a little excitement in her life—though that should be your department, shouldn't it?"

"That's a crude remark."

"So I'm having a crude night. It happens in my line of work, you get a lot of crude nights."

A light went on in the hall and a few seconds later Dave Brant opened the door. He was still wearing the clothes he'd had on the previous night, jeans and a sweatshirt, dirty and covered with bloodstains now dried to the color of chocolate. The hand he'd injured in a fall was covered with a bandage that looked as though he'd put it on himself.

He was gray-faced, gray-voiced. "It there any news?"

Gallantyne shook his head. "Sorry. May we come in?"

"I guess so."

"You remember Mr. MacPherson, don't you?"

"Yes."

"I'd like to talk to you for a few minutes, Mr. Brant."

"I've told you everything."

"There may be one or two little items you forgot." Gallantyne closed the door. "Or overlooked. Are you alone in the house?"

"I sent my son Michael to spend the night with a friend. My wife is asleep. The doctor was here half an hour ago and gave her a shot."

"Did he give you anything?"

"Some pills. I didn't take any of them. I want to be alert in case—in case they find Jessie and she needs me. I may have to drive somewhere and pick her up, perhaps several hundred miles away."

"I suggest you take the pills. Any picking up can be done by the police—"

"No. I'm her father."

"—in fact, must be done by the police. If Jessie turns up now, at this stage, it won't simply be a matter of putting her to bed and telling her to forget the whole thing."

"You mean she will be questioned?"

"She will be questioned if she's physically and mentally able to answer."

"Don't say that, don't—"

"You asked."

Gallantyne hesitated, glancing uneasily at Mac. The hesitation, and the doubt in his eyes, made it clear to Mac why he'd been invited to come along. Gallantyne needed his support; he was getting older, more civilized; he'd learned to see both sides of a situation and the knowledge was destroying his appetite for a fight.

"Perhaps we'd all better go in the living room and sit down," Mac said. "You must be tired, Mr. Brant."

"No. No, I'm alert, I'm very alert."

"Come on."

The single lamp burning in the living room was behind an imitation leather chair. On the table beside the chair, pictures of Jessie were spread out: a christening photograph taken when she was a baby, classroom pictures, snaps of Jessie with Michael, with her parents, with the Arlingtons' dog; Mary Martha and Jessie, arms self-consciously entwined, standing on a bridge; Jessie on the beach, on her bicycle, in a hammock reading a book.

Silently, Dave bent down and began gathering up the pictures as if to shield Jessie from the eyes of strangers. Gallantyne waited until they were all returned to their folders. Then he said, "You asked me before, Mr. Brant, if I had any news. I told you I hadn't, and that's true enough. I do have something new, though. A man claims to have seen Jessie at 10:30 last night."

"Where?"

"Coming out of the Arlingtons' house. Would you know anything about that, Mr. Brant?"

"Yes."

"What, for instance?"

"It's not—not true."

"Now why do you say that? You weren't anywhere around at that time, were you? I understand you were out searching for Mr. Arlington, who'd left here after a quarrel with his wife."

"Yes."

"Where did you go?"

"A few bars, some cafés."

"And after that?"

"Home."

"Whose home?"

Dave turned his head away. "Well, I naturally had to check in at Virg—at Mrs. Arlington's house to tell her I hadn't been able to find Howard."

"This checking in," Gallantyne said softly, "was it pretty involved? Time-consuming?"

"I told her the places where I had looked for Howard."

"It took you exactly two seconds to tell me."

"We discussed a few other things, too. She was worried about Howard, he'd been acting peculiarly all evening."

"In what way?"

"He seemed jealous of the attention Virginia paid to Jessie."

"Did he have any other cause for jealousy?"

"I don't know what you're getting at."

"It's a simple enough question, surely."

"Well, I can't answer it. I don't know what was going on in Howard's mind."

"I'm talking about *your* mind, Mr. Brant."

"I've—I've forgotten the question. I'm—you're confusing me."

"Sorry," Gallantyne said. "I'll put it another way. How did you feel when Mr. Arlington walked out of here last night?"

"We were all upset by it. Howard had never done anything like that before."

"What time did he leave?"

"Between 9:30 and ten."

"What happened after that?"

"I took Virginia home. Then I decided I'd better try and find Howard."

"You decided, not Mrs. Arlington?"

"It was my idea. She was too depressed to be thinking clearly."

"Depressed. I see. Did you attempt to cheer her up in any way?"

"I went looking for her husband."

"And you returned to her house at what time?"

"I'm not sure. I wasn't wearing a watch."

"Well, let's try and figure it out, shall we? You know what time you discovered Jessie missing from her room."

"Eleven. She has a clock beside her bed."

"Very well. At ten, your wife retired for the night. Half an hour later Jessie was seen leaving the Arlington house."

Dave kept shaking his head back and forth. "No, I told you that's not true. It's a—a terrible impossibility."

"Impossibilities can't be terrible, Mr. Brant. By definition, they don't exist. Possibilities are a different matter. They can happen, and they can be quite terrible, like the one you're seeing now."

"No. I don't, I *won't.*"

"You have to," Gallantyne said. "I suggest that Jessie went over to the Arlingtons' place between ten and 10:30. The house was always open to her, she could come and go as she liked, according to Mrs. Arlington. She entered by the back door—"

"No. It was locked, it must have been locked."

"Did you lock it yourself?"

"No."

"That was a pretty serious mistake, wasn't it, Brant? Or are you so casual about that sort of thing you don't mind an onlooker?"

"She didn't see us, she couldn't—"

"I think she did. She saw her father, and the woman she called her aunt, in an attitude that shocked and frightened her so badly that she dashed out into the street. I don't know what was in her mind, perhaps nothing more than a compulsion to escape from that scene. I do know there was a man waiting for her in a car. Perhaps he'd been waiting a long time, and for many nights previously, but that was the night that counted because Jessie's guard was down. She was in a highly emotional state, she didn't have sense enough to cry out or to run away when the man accosted her."

Dave's body was bent double, his forehead touching his knees, as though he was trying to prevent himself from fainting.

Mac crossed the room and leaned over him. "Are you all right, Brant?"

"Aaah." It was not a word, merely a long, painful sigh of assent: he was all right, he wished he were dead but he was all right.

"Listen, Brant. It didn't necessarily happen the way Lieutenant Gallantyne claims it did."

"Yes. My fault, all my fault."

"Tell him, Gallantyne."

Gallantyne raised his eyebrows in a show of innocence. "Tell him what?"

"Can't you see he's in a bad way and needs some kind of reassurance?"

"All right, I'll give him some." Gallantyne's voice was quiet, soothing. "You're a real good boy, Brant. You had nothing to do with your daughter's disappearance. A little hanky-panky with the dame next door; well, Jessie was nine, old enough to know about such things. She shouldn't have been shocked or scared or confused. Don't they teach these matters in the schools nowadays? The birds and the bees, Daddy and Aunt Virginia . . . Now, you want to tell me about it?"

Slowly and stiffly, Dave raised his head. "There's nothing to tell except it—it happened."

"Not for the first time?"

"No, not for the first time."

"Did you plan on divorcing your wife and marrying Mrs. Arlington?"

"I had no plan at all."

"What about Mrs. Arlington?"

"If she had one, I wasn't the important part of it."

"Who was?"

"Jessie. Jessie seems to be a projection of herself. She's the child Virginia was and all the children Virginia will never have."

"When did you find this out?"

"Today. I started thinking about it today."

"A bit late, weren't you?" Gallantyne said. "Too late to do Jessie any good."

"You—are you trying to tell me Jessie is—that she's dead?"

"The man who was waiting for her in the car has a history of sexual psychopathy. I can't offer you much hope, Brant."

Not any hope except that the other child in his history managed to survive.

He was moving toward the sea as inevitably as a drop of water. There were stops for traffic lights, detours to avoid passing places where Ben or Louise sometimes went; there were back-trackings when he found himself on a strange street. These things delayed him but they didn't alter his destination.

He passed the paper company where he worked. A light was burning in the office and he went over and peered into the window, hoping to see Mr. Warner sitting at his desk. But the office was empty, the light burning only to discourage burglars. Charlie was disappointed. He would have liked to talk to Mr. Warner, not about anything in particular, just a quiet, calm conversation about the ordinary things which ordinary people discussed. To Mr. Warner he wasn't anyone special; such a conversation was possible. But Mr. Warner wasn't there.

Charlie went around the side of the building to the loading zone, which was serviced by a short spur of railroad track. He followed the spur for no reason other than that it led somewhere. He took short, quick steps, landing on every tie and counting them as he moved. At the junction of the spur and the main track he stopped, suddenly aware that he was not alone. He raised his head and saw a man coming toward him, walking in the dry, dusty weeds beside the track. He looked like one of the old winos who hung around the railroad jungle, waiting for a handout or an empty boxcar or an even break. He was carrying a paper bag and an open bottle of muscatel.

He said, "Hey, chum, what's the name of this place?"

"San Felice."

"San Felice, well, what do you know? I thought it seemed kinda quiet for L.A. It's California, though, ain't it?"

"Yes."

"Not that it matters none. I been in them all. They're all alike, except California has the grape." He touched the bottle to his cheek. "The grape and me, we're buddies. Got a cigarette and a light?"

"I don't smoke but I think I have some matches." Charlie rummaged in the pocket of his windbreaker and brought out a book of matches. On the outside cover an address was written: 319 Jacaranda Road. He recognized the handwriting as his own but he couldn't remember writing it or whose address it was or why it should make him afraid, afraid to speak, afraid to move except to crush the matches in his fist.

"Hey, what's the matter with you, chum?"

Charlie turned and began to run. He could hear the man yelling something after him but he didn't stop until the track rounded a bend and a new sound struck his ears. It was a warning sound, the barking of dogs; not just two or three dogs but a whole pack of them.

The barking of the dogs, the bend in the tracks, the smell of the sea nearby, they were like electric shocks of recognition stinging his ears, his eyes, his nose. He knew this place. He hadn't been anywhere near it for years, but he remembered it all now, the boarding kennels behind the scraggly pittosporum hedge and the grade school a few hundred yards to the south. He remembered the children taking the back way to school because it was shorter and more exciting, teetering along the tracks with flailing arms, waiting until the final split second to jump down into the brush before the freight train roared past. It was a game, the bravest jumped last, and the girls were often more daring than the boys. One little girl in particular seemed to have no fear at all. She laughed when the engineer leaned out of his cab and shook his fist at her, and she laughed at Charlie's threats to report her to the principal, to tell her parents, to let some of the dogs loose on her.

"You can't, ha ha, because they're not your dogs and they wouldn't come back to you and a lot of them would have babies if they got away. Don't you even know that, you dumb old thing?"

"I know it but I don't talk about it. It's not nice to talk about things like that."

"Why not?"

"You get off those tracks right away."

"Come and make me."

For nearly an hour Virginia had been standing at the window with one corner of the drape pulled back just enough so that she had a view of the front of the Brant house and the curb where the black Chrysler was parked. She had seen Gallantyne and the lawyer getting out of it and had stayed at the window watching hopefully for some sign of good news. Minute by minute the hope had died but she couldn't stop watching.

She could hear Howard moving around in the room behind her, picking up a book, laying it down, straightening a picture, lighting a cigarette, sitting, standing, making short trips to the kitchen and back. His restless activity only increased her feeling of coldness and quietness.

"You can't stand there all night," Howard said finally. "I've fixed you a hot rum. Will you drink it?"

"No."

"It might help you to eat something."

"I don't want anything."

"I can't let you starve."

For the first time in an hour she turned and glanced at him. "Why not? It might solve your problems. It would certainly solve mine."

"Don't talk like that."

"Why not? Does it hurt your ego to think that your wife would rather die than go on living like this?"

"It hurts me all over, Virginia. Without you I have nothing."

"That's nonsense. You have your work, the company, the customers—you see more of them than you do of me."

"I have in the past. The future's going to be different, Virginia."

"Future," she repeated. "That's just a dirty word to me. It's like some of the words I picked up when I was a kid. I didn't know what they meant but they sounded bad so I said them to shock my aunt. I don't know what future means either but it sounds bad."

"I promise you it won't be. I called the boss in Chicago this morning while you were still in bed. I didn't mention it to you because I would have liked the timing to be right but I guess I can't afford to wait any longer. I resigned, Virginia. I told him my wife and I were going to—to adopt a baby and I wanted to spend more time at home with them."

"What made you say a crazy thing like that?"

"I hadn't planned to, it just popped out. When I heard my-self saying it, it didn't seem crazy. It seemed right, exactly right, Virginia."

"No. You mustn't—"

"He offered me a managerial position in Phoenix. I'd be on a straight salary, no bonuses for a big sale or anything like that, so it would mean less money actually. But I'd be working from nine to five like anybody else and I'd be home Saturdays and Sundays. I told him I'd think about it and let him know by the end of the week."

She had turned back to the window so he couldn't see her face or guess what was passing through her mind.

"Maybe you wouldn't like Phoenix, Virginia. It's a lot bigger than San Felice and it's hot in the summers, really hot, and of course there's no ocean to cool it off."

"No—no fog?"

"No fog."

"I'd like that part of it. The fog makes me so lonely. Even when the sun's shining bright I find myself looking out to-wards the sea, wondering when that gray wall will start moving towards me."

"I guarantee no fog, Virginia."

"You sound so hopeful," she said. "Don't. Please don't."

"What's wrong with a little hope?"

"Yours isn't based on anything."

"It's based on you and me, our marriage, our life together."

She took a long, deep breath that made the upper part of her body shudder. "We don't have a marriage any more. Remember the nursery rhyme, Howard, about the young woman who 'sat on a cushion and sewed a fine seam, and fed upon strawberries, sugar and cream'? Well, the sitting bored her, the cream made her fat, the strawberries gave her hives and her fine seams started getting crooked. Then Jessie came to live next door. At first her visits were a novelty to me, a break in a dull day. Then I began to look forward to them more and more, finally I began to depend on them. I was no longer satisfied to be the friend next door, the pseudo-aunt. I wanted to become her mother, her legal mother. . . . Do you understand what I'm trying to tell you, Howard?"

"I think so."

"I saw only one way to get what I wanted. That was through Dave."

"Don't say any more."

"I have to explain how it happened. I was—"

"Even if Phoenix is hot in the summer, we can always buy an air-conditioned house. We could even build one from scratch if you'd like."

"Howard, listen—"

"We'll look around for a good-sized lot, make all our own blueprints or hire an architect. They say it's cheaper in the long run to hire an architect and let him decide what we need on the basis of what kind of life we want and what kind of people we are."

"And what kind of people are we, Howard?"

"Average, I guess. Luckier than most in some things, not so lucky in others. We can't ask for more than that. . . . I've forgotten exactly what the phoenix was. Do you recall, Virginia?"

"A bird," she said. "A bird with gorgeous bright plumage, the only one of his kind. He burned himself to death and then rose out of his own ashes as good as new to begin life again."

She turned away from the window, letting the drape fall into place. "Lieutenant Gallantyne is leaving the Brants' house. Ask him to come in here, will you, Howard?"

"Why?"

"I want to tell him everything I didn't tell him before, about Jessie and my plans for her, about Dave, even about the twenty dollars you gave Jessie. We can't afford to hide things any more, from other people or each other. Will you ask the lieutenant to come in, Howard?"

"Yes."

"It will be a little bit like burning myself to death but I can stand it if you can."

She sat down on the davenport to wait, thinking how strange it would be to get up every morning and fix Howard's breakfast.

The girl was coming toward him around the bend in the tracks. She was taller than Charlie remembered, and she wasn't skipping nimbly along on one rail in her usual manner. She was walking on the ties between the rails slowly and awkwardly, pretending the place was strange to her. She had a whole bundle of tricks but this was one she'd never pulled before. The night made it different, too. She couldn't be on her way to or from school; she must have come here deliberately looking for him, bent on mischief and not frightened of anything—the dark, the dogs, the winos, the trains, least of all Charlie. She knew when and where the trains would pass, she knew the dogs were confined and the winos wanted only to be left alone and Charlie's threats were as empty as the cans and bottles littering both sides of the tracks. She always had an answer for everything: he didn't own the tracks, he wasn't her boss, it was a free country, she would do what she liked, so there, and if he reported her to the police she'd tell them he'd tried to make a baby in her and that would fix him, ha ha.

He was shocked at her language and confounded by her brashness, yet he was envious too, as if he wanted to be like her sometimes: *It's a free country, Ben, and I'm going to do what I like. You're not my boss, so there*— He could never speak the words, though. They vanished on his tongue like salt, leaving only a taste and a thirst.

He stood still, watching the girl approach. He was surprised at how fast she had grown and how clumsy her growth had made her. She staggered, she stumbled, she fell on one knee and picked herself up. No, this could not be pretense. The nimble, fearless, brash girl was becoming a woman, burdened by her increasing body and aware of what could happen. Danger hid in dark places, winos could turn sober and ugly dogs could escape, trains could be running off schedule and Charlie must be taken seriously.

"Charlie?"

During her time of growing she had learned his name. He felt pleased by this evidence of her new respect for him, but the change in her voice disquieted him. It sounded so thin, so scared.

He said, "I won't hurt you, little girl. I would never hurt a child."

"I know that."

"How did you find out? I never told you."

"You didn't have to."

"What's your name?"

"Louise," she said. "My name is Louise."

Gallantyne let Mac off in the parking lot behind police headquarters.

Mac unlocked his car and got in behind the wheel. The ugliness of the scene with Brant, followed by Virginia Arlington's completely unexpected admissions, had left him bewildered and exhausted.

"Go home and get some sleep," Gallantyne said. "I don't think you were cut out for this line of work."

"I prefer to function in the more closely regulated atmosphere of a courtroom."

"Like a baby in a playpen, eh?"

"Have it your way."

"The trouble with lawyers is they get so used to having

everything spelled out for them they can't operate without consulting the rule book. A policeman has to play it by ear."

"Well, tonight's music was lousy," Mac said. "Maybe you'd better start taking lessons."

"So you don't approve of the way I handled Brant."

"No."

"I got through to him, didn't I?"

"You broke him in little pieces. I suggest you buy yourself a rule book."

"I have a rule book. I just keep it in my Sunday pants so it doesn't get worn out. Now let's leave it like that, Mac. We're old friends, I don't want to quarrel with you. You take things too seriously."

"Do I."

"Good night, Mac. Back to the playpen."

"Good night." Mac yawned, widely and deliberately. "And if you come up with any more hot leads, don't bother telling me about them. My phone will be off the hook."

He pulled out of the parking lot, hoping the yawn had looked authentic and that it wouldn't enter Gallantyne's head that he was going anywhere but home.

The clock in the courthouse began to chime the hour. Ten o'clock. Kate would be asleep inside her big locked house from which everything had already been stolen. He would have to awaken her, to talk to her before Gallantyne had a chance to start thinking about it: how could she have known about the affair between Brant and Virginia Arlington? She didn't exchange gossip with the neighbors, she didn't go to parties or visit bars, she had no friends. That left one way, only one possible way she could have found out.

He expected the house to be dark when he arrived, but there were lights on in the kitchen, in one of the upstairs bedrooms and in the front hall. He pressed the door chime, muted against Sheridan as the doors were locked against Sheridan and the blinds pulled tight to shut him out. *Yet he's here,* Mac thought. *All the steps she takes to deny his existence merely reinforce it. If just once she would forget to lock a door or pull a blind, it would mean she was starting to forget Sheridan.*

Mary Martha's voice came through the crack in the door. "Who's there?"

"Mac."

"Oh." She opened the door. She didn't look either sleepy or surprised. Her cheeks were flushed, as if she'd been running around, and she had on a dress Mac had never seen before, a party dress made of some thin, silky fabric the same blue as her eyes. "You're early. But I guess you can come in anyway."

"Were you expecting me, Mary Martha?"

"Not really. Only my mother said I was to call you at exactly eleven o'clock and invite you to come over."

"Why?"

"I didn't ask her. You know what? I never stayed up until eleven o'clock before in my whole, entire life."

"Your mother must have had a reason, Mary Martha. Why didn't you ask her?"

"I couldn't. She was nervous, she might have changed her mind about letting me stay up and play."

"Where is she now?"

"Sleeping. She had a bad pain so she took a bunch of pills and went to bed."

"When? When did she take them? What kind of pills?"

The child started backing away from him, her eyes widening in sudden fear. "I didn't do anything, I didn't do a single thing!"

"I'm not accusing you."

"You are so."

"No. Listen to me, Mary Martha." He forced himself to speak softly, to smile. "I know you didn't do anything. You're a very good girl. Tell me, what were you playing when I arrived?"

"Movie star."

"You were pretending to be a movie star?"

"Oh no. I was her sister."

"Then who was the movie star?"

"Nobody. Nobody real, I mean," she added hastily. "I used to have lots of imaginary playmates when I was a child. Sometimes I still do. You didn't notice my new dress."

"Of course I noticed. It's very pretty. Did your mother make it for you?"

"Oh no. She bought it this afternoon. It cost an enormous amount of money."

"How much?"

She hesitated. "Well, I'm not supposed to broadcast it but I guess it's O.K., being as it's only you. It cost nearly twenty dollars. But my mother says it's worth every penny of it. She wanted me to have one real boughten dress in case a special occasion comes up and I meet Sheridan at it. Then he'll realize how well she takes care of me and loves me."

In case I meet Sheridan. The words started a pulse beating in Mac's temple like a drumming of danger. He knew what the special occasion would have to be, Kate had told him a dozen times: *"He'll see Mary Martha over my dead body and not before."*

"Louise?" Charlie peered at her through the darkness, shielding his eyes with one hand as though from a midday sun. "No. You don't look like Louise."

"It's dark. You can't see me very well."

"Yes, I can. I know who you are. You get off these tracks immediately or I'll tell your parents, I'll report you to the school principal."

"Charlie—"

"Please," he said. "Please go home, little girl."

"The little girls are all at home, Charlie. I'm here. Louise."

He sat down suddenly on the edge of one of the railroad ties, rubbing his eyes with his fists like a boy awakened from sleep. "How did you find me?"

"Is that important?"

"Yes."

"All right then. I could see you were troubled, and sometimes when you're troubled you go down to the warehouse. You feel secure there, you know what's expected of you and you do it. I saw you looking in the window of the office as if you wanted to be inside. I guess the library serves the same purpose for me. We're not very brave or strong people, you and I, but we can't give up now without a fight."

"I have nothing to fight for."

"You have life," she said. "Life itself."

"Not for long."

"Charlie, please—"

"Listen to me. I saw the child last night, I spoke to her. I don't—I can't swear what happened after that. I might have frightened her. Maybe she screamed and I tried to shut her up and I did."

"We'll find out. In time you'll remember everything. Don't worry about it."

"It seemed so clear to me a couple of hours ago. I was the witness then. It felt so good being the witness, with the law on my side, and the people, the nice people. But of course that couldn't last."

"Why not?"

"Because they're not on my side and never will be. I can hear them, in my ears I can hear them yelling, *get him, get him good, he killed her, kill him back.*"

She was silent. A long way off a train wailed its warning. She thought briefly of stepping into the middle of the tracks and standing there with Charlie until the train came. Then she reached down and took hold of his hand. "Come on, Charlie. We're going home."

Even before Mac opened the door he could hear Kate's troubled breathing. She was lying on her back on the bed, her eyes closed, her arms outstretched with the palms of her hands turned up as if she were begging for something. Her hair was carefully combed and she wore a silky blue dress Mac had never seen before. The new dress and the neatness of the room gave the scene an air of unreality as if Kate had intended at first only to play at suicide but had gone too far. On the bedside table were five empty bottles, which had contained pills, and a sealed envelope. The envelope bore no name and Mac assumed the contents were meant for him since he was the one Mary Martha had been told to call at eleven o'clock.

"Kate. Can you hear me, Kate? There's an ambulance on the way. You're going to be all right." He pressed his face against one of her upturned palms. "Kate, my dearest, please be all right. Please don't die. I love you, Kate."

She moved her head in protest and he couldn't tell whether she was protesting the idea of being all right or the idea of his loving her.

She let out a moan and some words he couldn't understand.

"Don't try to talk, Kate. Save your strength."

"Sheridan's—fault."

"Shush, dearest. Not now."

"Sheridan—"

"I'll look after everything, Kate. Don't worry."

The ambulance came and went, its siren loud and alien in the quiet neighborhood. Mary Martha stood on the front porch and watched the flashing red lights dissolve into the fog. Then she followed Mac back into the house. She seemed more curious than frightened.

"Why did my mother act so funny, Mac?"

"She took too many pills."

"Why?"

"We don't know yet."

"Will she be gone one or two days?"

"Maybe more than that. I'm not sure."

"Who will take care of me?"

"I will."

She gave him the kind of long, appraising look that he'd seen Kate use on Sheridan. "You can't. You're only a man."

"There are different kinds of men," Mac said, "just as there are different kinds of women."

"My mother doesn't think so. She says men are all alike. They do bad things like Sheridan and Mr. Brant."

"Do you know what Mr. Brant did?"

"Sort of, only I'm not supposed to talk about the Brants, ever. My mother and I made a solemn pact."

Mac nodded gravely. "As a lawyer, I naturally respect solemn pacts. As a student of history, though, I'm aware that some of them turn out badly and have to be broken."

"I'm sleepy. I'd better go to bed."

"All right. Get your pajamas on and I'll bring you up some hot chocolate."

"I don't like hot chocolate—I mean, I'm allergic to it. Anyway, we don't have any."

"When someone gives me three reasons instead of one, I'm inclined not to believe any of them."

"I don't care," she said, but her eyes moved anxiously around the room. "I mean, it's O.K. to tell a little lie now and then when you're keeping a solemn and secret pact."

"But it isn't a secret any more. I know about it, and pretty soon Lieutenant Gallantyne will know and he'll come here searching for Jessie. And I think he'll find her."

"No. No, he won't."

"Why not?"

"Because."

"He's a very good searcher."

"Jessie's a very good hider." She stopped, clapping both hands to her mouth as if to force the words back in. Then she began to cry, watching Mac carefully behind her tears to see if he was moved to pity. He wasn't, so she wiped her eyes and said in a resentful voice, "Now you've spoiled everything. We were going to be sisters. We were going to get a college education and good jobs so we wouldn't always be waiting for the support check in the mail. My mother said she would fix it so we would never have to depend on bad men like Sheridan and Mr. Brant."

"Your mother wasn't making much sense when she said that, Mary Martha."

"It sounded sensible to me and Jessie."

"You're nine years old." *So is Kate,* he thought, picturing the three of them together the previous night: Jessie in a state of shock, Mary Martha hungry for companionship, and Kate carried away by her chance to strike back at the whole race of men. That first moment of decision, when Jessie had appeared at the house with her story about Virginia Arlington and her father, had probably been one of the high spots in Kate's life. It was too high to last. Her misgivings must have grown during the night and day to such proportions that she couldn't face the future.

There was, in fact, no future. She had no money to run away with the two girls and she couldn't have hidden Jessie for more than a few days. Even to her disturbed mind it must have been clear that when she was caught Sheridan would have enough evidence to prove her an unfit mother.

The three conspirators, Kate, Mary Martha, Jessie, all innocent, all nine years old; yet Mac was reminded of the initial scene of the three witches in *Macbeth—When shall we three meet again?*—and he thought, with a terrible sorrow, *Perhaps never, perhaps never again.*

He said, "You'd better go and tell Jessie I'm ready to take her home."

"She's sleeping."

"Wake her up."

"She won't want to go home."

"I'm pretty sure she will."

"You," she said, "you spoil everything for my mother and me."

"I'm sorry you feel that way. I would like to be your friend."

"Well, you can't be, ever. You're just a man."

When she had gone, he took out the letter he'd picked up from Kate's bedside table before the ambulance attendants had arrived. She had written only one line: "You always wanted me dead, this ought to satisfy you."

He realized immediately that it was intended for Sheridan, not for him. She hadn't even thought of him. First and last it was Sheridan.

He stood for a long time with the piece of paper in his hand, listening to the old house creaking under the weight of the wind. Over and beyond the creaking he thought he heard the sound of Sheridan's footsteps in the hall.

ABOUT THE AUTHOR

Margaret Millar was born in Kitchener, Ontario, Canada, and educated at the Kitchener Collegiate Institute and the University of Toronto. In 1938 she married Kenneth Millar, better known under his pen name of Ross Macdonald, and for over forty years they enjoyed a unique relationship as a husband and wife who successfully pursued separate writing careers.

She published her first novel, *The Invisible Worm,* in 1941. Now, over four decades later, she is busily polishing her twenty-fifth work of fiction. During that time she has established herself as one of the great practitioners in the field of mystery and psychological suspense. Her work has been translated into more than a dozen foreign languages, appeared in twenty-seven paperback editions and has been selected seventeen times by book clubs. She received an Edgar Award for the Best Mystery of the Year with her classic *Beast in View;* and two of her other novels, *The Fiend* and *How Like an Angel,* were runners-up for that award. She is a past President of the Mystery Writers of America, and in 1983 she received that organization's most prestigious honor, the Grand Master Award, for lifetime achievement.